Julia Justiss wrote her [...] stories in her third-grad[...] writing ever since. After publish[...] she turned to novels. Her Regency historical [...] have won or been placed in contests by the Romance Writers of America and *RT Book Reviews* as well as in the Readers' Choice Award and the Daphne du Maurier Award. She lives with her husband in Texas. For news and contests, visit juliajustiss.com.

THE NEW EARL'S CONVENIENT WIFE

Julia Justiss

MILLS & BOON

First published in Great Britain 2026
by Mills & Boon, an imprint of HarperCollins*Publishers* Ltd,
1 London Bridge Street, London, SE1 9GF

www.harpercollins.co.uk

HarperCollins*Publishers*, Macken House, 39/40 Mayor Street Upper,
Dublin 1, D01 C9W8, Ireland

The New Earl's Convenient Wife © 2026 Janet Justiss

ISBN: 978-0-263-41864-4

01/26

MIX
Paper | Supporting
responsible forestry
FSC
www.fsc.org
FSC™ C007454

This book contains FSC™ certified paper
and other controlled sources to ensure responsible forest management.

For more information visit www.harpercollins.co.uk/green.

Printed and Bound in the UK using 100% Renewable Electricity
at CPI Group (UK) Ltd, Croydon, CR0 4YY

To the Belles,
who provide endless encouragement,
sage advice and priceless friendship. Love you!

Chapter One

Thorne Hall, Lake District, March 1814

Slipping into a pew, Lieutenant Rafael Tynesley knelt and bowed his head as multicolored light from the ancient stained glass windows washed over him in tints of blue and red, darkening his deep auburn hair to a burnished sienna and turning the sleeve of his uniform coat a glowing blue. After being away at war almost continuously for the last five years, the family pew in the medieval village church seemed both familiar, yet strange.

Not nearly as strange as the tragedy that had brought him home, he thought, a grief mingled with disbelief once again swirling through him. Who could have imagined that what his brother's last letter had described as a 'mild autumn cold' could have turned into a putrid infection of the lungs virulent enough to cause Ian's death?

He'd intended to say a prayer for his brother's soul

before crossing through the woods and gardens to the house, a way to ease himself back into a place and position he'd never expected to fill. But with his mind clouded by regret or dull with incomprehension, words failed to come.

Not that he'd expected to be inspired by a tide of memories. He'd loved his brother and respected him, but they'd never been close. Ian had been quiet, bookish, musical like their father, while Rafe was the noisy, boisterous one, always eager to leave the house for the fields or the forest, keen on the riding, hunting, and fishing in which his older brother had little interest. The one who always seemed to get into mischief, returning with muddied clothes or skinned knees. When they'd gone away to school, it had been Rafe who shielded Ian, pugnaciously daring anyone to bully his sibling and ever ready to back up that dare with his fists.

He'd always thought, if he survived until the war against Napoleon was finally won, when he returned to Thorne Hall, Ian would be married to his long-time fiancée, Juliana Waverton, the father of an heir and a band of other offspring. He'd go on absently overseeing the estate in the same detached manner as the father he so closely resembled, while between visits, Rafe, as a younger son, would be seeking his fortune elsewhere.

But somehow, that wedding had never happened.

Ian had died single and childless, leaving Rafe with no family closer than a second cousin. And making him the new Earl of Thornthwaite.

Earl of Thornthwaite. Shaking his head at how oddly that rang in his ear, he managed to find a few words asking the Lord's blessing on Ian and rose wearily to his feet. As soon as news of his brother's death reached him, he'd come home directly from where his unit, the 16th Queen's Light Dragoons, had been blockading Bayonne while the bulk of the army headed for Toulouse. Stopping only briefly in London to inform the Horse Guards of his intention to resign his commission, he'd not even lingered long enough to obtain new civilian clothing.

He figured the minimal bits of kit he'd left at Thorne Hall would be adequate until he had time to get new garments made up. It wasn't as if he'd be on display as chief mourner at his brother's funeral; obviously, that event couldn't have been delayed for the uncertain length of time it would take for news of Ian's death to reach him and for him to return to England.

His haste had been prompted more from a sense of lingering disbelief—perhaps he'd return to find the message had been premature, that Ian had recovered after all—and uncertainty about what his position as earl—a rank he'd never expected to receive and a responsibility for which he'd never been trained—would entail.

An uncertainty that made a return to the family home, which should have been familiar and easy, seem even more strange and uncomfortable, as if he were trying to run after inadvertently donning someone else's boots.

An apt analogy, he thought wryly as he walked out of the church, closing the heavy door gently. He would be running in someone else's boots—his brother's.

Why had Ian's engagement not ended in marriage several years ago? Rafe wondered again as he headed towards the family plot to pay his respects at his brother's tombstone. He hadn't imagined he'd be able to attend the wedding, being rather occupied with Wellington's forces in the Peninsula, but he'd long been expecting to hear about it, either in one of his brother's brief and infrequent missives, or from the bride herself.

And what of that bride? he wondered suddenly. The two respective families, owning neighbouring estates, had planned since childhood for the Earl of Thornthwaite's son to marry Baron Waverton's daughter. At first the proposed bride had been the elder daughter, but with nothing formally settled before Agatha went to London for her first Season, where she snagged a marquess's son, with no objection from either party, the role of bride devolved upon her younger sister.

Juliana must be…what, four-and-twenty by now? he thought, frowning. An age considered truly on the shelf. Or had something happened he'd not been informed of and she'd married someone else? If not…

Musing about her current whereabouts, as he rounded the side of the church, he spotted a short, slender figure rising from behind a new tombstone before which she'd just laid a wreath of spring flowers. As she straightened and caught sight of him, her hauntingly familiar dark brown eyes widened in shock, her pale face going whiter still. With a gasp, she reached out to clutch the top of the tombstone, as if to keep from falling.

Recognition registered in a flash. 'Mouse!' he exclaimed, surprise at seeing her so unexpectedly sending her old nickname to his lips. Concern immediately submerging surprise, he hastened to assist her.

Sliding to a halt, he reached out to steady her, immediately suppressing an odd tingle his mind refused to identify. Concentration back on Juliana, he thought for a moment she would throw herself into his arms before, with a ragged sigh, she gently edged out of his hold and gave him a tremulous smile. 'Rafe! I'm so glad you are home at last.'

She looked so careworn and vulnerable, every protective instinct urged him to pull her close and shelter her against his chest. But this was no longer the little girl he'd rescued from tree branches and whose scratches he'd patched up after they'd roamed through the woods. Noting the self-possession and a quaint dignity in her expression, instead, he said, 'Juliana, I'm so sorry for your loss.'

'Your loss, too. As tragic as the circumstances are I can only be thankful you were called home and out of war's danger still intact.'

'You worried about me?'

'Of course!' she replied, looking a bit affronted. 'You've been my best friend since I was seven. Brave and valiant as I know you are, surviving takes luck, too. How could I not worry and pray for your safe return? But you've had a long ride and must be longing for a warm fire and some hot tea. Shall we go?'

Nodding, Rafe offered his arm, which she took with a bit of reluctance, a wave of sympathy for her muting the slight frisson induced by that contact. How odd must it seem to her, so long affianced to his brother, to touch or accept assistance from any other man? Even from him, who truly had been a dear friend since their youth.

'My return has been expected, I'm sure,' he said as, after giving his brother's grave a quick salute, he turned her down the pathway towards the Long Walk leading back to the Hall. 'How do you come to be at Thorne Hall? And wherever is your maid or groom?' he asked, only belatedly realizing she appeared to be entirely alone. 'Your family should never have let you visit here unprotected!'

'My nurse-turned-maid, Baxter, is back at the

Dower House. Where we have been staying. As you know, it's only a short walk from there to the church and I wanted solitude.'

To mourn, he thought with another wave of grief and sympathy. 'You always were a solitary creature,' he teased, trying to lift her spirits. 'But—you said you'd been "staying" there? Are your parents visiting as well?' The family would certainly be welcome, but as their home, Edgerton Manor, was only a several-hour journey by coach, it seemed odd that they would prefer the accommodations available at the Dower House, which Rafe vaguely remembered as old-fashioned and sparsely furnished, to the comforts of their own house.

Juliana gave a derisive sniff, but bit back the acid rejoinder it appeared she'd been about to utter. 'I've been here some time, and their duties at home precluded either Mother or Papa from accompanying me.'

Distracted at first by his irritation at this most recent example of the slighting fashion in which her family had always treated their younger daughter— a strange woodland sprite who either would not or could not adapt herself to the habits and behaviour of a 'proper' young lady—Rafe only belatedly realized the implication of her remark. 'You've been here for some time?' he echoed.

With a sigh and another tremulous smile, she nodded. 'I'll tell you the whole. But first, I must give you some…warning. I'm afraid you'll find Thorne Hall sadly changed from the way you remember it.'

Surprised, he'd been about to ask in what way, but as they left the woodland path and passed through the brick gatepost into the Long Walk, he understood immediately what she'd meant.

The Tudor-designed brick-walled enclosure had been his late mother's chief delight. Arranged around a central walkway were rectangular beds planted in ornamentals, alternating with square areas intended for herbs and vegetables, with espaliered fruit trees on the brick walls beyond the pathways that outlined the whole expanse. Graceful carved statues of wood sprites and smiling maidens decorated some of the corners, fancifully shaped topiary shrubs as their backdrop, while the outside edges of the beds were bordered by low-clipped boxwood hedges.

At least, that's the way the garden had looked the last time he'd strolled through it. After his mother's passing while he was still a teen, his father and then his brother had maintained it according to her design.

She'd hardly recognize it now.

Walkways were still visible, but the grass that had once been low-cut and even now grew in untidy clumps. Weeds surrounded the hardy herbs in the vegetable plots and a haphazard mix of roses and cottage garden flowers filled the ornamental beds, the most aggressive ones leaning out over the uneven boxwood borders into the pathway, as if to grab at the heels of passers-by. An unrecognizable sprawl of greenery spread in all directions behind the statues, while untrimmed extra branches reached out like beseeching arms from the untended espaliers on the walls. The whole area gave an impression of forlorn abandonment.

Rafe turned to Juliana in dismay. 'Is the house as bad as this?'

Her expression solemn, she said, 'Not quite. But the evidence of neglect is still apparent. Which is why we'll go to the Dower House first, where we can be sure of a warm fire in the hearth, hot tea and something edible to accompany it. As no one tried to interfere, Baxter and I saw to putting it in order right after we arrived.'

'If the house looks anything like the Long Walk, I'll need sterner sustenance before I see it,' he replied grimly. 'But why is everything in such disarray? Ian was no more enthusiastic about estate management than our father, but surely he tended things better than this! Or his staff should have. I'd understand it better if he had been ailing for years, but he only fell ill last autumn, didn't he? How could so much damage occur in just a few months?'

'First, tea and a warm fire. Then I'll explain.'

A short while later, Rafe was seated in front of a snug fire in the small front parlour of the Dower

House. He wasn't much acquainted with the dwelling, for the place had been shut up for decades, there being no Dowager Countess who had required separate living quarters since well before his lifetime.

He looked up as Juliana walked in with a plate of cakes, her maid following to deposit a tea tray before withdrawing with a curtsey. 'Is Baxter not remaining to observe the proprieties?' Rafe asked as the maid exited. 'No one batted an eyelid when you roamed the woods with me when you were ten years old, but you're a grown woman now, Mouse. And quite a pretty one.'

Grimacing, Juliana waved off the compliment. 'If we were anywhere we could be observed, Baxter would have remained. But as it's highly unlikely we will be disturbed, she can safely leave. And though I may be grown now, you needn't pay me empty compliments. I'm no more proper or conventional than I was when we roamed the woods together.'

'Still crawling into hollow logs to observe the wildlife and mimicking bird calls, with the bright observant eyes and quick movements that won you your nickname?'

'You were the only one who ever called me "Mouse." I thought it rather apt, though Mama was horrified when my sister tattled about it. Darling Agatha. The perfect, pretty, maidenly paragon Mama tried so hard and vainly to force me to become. How fortunate that

Aggie snared her courtesy earl and Ian agreed to take me in her place, sparing me further aggravation and Mama the frustration of trying to turn me into something I could never become.'

'That union was agreed upon almost six years ago, just before I left for the Army,' Rafe said, abandoning his concern over the estate's condition to seize instead the opportunity she'd just handed him to discover what had happened between her and his brother. 'So why... why am I talking to Ian's fiancée instead of his wife?'

'Well, neither of us were in any particular hurry to wed. Though Mama occasionally taxed me about setting a date, with the engagement announced and the settlements drawn up, making the match almost as official as if we *were* wed, she was content to pursue her own interests and leave us alone.'

'Ian, like your father, was much more interested in books than in people. He was also the only one besides you who ever accepted me as I am, tolerant of my disinterest in society and my preference for exploring the outdoors and its creatures. He was the kindest, gentlest man I kn-knew.' Her voice breaking, she swallowed hard, a sheen of tears augmenting the glisten of her bright eyes. 'We weren't a...conventional couple, but we loved each other in our own ways. I will miss him t-terribly.'

A hollow pang of grief reverberating in his own chest, this time Rafe followed his instincts, rising to pull Juliana into his arms, compassion for her muting that unexpected physical response. 'I'll miss him, too, Mouse,' he whispered, stroking her hair, his heart aching for her. 'But you still have me to watch out for you.'

After clinging fiercely for a moment, she pushed him away, brushing the tears from her eyes with one impatient hand as she walked over to seat herself on the sofa. 'Y-yes. You will always be my dearest friend,' she said, an odd note in her voice as she looked away to begin pouring tea.

Not sure what that intonation meant, Rafe followed to take the armchair she indicated. Any other bereaved maiden might have clung to him, weeping, but Juliana had always been oddly independent. Holding herself apart, observing, her bright, sharp eyes taking in everything. She used to silently creep after him and Cary, one of the farm boys with whom he'd rousted about, when they went fishing or hunting, the boys unaware of her scrutiny until Rafe caught a glimpse of those dark, shining eyes. Often she'd try to scurry away before he could hail her—another reason he'd bestowed the nickname, though he'd been more concerned about her safety, especially if they were hunting, than annoyed that she'd followed them.

He'd also witnessed enough interactions between her and her mother, who made ceaseless and sometimes abusive efforts to force her daughter into the conventional mold her older sister fit so well, to believe that he and Ian had been the only ones to appreciate her.

What would her family do with her now that she was no longer affianced to an earl? And how to discover the answer without intrusive questions that might upset her even more?

But pressed by the imperative to find out, he said, as delicately as he could, 'I know it's early days yet, and you may well not know your own mind. But…do you have any plans for the future?'

'It's been several months since Ian's passing, so I've had time to think. It had already become evident by that last month that he was not going to recover—which is why I'm here, by the way. Baxter's cousin, Thomas Sterling, is a tenant on one of the farms and sent her word when he began to fail. When I learned he was here alone, with no one to help him, I gathered Baxter and came immediately.'

'Ian had written that he'd been suffering a cold. How and when did it turn fatal? Did he not take care of himself, and when it grew worse, he didn't seek treatment?'

She nodded. 'Margary, your old Nurse, who's retired to a cottage on the estate, told me after I'd arrived that he'd gone out walking, alone. It was early October, but a foul day with a sharp wind blowing in cold rain. He was away for hours, she said, and returned soaked to the skin, his lips blue and shuddering with cold. By the next morning, he'd developed a cough and a fever. Once Sterling let me know, I came at once.'

'Your parents approved your coming to nurse him, with no one but your maid as chaperone?'

'As we were already affianced, it wasn't as if I could be compromised. Or, if any gossip did occur, Mama would have been only too happy to call for an immediate wedding. She'd been pressing for it for years.'

'I'm sure she was!' he retorted. 'With good cause, as it turned out.'

Ignoring that comment, she continued, 'I arrived to find him already very ill. I summoned the local physician, who listened to his cough, shook his head and told me the lungs were compromised. He had the apothecary make up some medicine to relieve the congestion. But his condition didn't improve.'

'But Ian was young, strong. I should think he could have fought it off.'

She paused a moment before replying, 'I'm sure he did fight, as much as he was able. He was never as robust as you, remember. You, who grew up going out in all weathers, coming in drenched, and never seeming the worse for it. A quality that stood you in good stead in the army, I imagine.'

'It did. But don't try to distract me. I'm trying to allow for illness, but I still fault Ian for not insisting on wedding you, protecting you, while he still could.'

She shook her head. 'By the time I arrived, his fever

was so high, he was delirious much of time, too weak to even sip the broth I offered. I suppose I could have pushed for the wedding, though I'm not sure any man of the cloth would have agreed to it, with Ian not always coherent. How could a vicar swear Ian was of sound enough mind to agree to plight his troth, with him in such a condition?'

Rafe shook his head. 'Maybe so, but I must agree with your mother. Much as I loved my brother, I can't help thinking he used you ill. He *should* have married you long since. As the widow of an earl, even without the blessing of children, you'd have status no one could take away. And more important, you'd have an income that would make you permanently independent of your parents. You could have remained in the Dower House officially as long as you liked.' He smiled fondly at her. 'Studied nature to your heart's content, with my blessing.'

'You mustn't worry about me,' she said quickly. 'I've had quite a bit of time to contemplate my future, and I don't intend to spend it under my mother's thumb. I do have…prospects, actually.'

'"Prospects"?' Rafe echoed. 'Hiring yourself under a false name onto some Royal Society scientific expedition? Or has some sly young gentleman, observing the length of your endless engagement, tried to tempt you into breaking it? It would have served Ian right if one had!'

She smiled noncommittally. 'Would that there might be a scientific expedition to sign onto! And I would never have served Ian such a turn. But more to the point, I stayed on at the Dower House awaiting your return so I might show you around the estate, give you some explanation about what happened and my recommendations going forward. As I mentioned, Baxter's cousin Sterling is a tenant, so we are aware of the conditions here.'

She'd ever been independent, unlike most females he'd encountered, not given to disclosing her thoughts and emotions or asking for help or even sympathy with her problems. Rafe only knew about the difficulties she'd had with her mother because he'd personally observed some of the confrontations between them.

Relieved that she seemed to have some viable options for her future—and as concerned about the condition of the estate as he was about Juliana's security—Rafe tacitly accepted her change of subject. 'I very much appreciate your staying on and will be most interested in your comments and suggestions. So why has the property fallen into such a state? As I mentioned, I knew Ian had little interest in managing it, but I'm shocked that he would have let it…decline to such an extent.'

'The answer is…somewhat complicated.' She paused, as if trying to choose her words carefully. Which she probably was. It would be difficult to answer his inquiry without showing his brother in a negative light, and given her love for Ian, Rafe knew she'd want to avoid doing that.

'You know Ian has always been a dreamer, more at home in the world of his books than with real people. Inclined to…melancholy.' She gave him a brief, strained smile. 'One reason we got on so well—I never taxed him to go to parties or mingle in local Society, as my sister used to before she went for her Season in London and married someone more amenable. As I mentioned, I was in no hurry to wed, content myself with my own books and my wanderings in the fields and forest. But as Ian's melancholy deepened, he began to shut himself off, even from me. He started spending days, then weeks, alone in his rooms. Sometimes neglecting to send for meals or leaving them untouched outside his door if they were brought. Of course, with him already distressed, I couldn't think of pressing him to schedule a wedding, even a very private one. As his isolation increased, he gradually ceased overseeing the estate. Taylor, the former estate manager, had retired by then and Ian had accepted Taylor's recommendation to have his nephew replace him.'

Restless, a militant gleam in her eyes, she rose and began pacing. 'Young Taylor, Sterling quietly informed us after the man had been at Thornthwaite for several months, possessed nothing close to the character or expertise of his uncle, who died shortly after his retirement. But he was crafty, and noting how little supervision he was given, gradually began, Sterling believes, to pocket much of the rents he collected. It's certain very little was invested back into the farms, the tenants' requests for seeds, materials or repairs going unheeded. I noticed myself on my visits here how the estate was declining. But once again, if Ian agreed to see me—and sometimes he would not—he appeared so nervous and preoccupied, I didn't feel I could bring up the matter of the estate. By this time, most of the servants who'd been here for years were gone—discharged, rumour claims, by Young Taylor, and not replaced. Except for the new housekeeper, Mrs Higgins, whom another rumour says is his mistress. Certainly from what I've observed, she hasn't much skill at housekeeping,' she added acerbically.

Rafe had been listening with growing concern— and increasing anger. He was about to furiously demand how his brother could possibly have let things come to such a point when she turned to face him, tears dripping down her cheeks. 'Oh, Rafe, I'm so sorry! I tried to intervene as much as I could, but I… I had no authority to order anything, which both Taylor and Higgins knew. All I could do was watch and note everything that had been done, or not done, so I might give you the fullest and most complete account when you returned. I was Ian's almost-wife,' she continued after a moment, her earnest tone softening to a murmur. 'I'm…ashamed that I wasn't able to leave Thornthwaite in better condition for you.'

Rafe's anger dissolved at her evident distress. 'Mouse, Mouse, you mustn't blame yourself,' he soothed, once again pulling her into his arms. 'How could you do anything, when, with no marriage lines, you had no legal authority to intervene?'

This time, she let herself lean into his strength, not moving away until the tremors in her body ceased. 'I did contemplate shooting Taylor,' she admitted as she stepped away. 'Or setting a trap for him to fall into. But I've never harmed a fellow creature in my life and I couldn't bring myself to, even one as despicable as Taylor.'

In the course of discharging his army duties, Rafe had caused plenty of harm to fellow creatures. Murder might be out of the question, but if conditions in the house matched the general disintegration of the grounds, he wasn't one bit concerned about the damage it might cause the man if he discharged the venal agent and his lazy paramour on the spot. And followed that up with legal prosecution for fraud and embezzlement if he could gather enough evidence to support the charges.

'There now, dry your eyes and finish your tea. I'm home now, and I do have authority over everything. I shall certainly call on your notes and observations to suggest ways of putting things to rights.'

She nodded. 'I'm happy to help in any way I can. Although I lack most of the skills a gently bred female is supposed to possess, once Ian and I were engaged, I did pay close attention to Mama's instructions on managing a household and an estate—knowing Ian would have little interest in doing so. I'm hoping you will find my observations and suggestions useful.'

'They will be welcome. My training as a soldier will have marginal use in governing the estate,' he said ruefully.

'You may find it more useful than you think. After all, I imagine that managing troops and strategizing battles requires a good deal of organizational skill.'

'We shall see.'

After taking another sip of tea, Juliana turned her dark brown eyes on him, her expression almost… pleading. 'Rafe…you mustn't think too badly of Ian. He didn't *want* to remain so dreadfully paralyzed and unhappy. He would have pulled himself out of it if he'd found any way to do so. Every time I visited, he apologized for not feeling up to having the wedding.' She swallowed hard. 'I'd remember the sweet, shy boy he used to be and would be so overcome with sorrow for his pain, all I could do was assure him I was fine and would wait for him as long as it took. I think… I believe you would have had compassion for him too, if you'd seen how overcome he was.'

Rafe had seen men break under fire. Turn their faces

to the tent wall, refusing to eat or drink once they realized the wounds they'd sustained were mortal. As far as he knew, his brother had never suffered any such extreme circumstances.

But he'd been gone for years, and who knew the depths of despair a mind might become prey to? Straightforward, prosaic Juliana wasn't given to dramatics or exaggeration. If she thought Ian's suffering had been genuine and deep, whatever caused it, it probably was.

In any event, his brother was beyond blame or explanation.

Managing the estate was his burden now.

After finishing the last of his tea, he set down his cup. Looking over at Juliana's troubled face, Rafe had the sudden feeling that she knew more about the circumstances of his brother's condition than she'd just related. He couldn't pinpoint what prompted that niggle of doubt, nor could he imagine what she could possibly be concealing.

But her revelations had laid out the problem before him, and it was time to address it. Letting go of his conflicted feelings about his brother, he stood. 'I've delayed long enough. I'd better gird my loins and return to the house.'

'Would you like me to accompany you?'

He shook his head. 'I imagine most of the depredations will be pretty obvious. I'd better face the shock alone.' *And confront the perpetrators alone, so they cannot accuse you of informing on them.* 'I would like to take you up on the offer of consulting later, though.'

'Of course. I'm anxious to do whatever I can to help. Then, once you know the whole and have listened to my recommendations, I'll return to Edgerton Manor and trouble you no further.'

'Return to "pursue your other options?"' he suggested with a smile.

She said nothing, merely nodding noncommittally.

'I'll be going, then. Thank Baxter for the tea. And Juliana—you'll never be a "trouble" to me. Only a delight.'

Her lips trembling, she nodded, blinking hard against a glaze of tears. After recovering her composure, she said as she walked him to the door, 'I'll remind you of that the next time you're annoyed with me.'

Smiling briefly, Rafe squared his shoulders and set off to discover just how dilapidated his inheritance had become.

Chapter Two

For a long time after Rafe walked out the door, Juliana lingered on the salon's threshold, trying to master the tumultuous feelings his reappearance had engendered.

Not that she was surprised by his return; she'd been anticipating it for several weeks. Long resigned to her position in his life, she'd felt confident she'd armored herself against any excess of emotion. But when he'd suddenly and unexpectedly materialized in front of her in the churchyard, that supposed control had vanished.

As she looked up from placing the flowers on Ian's grave and spotted him, her heart skipped a beat and her chest grew so tight she couldn't breathe. Suddenly dizzy, she staggered to catch herself, then stood frozen as he hurried to her, her gaze taking in every detail of his dear, well-remembered face.

A tanned face, with lines etched upon his brow by years of soldiering in the fierce Peninsular sun now matching the crinkle of smile lines beside his compelling dark eyes. He looked taller, his solid body thinner, evidence of the uncertain supply of victuals available to an army on campaign. His dark auburn hair, a bit longer than he usually wore it, curled around his ears, the thick wave of it she'd once dreamed of brushing aside with her fingertips shadowing his forehead, just as she remembered. He'd always been a commanding figure, but he now had an additional air of authority that added to the sense of gravity he'd always possessed, a seriousness balanced by the bent to find amusement he'd so often demonstrated when they'd roamed the hills and forests together as children.

She'd only just kept herself from hugging the breath from him, so relieved and happy was she to have him returned to Thornthwaite, hale and whole. Until she remembered how important it was now, more than ever, to keep such feelings buried.

Still shaken when she recalled the intensity of her reaction to him, she wandered back into the salon and dropped into a chair.

She'd have to be careful, much more careful than she'd anticipated. Once he'd dealt with Taylor and Higgins and took up her offer of consulting with him, she'd see him often. Sooner or later he'd have time to reflect on the matter of the wedding that never happened and wonder at the thinness of her excuses for delaying it.

In worldly terms, though she'd not exaggerated the depth of Ian's despondency, it made no sense that she'd not pushed harder for a marriage that would have offered her status and security. But at the end, after the reductions Taylor had made to the estate's income and profitability, she knew if she married Ian, the settlements agreed upon at their engagement years ago when the estate had been thriving would strip Thornthwaite of much of the resources Rafe would need to bring it back to profitability.

He must never suspect that she'd refused Ian's deathbed offer of marriage, for doing so would either make her look so unworldly as to be demented. Or reveal the truth.

The truth was that she'd fallen in love with Rafe Tynesley as a ragged child tagging after one of the few people who didn't scorn or dismiss her. One who'd shared her fascination with the natural world and been patient with her zeal to examine fish, rocks, insects, birds, mammals and all their actions and habits. The one person who never made her feel she was the oddity she knew herself to be, the 'unnatural' girl her mother always railed at.

As she'd grown from child to girl, she'd become increasingly aware of his dynamic physical presence, her love deepening with an attraction that tempted her to linger near him, touch his arm, clasp his hand...dream of having him kiss her.

Dreams that were crushed when she'd watched from afar as he fell desperately in love with Society beauty

Thalia Heathcote. She remembered his shock, apathy and a lassitude worse than anger when he lost that love, his beloved's family forcing her to wed a man of higher status and greater fortune. She'd ached, watching him leave, but understood completely the impetus that propelled him to join the army and seize the chance to quit England and distance himself from the pain, grief, anger and heartache.

If only she could have escaped her own heartache and grief.

As she knew from her own experience, such all-consuming love happened only once in a lifetime, whether or not one was fortunate enough to wed one's beloved. There would never be anyone for her but Rafe.

So she'd hidden that love away—and until seeing him today, thought she'd successfully locked away that distant, bittersweet unrealized dream.

She'd have to make sure she reincarcerated it.

After his departure, she'd resolutely moved on, content to take her sister's place and marry Ian, for though her love might be unrequited, she still cared deeply for Rafe's welfare. She could never reveal to him the secret that she'd agreed to marry Ian partly because she knew there would be no children, that sooner or later, the family property would become Rafe's. With his brother indifferent to estate matters, she could protect Thornthwaite's heritage for him, see him on his occasional trips home and write to him on her husband's behalf. But shielded from a resurgence of her feelings by her marriage and her position as his sister-in-law, she could salvage some closeness to him by remaining the odd little girl he'd always treated with indulgent affection.

She'd agreed to be engaged to Ian to protect *him* as well, knowing the enormous pressure to wed he would face as the heir to property and title. With the wordless understanding between two individuals, neither of whom conformed to Society's expectations, she knew their union would shield the gentle man of whom she was so fond from the sort of marriage that would have been a horror for him.

But with Ian gone, this afternoon's surge of emotion had demonstrated with shocking clarity that she would have to swiftly and brutally resubmerge her feelings. After she helped Rafe back on the path to restoring Thornthwaite and if her tentative plans worked out, she could then escape and live the rest of her life in quiet exile from Society, her mother's thwarted expectations and the seductive urge to try to be more to Rafe than the engaging child he now regarded her as.

She was reasonably sure she could keep her emotions bottled up, at least for the length of time it took to sketch out the plans for restoring Thornthwaite. But she'd have remain on guard to resist her still-smoldering desire for him when they were closeted together, probably often alone, over the next few days or weeks.

The best, the only, thing she could do for him now was to equip him to restore his birthright and quietly slip back out of his life. Distancing herself forever from temptation, as he had in the army outrun his heartache and grief.

Pulling herself from her reverie, she told herself tartly that the more immediate thing she could do for him was consult Baxter about dinner. She was confident, after his clash with Taylor, he would return to the Dower House for company and consolation. Which was all she must allow herself to give.

Juliana was proven correct, and sooner than she'd expected. Night had barely fallen when she heard a knock at the front door, followed a moment later by Rafe, ushered into the salon by their borrowed man-servant. 'Thank you—Mason, isn't it?' he said, nodding to the retainer.

'It is, my lord. Good of you to remember,' the man said, before bowing himself out.

As he crossed the room to her, an apologetic smile replacing the anger she'd seen on his face as he entered, she thought ruefully that she might be able to school her expression to calm, but she failed completely to forestall the leap of her heart or the stir to her senses.

Thank heaven neither reaction *was* visible. But she was going to have to do much, much better.

'Sorry to return so soon, like a bad penny. Could I prevail upon you for another round of tea? As that will likely be all that's available for my dinner.'

'Of course!' she said, waving him to a seat on the sofa. 'Though I expect by now you might prefer something a bit stronger than tea.'

'Indeed,' he admitted with a sigh.

'We can do better for dinner, too,' she said, as she rose to pour him a glass of wine. 'The kitchen maid I harangued Taylor into lending us along with Mason hasn't quite graduated to performing like a true cook, but she can prepare simple dishes. We're having stew tonight, and there will be plenty, if you'd care to join us.'

'Thank you. I'd appreciate both the food and the company. But—you had to *argue* with Taylor to obtain staff to serve the Dower House?'

'Oh, my, yes,' she replied, handing him the glass, careful not to let her fingers touch his, vividly conscious of even that slight proximity. 'I caused such a ruckus it roused Ian from his sickbed to brush aside Taylor's protest that the Hall was already short-staffed and order him to grant my request.'

'If the house is short-staffed, that was his doing,' Rafe retorted. 'That he would treat my brother's affianced wife with so little respect makes me doubly glad I just gave him his congé—and his reputed paramour as well. She answered my request for food and wine by bringing the most inedible cakes I've ever had the misfortune to taste! The rocks in Portugal would have more flavor. I told them both to be off Thornthwaite land by first light tomorrow, or I'd have them prosecuted for trespassing.'

'I hope you removed the coins in the office strongbox before you issued that ultimatum,' she said, seating herself a safe distance away on the sofa.

'Indeed I did. I'm glad now that I did not send advance warning of my return. I was able to remove the books, the strongbox and all the keys before Taylor realized I was on the premises. Where is Duxford, by the way? Retired or replaced, along with Mrs Henderson and Mrs Waverly?'

'I'm afraid so. Sterling said the butler was the first to go, but as Duxford was getting on in years, his departure didn't ring any alarm bells. Until Taylor neglected to replace him—and then discharged both Mrs Henderson and Mrs Waverly. Afraid for their own tenure after the departure of the housekeeper and the cook, several of the maids and kitchen staff left, too.'

'He got rid of senior staff first, then—anyone who might have the standing to challenge his authority,' Rafe surmised.

'Yes. It was only then, Sterling told us, that tenants around the estate began to question what was happening. You have the estate books, you say? Perhaps after going through them, you'll find enough evidence of malfeasance that you can have Taylor prosecuted, wherever he may flee.'

'At least he won't have Thornthwaite cash, such as there was, to flee with. Unless he had some hidden away outside the house,' Rafe said grimly, taking a long sip of his wine.

'So you've discharged the villains, taken up the reins and assumed mastery of the estate? Excellent achievements for your first few hours home, Rafe! Though I suppose you are "Rafe" no more; it must be "Thornthwaite" now.' Referring to him by title would be a good first step in putting him at a distance, she thought.

He gave an impatient shake of his head. 'I'll always be "Rafe" to you, Mouse. Although you are changed now, too. Quite the grown-up lady! I suppose I should address you as "Miss Waverton."'

'I was already grown-up six years ago when Ian and I became engaged,' she pointed out. 'And I will always be "Mouse" to you, dear friend. Just that strange little girl who prowled the woods and fields collecting specimens.'

He gave her an odd, almost assessing look that sent a ripple of…something across her skin. As if he'd drawn a finger along her bare hand or arm, it made her stomach contract and set off a tingling deep inside her, warming her face and rendering her breathing shaky.

'No, I mustn't forget that you *are* grown,' he continued after a moment. 'Once you've helped me untangle the mess that is currently Thornthwaite, we shall have to untangle the future for Miss Waverton.'

Though formality might reinforce the distance she should maintain between them—and perhaps temper the strong physical pull he exerted on her—she couldn't quite make herself relinquish the nickname born of his fondness. 'Please don't call me "Miss Waverton"! I spent most of my life as "Miss Juliana", at least on the few occasions when anyone could be bothered to refer to me formally. With you, I much prefer "Mouse."'

The strange, heated look that both excited and alarmed her fading from his eyes, he said, 'Then "Mouse" you shall remain, at least when we are alone. I suppose in company it must be "Thornthwaite" and "Miss Waverton."'

She nodded, trying to settle her disturbed senses. 'That would be more proper. Mama always said "A lady must show suitable respect for the titled, especially titled gentlemen." And speaking of Mama, I must warn you at once that we must be especially careful, once word spreads that you've returned, in case my parents turn up. I'm hoping to give you my opinions of the way forward and return to Edgerton Manor before they learn you're here and decide to pay a visit. Mama, in particular, would like nothing better than to invent some reason to decide I'd been "compromised" and claim that you were honour-bound to marry me.'

He cocked his head to the side, as if arrested. 'It might not be such a bad idea, Mouse. I think we'd get along well together, don't you?'

She knew Rafe didn't love her—not the way she had once loved him, with total, passionate abandon. Still, she was surprised how much it hurt to have him mention the possibility of wedding her with all the ardor and enthusiasm he'd display in choosing between toast or beef for breakfast.

Hoping the pain didn't show on her face, she made herself say calmly, 'Wedding is one thing you can put off until later, once you're well on the road to restoring Thornthwaite. And your choice of a bride is a decision you shouldn't allow anyone to force.'

As heir, he would have to marry. She knew he'd not have the joy of marrying who he chose, but he would do his duty and treat his wife with courtesy and affection. Juliana was certain any number of lovely, charming, well-bred maidens would fight for the chance to secure the position and security that would accompany becoming his countess, even if her husband treated her with nothing warmer than respect.

That would be sufficient for most females—as long as his bride didn't need to conceal from him the passionate attachment she'd once felt—to say nothing of preventing it from recurring. Living with a man you once loved with every ounce of your heart and soul, who felt for you only a tepid affection, would be painful beyond enduring. Preventing him from reviving those feelings would be difficult enough for the relatively short time she anticipated remaining at Thornthwaite.

She wasn't sure she would have the strength to keep them bottled up, were they to be on intimate terms for a lifetime.

And if she could not…if Rafe were to become aware that his wife loved him with a true passion, being Rafe, he would feel guilty and regretful that he was unable to reciprocate her feelings. Destroying the friendship she treasured and creating an impossible, unhappy situation for them both.

Reason enough to thrust aside the very idea of wedding Rafe before the insidiously tempting possibility could plant its poisonous tentacles in her mind.

'You're right. I must put my house in order before I can think to tempt any sane female into taking on Thornthwaite,' he said ruefully.

Juliana shook her head at him. 'Don't be silly! You're not simple "Lieutenant Tynesley" any longer, but a peer of the realm. Ladies will be flocking to attract your attention when you next appear in London.'

'I suppose you're right. It hasn't yet quite sunk in that I'm now an earl.' He shook his head ruefully. 'What a coxcomb that makes me sound! I'm the same man I was six months ago, no more or less valuable or accomplished than when I was a younger son.'

'In your eyes, perhaps, but that's not the way of the world and you know it. You must prepare yourself to be flattered and deferred to—no matter how distasteful you will probably find it.'

He grimaced. 'Distasteful indeed! Maybe I could console myself in the company of my army mate, Hart Edmenton. He, too, came into a title unexpectedly, though his inheritance was a dukedom, and he has as little use for pretense and flattery as I have. However, I and our other army mate, Charles Marsden, teased him so much about his unexpected elevation in rank, he's more likely to chortle over my dilemma than sympathize.'

'You should have some months to accustom yourself,' Juliana said encouragingly. 'You'll want to take your seat sometime during this session of Parliament, but you needn't go to London immediately. And when you do, you'll be free to associate only with the company you choose.'

'Then I must surround myself with friends like you and Hart, who will keep me humble in the midst of the fawning attention.'

Was there any way she could help him then? 'I'd be happy to be of assistance, but there's little chance of my turning up in London,' she confessed.

Then mentally kicked herself for giving him an opening to discuss her future when he immediately responded, 'Will your parents not take you to the city for the Season? With Ian gone, they'll be looking to find you another husband, surely.'

Even if they were, I'd never have anyone but you, she thought. *And I can never have you.*

'I'm afraid a Season in London is out of the question. Papa even forbade Mama to go this year. Too many…financial reverses. And crop yields haven't been good.'

Rafe studied her a minute before saying, 'Is Carlisle accumulating debts again?'

Juliana felt little connection to the family that disdained her, but she wouldn't speak ill of them. 'I suppose he feels he must dress, entertain and gamble in the same manner as his Oxford friends.'

'Your father doesn't seek to limit his expenses— even when they put a strain on the estate?'

Juliana shrugged. 'With Aggie married and me, everyone thought, settled, Papa has no potential obligations other than Carlisle's. Both he and Mama are proud that a baron's son has friends from such high-born, influential families. As the heir, they feel it only right that he maintain his position among them. Which he couldn't do, Mama says, if he must be a nipfarthing about expenses.'

'He's not obligated to duplicate all their extravagances if his income won't support it,' Rafe retorted. 'I heard all too much complaining about such behaviour from fellow officers, younger sons all, with whom I served. They, risking life and limb for England, while their older brothers were squandering the family funds betting on which goose would cross the meadow first in Green Park. Your brother should take more care, especially as you now are no longer settled.'

'My family is unlikely to bestir themselves on my behalf now,' Juliana told him bluntly. 'They fault me for not having brought Ian to the altar when I could. Mama says if I'd had the least bit of physical charm or feminine allure, I'd have—' she broke off, seeing by the look on Rafe's face that she'd said too much. 'Well, no matter. A Season in London would almost certainly be wasted on me. Not even you, despite your f-fondness for me—' she forced herself to say the diminishing word '—could claim I possess any of the qualities trained into most young maidens entering the Marriage Mart. Deference to the prominent. The ability to pay flattering attention to gentlemen. A delight in social functions, fashion and gossip. And any desire whatever to beguile the highest-ranking and richest gentleman possible into wedding me.'

'You have other fine qualities, though,' he said stoutly. 'Honesty. Loyalty. Compassion. The expertise to manage an estate. To say nothing of a keen sense of observation, a quick wit and a superior talent at sketching and painting.'

Trying to resist being warmed by his praise, she said, 'Mama would not consider most of those traits desirable—especially honesty and quick wit. "A lady must never express an opinion, unless it is to agree with a gentleman's.'" She sighed. 'I was taken to task often enough for my frankness when Aggie's fiancé dined with us *en famille* after their engagement. Indeed, Mama threatened to banish me entirely from appearing at family dinners unless I learned to be silent. Which I did.'

Frowning, Rafe said, 'You were not "out" when your sister was presented, so that stricture seems a bit extreme. Lady Waverton couldn't have been worried that you might scare away potential suitors.'

'True, but with Aggie engaged, Mama was already counting on shortly seeing me betrothed to Ian in her stead. Eliminating the need for an expensive London Season or any requirement for me to appear "desirable," as long as my odd behaviour didn't alienate *Aggie's* intended.'

'What *does* your family intend for you, then?'

No point describing her mother's fury upon learning Ian had expired with them still unwed. Or the blistering scold that lady had administered before she broke down in tears and ordered Juliana from her presence after telling her she'd washed her hands of her and never wished to see her again. 'I don't think they *have* any plans. I do, however, and as Mama stopped short of forbidding me the house for my failings, once we finish going over estate matters, I'll return to Edgerton Manor only long enough to finalize them.'

'Forbid you the house?' Rafe echoed, bristling. 'I should hope not! You are still her daughter, whatever your mother thinks of your behaviour and prospects. And if she truly believes you possess neither charm nor allure, the woman is ignorant.'

Dear Rafe, trying again to bolster her self-esteem. But she'd listened to her mother catalogue the attributes men found attractive—a soft, womanly form, blond hair, blue eyes, a pretty deference to his superiority coupled with a pleasing, flirtatious manner— often enough to know she possessed none of them.

'You mustn't disturb yourself; I won't tarry long under Mama's roof. I do have those prospects, after all.'

Rafe studied her a long moment, while Juliana tried to keep her expression confident and reassuring. 'I'll try not to keep you at Thornthwaite too long, then. Whoever the astute young man who's captured your fancy is, I hope he won't carry you too far away. I expect I'll need to call on you for advice about the estate for some time, until I make the transition from soldier to farmer.'

'We can start discussing it tonight.' She'd guide him to talk about her observations and recommendations, steering him away from the dangerous topic of her future.

Which he obviously assumed involved a proposal from some other young man.

If he only knew how unlikely that possibility was, to say nothing of unappealing!

He'd also likely object if he knew her true intentions. Soon after Ian's death, she'd written about her loss to Lady Fallsham, an elderly woman she'd met in one of the botanical rooms at the British Museum during her sister's Season and with whom she'd struck up a friendship. The widow had swiftly replied, inviting Juliana to come live with her and the equally elderly cousin who currently served as her companion. An invitation Juliana had immediately accepted, asking only to delay until she might acquaint the new earl with the information he would need to assume management of his estate.

Lady Fallsham's country home, Fallsham Hall, would provide the perfect refuge. Juliana could assist a lady she admired, one who, unlike her own mother, approved of her interests and would encourage her to continue her studies and her sketching. She could immerse herself in assisting Lady Fallsham and in learning about and filling her sketchbooks with a new series of birds, insects and animals.

She could also establish a correspondence with Rafe. Advise him on estate matters when he asked and keep up with what was going on in his life—but from a safe distance.

Which consulting with him in person was not. Already temptation was whispering at her to scoot closer to him on the sofa, to use the excuse of making a point to tap his sleeve or press her hand against his. She suspected if she gave in and permitted herself those glancing contacts, her greedy senses would only crave more and more.

Spend too much time with him, and her fierce desire might overwhelm caution, propelling her into some irretrievable action—reacting to a brotherly kiss with unseemly passion or binding herself to him in a too-tight embrace—from which he would, in the best case, recoil. Or in the worst case, react with a revulsion that would lead him to sever any remaining bonds between them.

Best to leave soon, in honour and friendship that would allow friendship to continue. So if she could not share it, she would at least not be permanently exiled from his life.

Easier, too, to remain at a distance and suffer the pain of loneliness than stay close. Even as she told herself it was foolish beyond belief to allow each expression of tepid affection to cut so deeply, her heart slowly bleeding from every little wound.

Chapter Three

A month later, Rafe waited in the front parlour at Juliana's family home, Edgerton Manor, his second visit to his neighbour Lord Waverton's property since returning to England. The first time, he'd escorted Juliana home after a hectic week of consultations in which she'd first introduced him to Thomas Sterling, the long-time Thornthwaite tenant who'd kept his cousin Baxter, Juliana's maid, informed of what was transpiring on the estate. She'd then accompanied him and Sterling on visits to the estate's tenants, adding what she'd gleaned from Ian and her own visits about each farm and its workers to what Sterling knew. She'd assisted him in going over the account books, indicating what Old Taylor had done and pointing out the discrepancies in what his successor had recorded. With Sterling's and Baxter's help, they had located those of the former Thornthwaite staff still in the area and recommended the ones whom the estate had sufficient funds to rehire. Rafe hadn't needed Juliana's unspoken approval to immediately appoint Sterling as his new estate manager before she reluctantly allowed him to escort her home.

She'd argued against it, citing her mama's probable attempts to entrap him into marrying her. With no more wish than she to be forced into a commitment unless they were both ready, he assured her that, as a former infantry officer, he was quite capable of evading the enemy. And quickly demonstrated that ability by neatly sidestepping Lady Waverton's attempts to delay his departure or maneuver him into a compromising situation with her daughter. Once Juliana was safely returned to her family, he left her a whispered hope that her other 'prospects' might prosper and returned to confront the challenge of slowly restoring his estate.

After a month of hard work, he'd come back to Edgerton to report to her, pleased and proud of the beginning he'd made. She might not have had the authority to prevent the plundering wrought by the former estate manager—whom he'd reluctantly concluded he did not have enough evidence to prosecute—but she'd nonetheless felt responsible, even though she should not have. He wanted to let her know how helpful her careful observations and accurate assessment of what had transpired and recommendations on how he might repair the damages had been in beginning to reverse the decline. As responsible as she'd felt for the welfare of Thornthwaite, its tenants and his brother, he was certain she'd both appreciate and be pleased about the progress he'd made.

And, truth be told, he'd missed her.

He was also eager to discover whether the 'prospects' she'd assured him would allow her to escape her disapproving family had indeed come to fruition. If they had not, he felt ready to make more formal the offhand offer of marriage he'd made her before she left Thornthwaite.

Rafe didn't *disbelieve* in love, but after a wrenchingly unsuccessful love affair in his youth, he'd decided strong emotion wasn't the best basis to sustain a relationship for the long haul. He'd recently counselled his army friend, the new Duke of Fenniston, that a marriage based on admiration, respect, affection and mutual interests supported by physical compatibility was far more likely to offer lifelong happiness than one born of exalted feelings of passionate love that, in his observation, were unlikely to endure.

Smiling, he thought that perhaps it was the interest he'd expressed in the lady he'd advised his friend to seriously consider that had prompted Hart to suddenly see Mrs Hambleden in a new light. Most likely, their eventual union hadn't been all his doing, but he did feel quite satisfied that Hart had finally realized the answer to his need for not just a suitable duchess, but one who would make him happy for the rest of his days, was right before his eyes.

Was the answer to his own need for a suitable countess right before his?

True, it had been six years since he'd spent much time with Juliana, but he didn't think her basic character would have altered much in that time.

Certainly he felt respect, affection and admiration for her. Suddenly realizing his little Mouse had grown up into a Miss Waverton he found desirable had been a shock, though not an unpleasant one. She didn't have the statuesque beauty possessed by her mother and older sister; her figure was too short, lithe, and elfin to ever be considered 'voluptuous.' But when he'd embraced her, her firm, small breasts pressed against his chest, her lush little mouth eminently kissable, a purely erotic surge of sensation had overwhelmed what had initially been merely a brotherly desire to give comfort. Even as a child, he'd found her expressive brown eyes mesmerizing. Added to her unconscious grace and subtle sensual appeal, he knew without question that the satisfying physical intimacy he valued as an integral part of marriage was definitely possible, were Juliana to be his bride.

Perhaps he'd sensed that physical allure even when she'd first become engaged to Ian, but held on to his image of her as just an engaging child to avoid even thinking of his brother's future wife in sensual terms. But now that the link was broken…

She'd already demonstrated her competence, her sharp observations in noting what had happened to the estate and the remedies she'd suggested had been absolutely accurate. Rafe admired her zeal for the natural world and shared it, though not with the passion she felt. He also shared her disinterest in the dancing, gambling, socializing and general frittering away of time that occupied much of the London ton. He would be content, as he thought she would, to spend most of their time at Thornthwaite, overseeing the restoration and then the management of the estate while Juliana happily rambled about the woods and fields, observing animals, listening to bird calls, and making her sketches.

If he were truly honest, the main reason he'd come to update her on his progress was to discover how her own prospects had fared. And see if she were willing to discuss the possibility of a union between them.

Would she agree? And if she did not immediately accept him, should he continue to pursue her? He certainly didn't want to ruin the long friendship they'd shared. Would he be able to convince her that marriage would only add a richer, more satisfying depth to that friendship?

Lady Waverton walked in as he was pondering the question. 'Lord Thornthwaite, how kind of you to visit!

I know Juliana will be delighted to see you. I do hope you mean to grace us with a longer stay this time. No need to rush off!' she added, giving him a reproachful look. 'Besides, I'm sure you've been working far too hard at Thornthwaite. You deserve to take a break and let us entertain you.'

Rafe bowed, kissing the fingertips she offered. 'I'm grateful, as always, for your hospitality,' he replied noncommittally. 'How is Miss Waverton?'

Lady Waverton heaved a dramatic sigh that might have convinced Rafe she was deeply affected by her daughter's distress, had Rafe not been well aware of how little maternal sympathy her mother had ever displayed towards her. 'Juliana has been melancholy, as I'm sure you can appreciate, mourning your brother as she does. Your sympathy and understanding are such a comfort to her! The late earl's loss was so devastating…in so many ways.'

Devastating in that you didn't get her off your hands, Rafe thought uncharitably. 'Will she be joining us?'

'Her father asked her to work on a project for us. She's in the library—we've turned a corner of it into a sort of studio for her. I don't want to interrupt her— the sensibilities of an artist, you know! Let me escort you to her.'

'Her maid will join us there?'

'I'm sure there's no need to wait on Baxter. You are friends of long standing, after all.'

Before Rafe could protest that he'd be happy to await Juliana in the parlour or delay until her maid could join them, Lady Waverton seized his elbow and escorted him out of the room. Unwilling to break away and cause a scene, as she marched him down the hall, he rapidly considered how he might evade her plan to have him closeted with her daughter.

'She's just in there,' she said, halting and indicating the closed library door. 'I'll let you slip in quietly, so you don't disturb her work.'

A smiling Lady Waverton opened the door and gestured him in. But before he could protest or back away, Juliana jumped up, seized a china plate from the desk before her and hurled it against the wall. As it shattered into pieces, she whirled around, spotted them, reversed direction and fled out the French doors into the garden beyond.

'Oh, that *girl*!' her mother exclaimed furiously before, catching herself, she turned to Rafe. 'I'm so sorry, Lord Thornthwaite! Such unmaidenly behaviour! But then, she's never been quite the same after the shock of losing dear Ian, with all the promises he made her unfulfilled, all her hopes for the future destroyed!'

Rafe was shocked too, though not because he found Juliana's actions 'unmaidenly.' Never before had he seen her other than calm and controlled—and he'd witnessed several occasions where the verbal abuse she'd suffered would have merited a tantrum. His protective instincts alerted, knowing something must be drastically wrong, he brushed off Lady Waverton's continuing apologies, hurried through the library and ran out the door after her.

A short time later, Rafe discovered Juliana, as he'd suspected and hoped he might, at the edge of the pasture fence in a small glen of trees behind the horse barns. A place where he knew she'd often taken refuge throughout her childhood when escaping one of her mother's diatribes on her inadequacies.

'Juliana, what wrong?' he said urgently as he approached her. 'What happened to so upset you?'

She didn't respond, continuing to face away from him, breathing hard, her hands gripping the rail of the pasture fence so hard her knuckles showed white. Rafe put a tentative hand on her sleeve, his concern intensifying as he felt the trembling of her body. At first he thought she would pull away, but, to his relief, she allowed his touch. After several long moments, taking a deep breath, she stilled the trembling and turned to him.

'Rafe, how good to see you! Sorry for my…unfortunate behaviour. How are things at Thornthwaite? Has Sterling worked out well as estate manager? I hope your taking the time to visit means all is well in train.'

Tacitly accepting her change of subject—for the moment, for he had no intention of leaving Edgerton

Manor before he discovered what had provoked her flight—he said, 'Sterling has been a godsend. Not only does he know the needs of the farms—long unmet, as you know—he's held in such high esteem by the other tenants that, knowing he now has oversight of the estate, any resentment towards me they might with perfect justification have developed because of Ian's neglect has been blunted. True, they were initially skeptical of my assurance that I intended to remedy the deficiencies Taylor allowed, but with some careful management of the capital still remaining, we've been able to address the immediate shortfalls in equipment and repairs. I'm confident that they will continue to work with me, under Sterling's supervision, to do the hard work to restore the estate's buildings and increase its production.'

'I'm so pleased to hear it. Were you able to coax Mrs Henderson out of retirement to return as housekeeper?'

'Yes, thanks to your intervention. She recommended that Mason take over as butler and Jane, under her tutelage, continue training as cook. Since I'm the only one in residence and a former army officer used to the deprivations of campaign, she knows I don't require anything fancy in the way of meals. She's brought in two maids and a footman, about all the staff I can afford at the moment. Not enough to set Thorne Hall to rights as it was in my mother's day, but we're making a start.'

'Excellent! I appreciate you riding over to offer me a report.'

'Only what you deserve, after the care you took to set me on the right track. And let me emphasize again, you mustn't hold yourself responsible for what happened during Ian's…illness. I know you did whatever you could to prevent it. Your careful observations and astute recommendations have gone a long way towards equipping me to begin reversing the decline.'

An expression of sorrow briefly crossed her face. 'Thank you for that. Although I cannot help still feeling somewhat responsible. But shall we go in? You can probably safely remain for dinner, as long as you escape before Mama can contrive some way to keep you overnight.'

She turned to go, but Rafe caught her hand, the automatic tingle of response muted by his concern. 'I've given my report. What about yours? What just happened to upset you? Is your mother haranguing you again?'

He thought at first she would put him off again, but giving him a grimace of a smile, she said, 'Not Mama this time. Father said Carlisle would need gifts to give the hostesses at the house parties he'll be invited to over the summer and fall, after the *ton* leaves London. After having spectacularly failed to marry and now remaining a burden on the household, I should earn my keep by decorating some china plates for him, employing the "only feminine skill I possess," for otherwise, I was useless. *Useless*,' she repeated, tears sparkling at the edges of her eyes. 'I know I have a talent for painting and sketching. Even if he and Mama think drawing animals and birds is wasted effort.' She sighed. 'Now I've broken two of the plates. A fortunate circumstance that you've turned up, else I'd likely be sent to my chamber without supper—and provided with four more plates to decorate.'

'You *do* have a superior talent,' Rafe said, furious on her behalf at the blindness and insensitivity of the family who ought to value her and so obviously didn't. 'It's wasted on china plates. I'm glad you smashed one.'

That provoked a slight smile. 'Thank you. I'll use that thought to cheer me as I'm forced to paint half a dozen more.'

'Must you? Are your…prospects not close enough to fruition to spare you that?'

Her smile faded, such desolation in her expression that Rafe had great difficulty refraining from pulling her into his arms—an attempt at comfort he somehow knew she would resist.

'My…most promising one didn't work out,' she said softly. 'With enough time, I might be able to turn up a similar opportunity, but… Apparently my sister Agatha wrote to Mama telling her that her nursery-maid has taken ill and she needs help with the children. Although otherwise barely speaking to me, Mama informed me she intends to send me to Aggie as soon as I finish Carlisle's plates. With no money of my own, and nowhere else to go, I can't see any way to avoid it. Once there… I shall probably be entombed there forever. Certainly neither of my parents want me back here.'

Horrified by the prospect, Rafe said, 'What of your young man? Has he been so foolish as to withdraw his suit? Dishonourable to lead you on if his intentions were not serious!'

She uttered a strained laugh. 'It was nothing like that! There's no young man you need skewer on your saber for breaking a promise.'

'Then what?' he demanded.

At first, he thought she might put him off again. Instead, abject despair on her face before she closed her eyes, she shook her head as tears began slipping silently down her cheeks.

This time Rafe couldn't restrain himself. Gathering her close, he held her against his chest. 'What happened, Mouse?' he murmured. 'We've always been friends. You know you can confide in me and it will go no further. And I will do anything in my power to help you.'

After a few moments, she pulled away. 'Very well, I'll tell you, but you mustn't laugh. During Aggie's Season, I met an older lady while looking through the South Sea room exhibit at the British Museum.

We stuck up a conversation, which led to a friendship, which led to our maintaining a correspondence when I returned to Edgerton. She, like me, had a great interest in the natural world and enjoyed discussing it. She admired my sketches and encouraged me to continue my explorations. When I wrote to her to inform her about Ian's demise, she invited me to come live with her, as the elderly cousin who has long been her companion does not share any of these interests. After returning from Thornthwaite, I wrote to accept her offer. And heard nothing. I've just received a reply from her cousin informing me that Lady Fallsham passed away last month.'

'I'm so sorry,' Rafe murmured, too shocked by the nature of her 'prospect' to manage more.

'If I had more time, I could advertise for another position as a companion, if I could obtain funds to do so and find some way to insert such a notice in the London papers. I'd do better fetching and carrying for some older lady than putting up with the spoiled tantrums of my sister's children. It would have to be a companion, for even in my desperation, I couldn't in good faith advertise myself as a governess. With Mama believing "Book learning is of no use to a lady" and "Gentlemen deplore clever females", I was never taught more than the basic arithmetic necessary to running a household, to say nothing of more scholarly endeavours. My skill at the piano is limited and my needlework is such an abomination that, with Carlisle wasting so much of the estate's blunt, Mama barred me from further use of embroidery thread as a means of economy. I would have better luck cutting my hair, stealing some of Carlisle's old clothing and going off as a soldier; I'm a pretty good shot. But that's unlikely to happen, either. Options for a female are so limited.'

Swallowing hard, she turned to pat Rafe's hand. 'Sorry. I didn't mean to burden you with my difficulties. You have enough of your own, working long hours and saving every penny to put Thornthwaite back in order. Having cried on your sleeve, I'm better now. And speaking of better, we should return before Mama can contrive some excuse to declare me compromised.'

She turned to go, but Rafe caught her hand, his heart aching for her distress, for the bravery with which she pulled herself back from despair and tried to dismiss her nearly hopeless situation.

At she turned back to look at him inquiringly, compelled to seize the moment despite having not yet prepared a pretty speech, he began, 'There's another alternative to a life of servitude with Aggie—or hiring yourself out as a companion or governess. Or going for a soldier, God forbid! Marry me, Mouse. We've always dealt well together. We understand each other. We've been congenial companions since childhood, and I don't think the years we've been apart will have changed that. I admire and respect the talent your family underestimates and the wit your mother disparages. You could help me manage the estate and I'd be happy to let you study and sketch as much as you like, at least as much as you would have been able to do as a companion to Lady Fallsham.'

He halted, but as she remained frozen, her expression unreadable, he hurried on, 'To be honest, I need you. The job of restoring Thornthwaite will be long and difficult. And… I truly want you. You know I care about you. I've treasured you since you were a child. I can imagine us growing old together, a life lived in happy contentment. So…would you do me the honour of becoming my wife?' he concluded, belatedly dropping to one knee before her.

She looked down at him, still silent and motionless. Until that moment not realizing how much he truly wanted her to accept, he said, 'Is the prospect of marrying me…repugnant to you? Tell me honestly. I would never push you to do something you found… distasteful.'

Finally seeming to find her voice, she shook her head, saying faintly. 'It's not repugnant. Not at all.'

Encouraged, he said, 'I know my declaration may seem sudden, but I assure you, I've been giving the matter considerable thought since I first mentioned the possibility of our marriage that day at Thornthwaite. I would be honoured, relieved and very grateful if you'd at least seriously consider wedding me. Helping care for Thornthwaite, which I know you love. Taking care of each other. I think Ian would have approved.'

He shouldn't have added that, seeming to use her love for his brother to press her. But the more he talked about it, the more he wanted to persuade her to accept.

There'd be no tedious search later to find a competent, compatible lady to wed. No worries that some duplicitous female would echo all his thoughts and opinions just to win herself a countess's coronet. Marry Mouse, whose sterling character had been proved over the long years of their association, and he was certain they could create a happy life together.

Surely she'd conclude that remaining at Thornthwaite with him was preferable to being at the beck and call of a family that neither valued nor appreciated her.

That fact alone would be enough to prompt any other female into jumping to accept his offer. But odd, independent Juliana would make up her own mind. He couldn't pressure her, even if he'd wanted to.

'Please, get up, Rafe,' she said at last.

At least it wasn't an outright refusal. Trying to remain optimistic, he said, 'Take as much time as you need to consider. And don't worry; I won't breathe a word to your family, I know your mother would have you drugged tonight and onto a coach to Thornthwaite with a vicar waiting at the door if she knew I'd offered marriage. This will remain only between us until you make your decision. Though it will be a severe blow to my self-esteem if you decide you prefer tending your sister's children to marriage with me,' he added, trying to lighten the fraught moment.

'Are you sure, Rafe? Wed me now and you would be giving up any chance of marrying later someone for whom you felt a true passion. If…if after losing Thalia, you should encounter another such lady.'

Thalia. At the mention of her name, a brief but shockingly intense burst of the agony he thought long buried seared him, rendering him momentarily silent.

Shaking his head to clear it, he managed a smile. 'I'm not at all interested in another grand passion; one monumental heartache was quite enough for a lifetime, thank you! Having recovered from that unfortunate episode, what I wish for now in a wife is a woman I can respect and admire, someone who shares my preference for the country over London, someone intelligent, congenial and willing to work with me to restore Thornthwaite to what it once was. Someone, in short, exactly like you—who offers the additional blessing of being a lady for whom I already have a deep affection. With whom I share a friendship that is so much more comfortable and enduring than any "grand passion." But having sprung this declaration upon you with so little notice, I'll not press you for an answer before you are ready.'

Deciding it was time to retreat with whatever tattered dignity he could salvage, he offered his arm, ready to escort her back to the house.

But as she laid her hand on his sleeve, the contact sent a shiver over his skin, strong enough to make him catch his breath and spark a response deep in his loins. His Mouse was a woman now indeed, and he was shocked to realize again that he desired her as much as he wanted her.

She wrapped her fingers around his arm, intensifying the sensations coursing through him, and gazed up into his eyes.

Did she feel the connection sparking between them, he wondered, stunned by that possibility and the unexpected power of his response to her. He stood as if rooted, gazing back down at her, unwilling to move a muscle and risk breaking the sensual bond between them.

Finally she released her grip. As he struggled to refrain from reaching for her again, she said, 'Very well, Rafe. I will marry you.'

A surprisingly strong burst of elation filled him. 'You will? Are *you* sure?'

Her face clouded briefly and she closed her eyes, drawing in a sharp breath as if fighting some fierce inner struggle. He feared for an anxious moment she might withdraw her acceptance before she nodded. 'Yes, I will marry you.'

Deciding to overlook the fact that she hadn't confirmed she *was* sure, he said, 'Excellent. I suppose I must find your father and formally ask for your hand. When do you wish to marry? If it's agreeable to you, I'd like to remove you from Edgerton Manor as soon as possible.'

'I can agree to that!'

He smiled. 'I'd carry you off across my saddle bow this very day, if it wouldn't cause so much gossip. It's too far to go to London for a special license, but only a day's ride to obtain one from the bishop. We could be married at the parish church within the week. But before I leave to obtain one, I'd like to escort you and Baxter to stay at the Dower House until I can bring you into Thorne Hall as my bride. I don't want you to ever have to deal with your mother again.'

She nodded. 'A blessing devoutly to be wished.'

'We shall do it, then. You can pack some necessities while I speak with your father.'

It was only natural that she might have reservations, he reassured himself. For years she'd considered herself pledged to his brother, and her alternative upon losing him hadn't been marriage, but spinsterhood. But he'd make sure she never regretted choosing him. He'd do all he could to help her flourish and to make up to her for having been belittled, demeaned and criticized all her life by a family that didn't understand her or value her interests or her talents as he did.

'It's a bargain, then.' He leaned down to kiss her

hand—and on impulse, instead brushed a brief kiss across that tempting mouth. She sighed, her lips softening under his.

Rafe made himself pull away before the surge of desire her tentative reaction engendered induced him to deepen the kiss.

He reminded himself that she was still an innocent. Though the response he'd just sensed in her made him confident she would be ready at some point for intimacy, he would take his time and initiate her slowly. She'd already spent too much of her life pressured to conform to something she didn't want.

And he wanted her to want him. Was he being foolish?

Brushing away the thought, he offered his arm again and she took it, sparking another delicious tingle of attraction. Making Juliana his wife promised a wealth of previously unimagined possibilities.

Best of all, his heart would be *safe*; the support, stable affection and warm friendship they shared would never turn into the sort of dangerous, soul-shattering emotion he'd barely survived once and never wished to experience again.

He'd wed his best possible choice in only a week. He could hardly wait.

Chapter Four

Seven days later, Juliana stood nervously in her bed-chamber in the Dower House while Baxter pinned the circlet of silk roses atop her crown of braided hair. 'Now, you truly look like a bride,' the maid said proudly. 'And such a pretty one!'

Giving her image in the pier-glass a quick glance, Juliana acknowledged that she did appear to best advantage in her newest gown, the high waist and slender skirt making her short form appear taller and the forest-green hue complementing her soft brown hair and pale skin far better than the virginal white dress her mother had tried to foist on her.

She'd have only a few more minutes to calm herself and gather her thoughts before Mama, restrained from entering her chamber by the assurance that her maid was fully competent to assist her in dressing, would burst in to escort her to the carriage that would take her and her parents to the medieval village church.

The church where, little more than a month ago,

she'd first seen Rafe again, and he'd shaken her to the core and scattered her tidy assumptions about her future like spillikins flung down by an exuberant child. The church where he'd now be waiting to make her his wife.

A wave of mingled anxiety and delight sent a shiver through her.

At least there now *was* an anticipatory eagerness to temper the anxiety, she thought ruefully.

Thank heaven Rafe had suggested returning her to the Dower House the fraught day she accepted his proposal, removing her from what would have been a week of her mother's commands, instructions, and remonstrations on her shortcomings she was happy to have done without. Her father's initial protest that the village would think it scandalous for the bride to reside on the groom's property before the wedding she immediately squelched. During her engagement to Ian, she reminded her parents, she'd spent several months at the Dower House with only her maid as chaperone with their blessing—including ten days after she'd informed them that Rafe had returned from the army. Under her mother's barrage of chatter, which alternated between expressions of delight to Rafe and cautions to her about maintaining proper behaviour, she'd escaped Edgerton Manor.

She was soon to discover another reason to be grateful about relocating to the Dower House. But initially, as she rode with Rafe back to Thornthwaite, the relief over the grim future of family servitude from which he'd rescued her slowly turned to a feeling of panic.

Had she saved herself? Or had succumbing to his proposal in a moment of weakness condemned her to a lifetime of misery of another sort, having to forever restrain her emotions to guard against a revival of the love she'd suppressed, watching every word and action to ensure she never trespassed the bounds of friendship?

Of course, they had been separated for six long years; war might have made him into a different man than the one she'd once cherished. A man far easier to resist.

That reassuring thought faded, though, as she recalled that in the ten days she'd spent immediately upon his return, helping him sort through the problems he must address at Thornthwaite, she'd seen no evidence that the individual she so admired had fundamentally changed.

Whatever the current character of the man she'd pledged to marry, her acceptance could not be undone. She would never subject Rafe to the embarrassment of being left at the altar, even if she had somewhere else to go.

Still, by the time she spied the lights of the Dower House in the distance, she was almost speechless with anxiety, alarm and regret.

After turning the horses over to a groom, Rafe took her numb hand and walked her up the entry stairs. Pausing inside the door, he said, 'Now that we are to be wed, I can in good conscience do what I've been tempted to since almost the moment I first saw you at the church a month ago.'

So agitated she scarcely comprehended his words, she fumbled, 'D-do what?'

Smiling, he drew her closer. 'This,' he murmured. And kissed her.

At the soft brush of his mouth against hers, shock zinged from her head to her toes, immediately followed by a blaze of warmth that had her pressing closer. Murmuring encouragement, he deepened the kiss.

The hot wet touch of his tongue, gently probing her lips, sent another blast of sensation through her. Her hands going up to clasp his neck, she opened to him.

Exquisite was her last conscious thought before her mind yielded to sheer sensual pleasure.

Heat fired from deep within as his tongue caressed her mouth and laved her tongue with his own. Starbursts of delight exploded from that contact to radiate through her body, tightening her nipples, setting a pulse throbbing at her center.

She had no idea how long he kissed her, only that she would have continued the contact forever, had he not broken away to enfold her against him.

Bedazzled, she laid her head on his chest, feeling the drumming of his heart, hearing his breaths, as uneven and gasping as her own. Her brain still incapable of producing speech, she simply leaned into his embrace, feeling she would have been content to remain there forever.

At length, with a broken chuckle, he gently pulled away from her. 'Well…that was quite a revelation. I was going to ask if my kiss pleased rather than alarmed you, but I suppose there's no need, is there?'

Still speechless, she shook her head.

He gazed intently at her for a moment, then shook his head wonderingly. 'Mouse, Mouse,' he murmured, bringing one of her hands up to kiss. 'I think we are going to deal very well together.'

'Will you kiss me again?' she asked, finally finding her voice.

He uttered a sound somewhere between a laugh and a groan. 'No, minx, I will not! Kiss me like that again, and bishop's license or no, I'd be hard-pressed to keep myself from carrying you to your chamber and claiming you as my bride this very night!'

She smiled shyly. 'Would that be…so awful?'

'Don't tempt me! No, Mouse, Ian did badly enough by you. I shall wait until we are well and truly wed before I make you my wife.' He smiled. 'An event I now anticipate with even greater eagerness.'

'So there can be no more kissing until the wedding?' she protested.

'Well… I won't promise that.' Touching the tip of his finger to her nose, he whispered, 'One kiss per day. Just one. To remember. And anticipate.'

'I will hold you to that.'

'Until tomorrow, then. I'll stop to see you before I set off for the bishop's. While I'm gone, consult with Baxter and Mrs Henderson about any changes you want to make in the household. I'm afraid funds won't permit taking you away for a wedding trip, but I'd like you to feel at home at Thornthwaite from the very first day.'

She shook her head. 'I wouldn't want to go any-where else.'

'Good. Until tomorrow.'

He leaned towards her, and for a moment she thought he might kiss her again despite his avowal. But even as she leaned towards him eagerly, he drew back, shaking his head again.

'No, I shall be prudent. Goodnight, my almost-wife.'

He left her then, standing still bemused in the en-tryway. She watched him ride away, feeling energy, vitality and comfort leave with him.

Only then did she realize that while she'd been kiss-ing him, she'd been aware of nothing but the intense delight of his nearness. Wholly consumed by delicious sensation, driven only by the imperative to get closer, kiss deeper, her whole body charged with a compulsion to touch and caress him.

There had been no fear, no worry, no anxiety. No upswelling of emotion—only sheer physical response.

And Rafe...had seemed pleased by that response.

She realized in that moment, with an upsurge of relief and anticipation, that physical desire might be the answer to the dilemma of wedding him. If Rafe were in fact still the man she'd once adored, by offering the passionate *lovemaking* he seemed to actually want from her, she could forestall any resurgence of passionate *devotion*.

He'd made it only too clear when he asked her to marry him that, having recovered from his "grand passion," he had no interest in experiencing such intense feelings again. Discovering she harbored any such emotion for him would doubtless cause him chagrin and dismay.

Had he truly recovered from his passion? For an instant after she mentioned Thalia's name, his face had gone blank and his body trembled. Despite what he'd assured her, it seemed not all the pain had dissipated.

All the more reason for her to concentrate on enjoying his caresses and closeness, so she might avoid emotion altogether, letting any feelings be buried beneath the overwhelming pressure of desire.

If occasionally those feelings tried to bubble up

again when he was not near enough to distract her, she'd just push them down and concentrate on the tasks at hand. It would take much diligent work to fully re-store Thornthwaite to what it had been, a task she was eager to help him with.

Her resolve strengthened by those reflections, she gave her image in the pier-glass mirror one last glance and put out of mind the lingering doubt. She'd focus on the delights ahead—the quiet ceremony in the church, the enjoyment of celebrating their lord's nuptials with the estate's tenants and then...best, most delicious of all, being able to give herself fully into Rafe's skill-ful hands.

A wave of warmth tingled through her at the thought.

She *could* do this, as she'd reassured herself that first night. Even if he still was every inch the man of her girlhood dreams, she could become Rafe's wife without ruining their friendship or causing heartache or distress to either of them. Hadn't she already tested that hypothesis when Rafe returned after obtaining the marriage license, claiming one kiss each of the last four days before the wedding? Each one more exqui-site, longer, more intense than the last.

Each one dispelling fear and blanking her mind to everything but pleasure.

Well, now she *must* do it.

No matter what the consequences turned out to be.

* * *

A clatter at the door followed by her mother's high-pitched tones put an end to her reverie. Thankfully, her sister was too preoccupied with her offspring and her husband's estate was located too far away for her to manage the trip to Thornthwaite in time, but she'd been unable to come up with a reason to exclude her parents. Little as the attendance of either of them would add to her day.

Certainly not her mother's gloating pride that she'd finally married off her disappointing daughter to a husband whose high rank would impress her friends. Or the presence of the father who would walk her down the aisle, who'd participated so little in her life that she might as well be escorted by a stranger.

Fortunately, the church would be filled with villagers and tenants, rallied by Baxter's cousin and new estate manager Mr Sterling. She'd come to know many of them during her visits to Ian, especially during the last year while she tried to minimize the damages the venal Taylor was inflicting on her distracted fiancé's estate. She *was* looking forward to beginning her new life surrounded by Thornthwaite's people, watching them enjoy the festivities and ready to accept their congratulations and good wishes.

And then, tonight, would come the best of all…

'Juliana, are you ready at last?' her mother asked as she swept into the room. 'Your father is impatient, the carriage is waiting and we don't want the horses to stand too long!'

'Yes, Mama, I'm coming,' she replied, stepping into the pelisse Baxter held out for her.

Lady Waverton looked her up and down critically. 'You'll do, I suppose. Though it would have been more proper to have worn the virginal white I recommended—though when have you ever followed my advice? Well, the green does suit you, and I suppose having known you so many years, Thornthwaite is well aware of your…eccentricities.'

Reminding herself she need endure only a few more hours of her mother's presence and then might afterwards see her only as frequently as courtesy demanded, Juliana bit her lip against a reply and walked out.

Her mother filling the short journey to St. Andrews Church with chatter to her father, Juliana was able to avoid any further conversation. Her senses sharpened as she stepped out of the carriage and entered the nave, soft colored light from the ancient windows dividing the stone space into dim brightness and dark shadow. But once she spotted Rafe standing beside the priest at the altar, the mingled voices hushed to a murmur, faces blurred, and she was conscious only of *him,* watching her walk towards him, a gentle smile on his face.

Despite her best efforts, a swell of emotion tightened her chest.

On this day she'd never believed possible, she would pledge her life to him. Even if she must never offer her heart.

Beating back emotion, she concentrated on taking even breaths as she proceeded calmly down the aisle. Yes, they would share a life, but nothing else between them had changed. Rafe hadn't experienced some momentous awakening of the heart; in wedding her, he looked to obtain a congenial wife and rescue a valued friend. Only that—no matter how exultant the tiny voice deep within that refused to be completely silenced.

But she was allowed to be happy, she told herself as they exchanged vows. She would be able to assist her dearest childhood friend revive his inheritance, help him finally offer real assistance to tenants too long neglected, and provide support and companionship to a man for whom she still cared deeply.

Hopefully, the lovemaking she anticipated with such eagerness would provide him a son and heir as well. Many sons, if they were so blessed. She'd not enjoyed tending her sister's indulged offspring, but the idea of watching over children born of their union, little beings who carried Rafe's essence within them that she'd be able to love openly and completely with all the passion she possessed…the prospect sent a wave of warmth welling up from deep within.

Yes, as his friend, helpmate and mother of his children, she could be happy.

After signing the parish register, they walked out to the cheers of the guests as they crossed to the green, where the wedding feast had been set out. Despite the estate's limited resources, Juliana was pleased that, with the help of Baxter and Sterling, they were able to offer their guests ale and a respectable selection of victuals.

Her mother, of course, was the first to rush over and seize her hand, her father trailing behind her. 'What a splendid day!' she enthused. 'We could not be happier, could we, Waverton, that dear Thornthwaite recognized his duty to us—and to Juliana—and wed her after all!'

While her father mumbled something incoherent, Rafe gave her mother a smile that didn't reach his eyes. 'Hardly only out of duty,' he said, clasping Juliana's hand in a tighter grip. 'I consider myself fortunate to have won so lovely and talented a bride.'

Lady Waverton batted his shoulder. 'What a charmer you are, to be sure. But 'tis my daughter who has the luck. Only think, Waverton, Juliana a *countess*! Who could be more unlikely? I only hope she doesn't cause you any…concern if she ever accompanies you to London.'

'I'll endeavour not to embarrass Thornthwaite if he is compelled to bring me to the City,' Juliana said evenly. Of course her mother would assume only duty would force a man as attractive as Rafe to marry her odd and disappointing daughter. She'd not even offered the concession that he might *like* her, she thought bitterly.

But determined not to let the woman spoil what was indeed a splendid day, Juliana said, 'You must excuse us so we may greet our other guests.'

'I would never find you an embarrassment—here or in London,' Rafe murmured as he maneuvered her away. 'Though I hope you already know that.'

She gave him a tremulous smile. 'I'll certainly do my best not to be.'

Shaking the hands that were offered, accepting the smiling congratulations of the tenants, they walked to the head of the table, where Rafe lifted a mug of ale. 'To my bride. And with her help, to prosperous days ahead for Thornthwaite and all who work her land.'

With cries of 'hear, hear,' the toast was drunk. Giving the crowd a wink, Rafe said, 'Now, for something even sweeter.' Depositing his mug, he bent down to give her a lingering kiss.

Her body responding instantly, Juliana barely heard the laughter, cheers and applause that erupted. Yes, *this* she could give him, without threat of embarrassment or regret.

All the kisses he desired. And so much more.

He released her, grinning broadly. Her cheeks

warmed with desire, her initial embarrassment at his public display of affection faded as she looked around at the merry, smiling faces. People who already accepted her and approved her taking her place among them.

Already Thornthwaite felt more like home than Edgerton Manor ever had.

She would revel in this celebration, delighted by the tenant's expressions of joy and support, warmed by Rafe's defense of her to her family, encouraged by this glimpse of what her future would be. And let sweet anticipation build about the wedding night to come.

Chapter Five

Several hours later, Rafe took Juliana's hand and waved as they bade their guests goodbye. The Wavertons had left shortly after the first toasts—probably not deeming the modest fare being offered his guests sufficient to tempt their discerning palates. The rest of the guests, having no such dainty scruples, continued to eat and imbibe with enthusiasm.

'I think it went off well, don't you?' she asked as they walked into Thorne Hall. 'Jerny and Westerbrook have brought their fiddles, so there should be dancing and merriment far into the night.'

'At least as long as the ale holds out. I do hope you didn't use the last of the estate's cash reserves to provide for this.'

Her eyes widening, she said, 'Of course not! I only—'

He put a hand to her lips. 'I'm teasing, Mouse. I'm proud of what a fine wedding feast you were able to organize, despite Thornthwaite's limited resources—

while expending far less to provide it than I would have thought possible.'

To his satisfaction, her face pinked with pleasure. 'Baxter and Sterling deserve much of the credit. And the merchants in the village, especially the brewmaster, who furnished the ale at cost.'

'Perhaps, but you were the one who planned and organized it. Already I've proof of what a clever lad I was, persuading you to marry me.'

It seemed to him that her smile dimmed, but before he could inquire what he'd said to distress her, she shook her head, her smile brightening again. 'And I know how clever I was to accept you…with our wedding night ahead.' Her smile fading, a blush tinged her cheeks. 'We've not gone beyond kissing, but I will not deny you your full conjugal rights, if…if you wish to claim them tonight. I know I'm not…attractive enough to inspire desire but I will endeavour to please you.'

'Did your mother tell you that tarradiddle, too?' Rafe asked, a rush of anger filling him at this new example of Lady Waverton's disparagement. 'I assure you, she could not be more mistaken! Men are enticed by more female features than just blond hair, a large bosom and rounded hips. Features like the slim beauty of your perfectly proportioned figure,' he said, running a finger from her shoulder down to her hip, delighted that her eyes widened and a gasp escaped her. 'The satin feel of your hair,' he continued, pulling through his fingers a strand that had come loose from her braided crown. 'The porcelain purity of your skin—' he stroked her cheek '—and those great, wide, all-seeing brown eyes, with such mystery and intelligence in their depths. But perhaps most of all,' he murmured, bending close, 'those plush, pert lips that make me want to kiss them every time I look at you.'

'Oh,' she said in a small voice, seeming disconcerted by his praise. But she recovered quickly, angling her head up. 'Then kiss me.'

He did, long and slow and deep, the mingling of tongues and taste of her now familiar, compelling, and this time, ah, this time, he could allow the desire her kisses inspired full rein.

Perhaps not full, he amended as he broke the kiss and took her hand to lead her upstairs. She was an innocent, unused to lovemaking. He must restrain himself and go slowly. Not for the world would he allow rampaging desire to frighten or hurt her; he wanted her to continue to respond to his touch with the same passionate enthusiasm she had for his kisses.

She halted abruptly as they entered the hallway leading to the bedchambers, her eyes going wide and her expression uncertain.

'I had Baxter transfer your things into the chamber that adjoins mine,' he said reassuringly. 'She'll be waiting to help you into your night-rail. I'll join you there in a few minutes.'

Nodding her consent, with a little huff of determination, she opened her chamber door and disappeared. Rafe entered his own room, shrugging out of his coat and making fast work of removing shoes, breeches, waistcoat, shirt and cravatte. Donning his banyan, his body throbbing with anticipation, he walked over to knock on the adjoining door.

He entered to find her sitting at her dressing table, Baxter brushing out the long brown hair whose sheen glistened in the candlelight. As Rafe held out his hand, Baxter curtseyed and handed him the brush. 'A goodnight to you, my lord, and to you, my dear lady,' she said, smiling as she exited the room.

Juliana sighed as Rafe continued to ply the brush, stroking through the soft curls that fell like a curtain to her waist. 'You have the most glorious hair,' he murmured, leaning down to kiss the top of her head. He moved the heavy mane aside and bent to place soft, damp kisses on the bared skin of her neck. She leaned into him, then accepted his hand as he helped her up and walked her to the bed.

'If I do anything you don't like, that alarms or hurts, you must tell me to stop,' he said as he sat her gently on the bed, then loosened the ties of her night-rail and slid it sideways to bare her shoulder. His fingers trembled now with the force of the desire thrumming through him, a roaring tide he must somehow restrain.

'Don't stop,' she whispered.

Encouraged, he laid her back against the pillows. She rose slightly to allow him to pull the garment from under her, up and over her head, though not wanting to alarm her, he kept the banyan belted, hiding the evidence of his own desire. 'Beautiful,' he murmured, devouring her with his eyes, desperately eager to claim the body she freely offered him.

Sitting beside her, he reached over to caress her breasts, hissing a breath as his body hardened further when her nipples peaked. Then she gasped and shuddered.

Dropping his hands, he moved back. *Slow down,* his brain tried to insist to his rampaging senses.

She seized his hands and placed them back at her breasts. 'Please, don't stop! That is…if…if you are truly sure you want me. If I am…enough.'

'More than enough, my sweet.'

She gave him a trembling smile. 'Then, I want more. I want…everything.'

Relief and delight joined the desire coursing through him. 'Then, dear wife, you shall have it all.'

Next morning, Rafe woke in a lazy haze of sensual satisfaction. Seeing Juliana curled beside him, the warmth amplified. His darling bride's innocent but tender responses had thrilled him. Despite his initial intention to initiate her into the wonders of lovemaking slowly, in the end, he had given her 'everything'.

He frowned; had he been carried away by her gentle submission to his increasingly passionate caresses? In the rational light of day, free from the magic of moonlight and desire, he realized she wouldn't have stopped him, whatever qualms she felt. With a wave of concern, he hoped he hadn't hurt or alarmed her.

Before that worrisome thought went any further, she yawned and slowly opened her eyes. Drowsiness disappeared as she spied him leaning over her. 'Last night was *wonderful*!' she murmured, giving him a rapturous smile.

Relieved, Rafe grinned and dipped her a bow. 'I'm so glad to have pleased you. Had your mother alarmed you with horror stories?'

'No, she said nothing except "A lady always allows her husband's pleasures". But as you know, I've done much observation in nature. The female of various species does not always appear to enjoy mating. To hear a mare scream, one might believe the business painful and unpleasant.'

Rafe laughed, half embarrassed, half astonished at her candor. Grasping for a response, he settled for, 'I'm glad to know this female didn't find it…too unpleasant.'

'There was some…discomfort at first,' she allowed. 'But nothing that would prompt me to scream like a mare.'

He laughed again, wondering if he should tell her

that human couples in the throes of rapture often screamed for quite other reasons.

Before he could decide, her smile faded and she looked thoughtful. 'I wondered…'

'What?' he asked, bemused by her previous disclosures and having absolutely no idea what she might say next.

'I wondered if we might…try it again? Just to be sure my first impression of its exceeding pleasure was not erroneous?'

His grin widened. 'Of course. And this time there should be little discomfort for you, only unspoiled pleasure.'

She gave him a glance that was pure, seductive Eve. 'Show me.'

For her first experience, he'd settled for only most the basic lovemaking, wanting to take her maidenhead at once and then let her body rest and recover, so that their future coupling might bring her only enjoyment. This time, he wanted it to be all for her.

He began with the kissing at which she already excelled. After a satisfying interval of deeply exploring her mouth, he moved his lips slowly down her body, nipping her shoulders and elbows, licking each finger. Holding in rigid check a body already primed for release, he noted her hardened nipples and moved his mouth to give them full and complete concentration while with his hand he massaged her hips and her mound.

As her breathing grew more labored and she began to twist beneath him, he urged her legs wider and slipped a hand down to trace the tender skin of her upper thighs. And finally, suckling harder, he let his fingers caress the sensitive bit of flesh at her center.

She reached up, as if to pull him over and into her. Much as he yearned to bury himself, promising his raging senses he would allow them fulfillment later, he bent instead to lave with his lips what his fingers had just caressed while moving those fingers into her passage to massage and withdraw, massage and withdraw.

Her breathing accelerated as she arched upward to him, moments later, and writhed as her climax overcame her. Leaving his fingers within, he leaned up to capture her cries in his mouth. Then, lay back on his pillows and cradled her against his chest, listening to the sweet sounds as her gasping breaths slowed and steadied.

He held her as she dozed, filled with tenderness and a masculine pride of knowing that he'd satisfied her. He still burned for his own release, but that could wait.

A few moments later she woke on a long sigh. Propping herself on his chest, she looked down at him with wonder. 'Oh. My. I never observed anything like *that* in nature.'

He chuckled. 'I'm no naturalist, but I understand that some such stimulation can occur in other species.'

'But…you are still just…*stimulated.*' He jumped, suppressing a groan as she moved her hand to caress his rigid member. 'Is it not time for you to be fulfilled?'

His body, already hard, quickened further. 'If my lady so desires.'

'She does.' Rolling to her back, she urged him over her, wrapping her legs around him as he entered her hot, slick passage. Groaning, no longer able to control passion too long restrained, instead of a slow, steady build of momentum, he found himself thrusting wildly.

By now he was too far gone in ecstasy to notice much, but she seemed to be encouraging him, lifting her hips to meet his thrusts, grasping his neck and pulling his head down for an endless kiss as he moved within her. She cried out again as he reached his own peak in a towering, body-and-soul-shattering intensity of release.

Afterwards, as they lay together in the contented haze after lovemaking, she snuggled against his shoulder with a sigh. 'Ah, had I known how delightful this could be, I might have pressed Ian harder for a wedding.'

'Minx,' he reproved, suddenly, possessively glad that wedding had never happened.

'Though I wouldn't have pushed him, not really. Not when I knew—' She stopped suddenly, eyes widening in alarm, then pasted a smile on her lips. 'It was delightful, husband. Can I tell you how contented I am to be your wife?'

'Gladly.' But something tickled the back of his mind, something about his brother. 'You wouldn't have pressed Ian because he was so…distressed those last months?'

She gazed at him for a moment. 'You…truly don't know?'

'Know what?'

She sat up, looking troubled—though to his delight, seeming entirely unconcerned that her movements caused the bed linens to fall to her waist, presenting him with the delightful view of the pert breasts he'd so recently tasted, whose pale skin still showed the marks of his passion.

Forcing his thoughts back to his brother, said, 'What about Ian should I have known?'

She sat for a few moments staring distractedly into the distance. 'I suppose I cannot now claim there was nothing?'

'There must have been. For you to regret having mentioned it now. For him to have been so "distressed". Can you not tell me?'

She remained silent while, both concern and curiosity now fully aroused, he checked the impulse to press her further. She would tell him, or not, but he must not try to force it from her.

Finally, shaking her head, she said, 'I suppose it is not a breach of his confidence to tell you now, with him gone. I know you loved him, too. But you must promise not to reveal what I tell you to anyone. And you must doubly promise that whatever I say, it will not alter the love you had for your brother.'

Rafe shrugged, puzzled, alarmed and unable to imagine what she could be so reluctant to reveal. 'Ian was my brother, and I did—do—love him. Nothing you could tell me would change that.'

'Very well—if you promise.' She heaved a sigh, her forehead puckered as if she weren't sure how to begin.

'Go on,' he coaxed.

'Ian…was not like most men. He didn't find women… appealing.'

It took a moment before her meaning penetrated. Shocked, Rafe said, 'He was a *molly boy*?'

'Never call him that!' she said sharply. 'One doesn't choose who or how one loves—as we both know well!'

A vision of Thalia flashed into his head, provoking another swift, fleeting stab of the pain from which he'd thought himself long ago recovered. Pushing away the image, he focused on putting together the clues Juliana had given him.

'I never guessed…never even imagined,' Rafe

said slowly, shaking his head. 'How could I not have known?'

'Ian loved you and cherished your opinion. He would have wanted to keep the truth from you, more than from anyone else. It would have destroyed him to have you think…less of him.'

'How did *you* know?' he demanded, torn between angry and aghast that she seemed to have known his brother so much better, it turned out, than he had.

'Whenever I could escape the house, I wandered the fields and forests, observing the wildlife, sketching and collecting specimens. Remember the little fishing hut, down by river that separates Thornthwaite land from Edgerton? We all played there as children, even Ian, though he was not much for fishing and preferred exploring the banks for interesting rocks.'

'Yes, of course. He'd slip away from our long riding expeditions, too, and hide away there, reading his books.'

'Exactly. While at Eton, Ian met another student with whom he shared…much in common. He often accompanied Ian to Thornthwaite on school breaks and continued to visit here frequently even after they left university.'

Searching his memory, Rafe pulled out a name. 'Eric Dickson? I always thought their friendship an odd pairing. I recall Eric being enthusiastic about joining us for the riding, hunting and sports Ian disdained.'

'Perhaps. But they also shared a deep love of literature and painting. And…a deep love. More than just a platonic one, as I learned one fall after you'd left for the army. I'd gone to the fishing hut to collect a gathering basket I'd left there and discovered them… being intimate.'

Rafe swallowed hard, still having difficulty getting his mind around that revelation. 'You must have been shocked.' He certainly was. 'What did you do?'

'Ran away, initially, uncertain what to think. Sheltered from life as I'd been, I hadn't previously known such things were…possible. Ian sought me out few days later, after Eric's departure. Apologetic, miserable, he wanted to explain. He said he knew he must have lost my respect and affection but begged me to keep his secret.'

'And you promised to do so?'

'Of course, and until this morning, I have. I also assured him that my…discovery did not alter the affection and esteem in which I'd always held him. How could it? From my own experience, I knew that we are what we are. Years and years of Mama haranguing me, criticizing, correcting, couldn't turn me into a perfect young lady like Aggie. The daughter she wanted me to be. How could I fault Ian for being who he was?'

She exhaled a little sigh, then continued, 'He also confided that he'd dreaded being married to Aggie and had been enormously relieved when she found another husband. We agreed then and there that bowing to our parents' desire for us to wed instead would work well for us both. Ian would be spared having to marry some unknown female, forcing himself into an intimacy that repelled him and having to constantly pretend to be something he wasn't. Making a respectable marriage would free me from my family's control and let me continue to be who I was as well.'

'But…you were willing to accept a *mariage blanche*?' Rafe asked, frowning.

She shrugged. 'I was a bit sad to abandon the idea of children, but that was the only disadvantage. I'd gain a safe and comfortable position while also being able to protect a friend about whom I cared deeply. Ian could continue to discreetly see the person he loved; I could enjoy my sketching, my studies and oversee Thornthwaite, a task that Ian didn't much enjoy, to ensure that it would pass to you and your heirs in good form.'

Rafe's frown deepened. 'It still wasn't a fair bargain for you! You deserved more—passion as well as companionship.'

She shook her head. 'I never expected passion. I wasn't the sort of girl to inspire it, as my mother always told me.'

'I think we've just proved her wrong about that,' Rafe said acidly.

Juliana smiled and touched his lips with a gentle fin-

ger. 'Thank you for that. But, not knowing then what
I know now, it would have worked...'

'So why didn't it? I can see why Ian might have been
distressed before you discovered his secret. But secure
in the bargain you'd made—however unfair to you I
think it—knowing you would protect him and permit
him to continue with his...relationship, why did he
fall into such a despondency that you never married?'

'Because early last spring, Eric was killed in an
accident. Ian was distraught. Not only had he lost the
person he loved most in the world, he'd lost all chance,
he believed, of being happy. Now a man grown, he felt
he might never encounter another of similar nature.
Someone with whom, though he could never share so
deep a love, he could at least quietly develop a relationship in which he could safely be himself. Now that he'd
inherited, as Earl, his movements were watched and
commented upon whenever he left Thornthwaite. If
his true nature were discovered, the shame and infamy
of it would destroy the reputation of both him and the
family. Nor could he bear the thought of the humili-
ation I would suffer as his wife. His initial grief for
Eric grew into a despondency that became ever deeper.
When he fell ill, I think he truly saw death as the only
way out of what for him had become an impossible
situation. His demise would free me from the possibility of disgrace, he told me. And he believed you would

be a better guardian of the estate, able to provide sons to carry on the family name as he could not.'

She paused, and when she began again, her voice dropped to little more than whisper. 'He would have been like other men if he could have. I know his…preferences tormented him, but we can only be who we are. I hope what I've revealed won't make you think less of him. I'll be furious with myself for stumbling into revealing his secret, if it does.'

'It's…a lot to take in,' Rafe admitted. 'But knowing the truth does make many puzzling factors clearer. Ian was my brother. I can't pretend to understand his inclinations, but it's not my place to judge them, either.'

He made a wry twist of the lips. 'After all, I know only too well how devastating it is to lose the one person who holds your whole heart. How hard it is to try to pick up the shattered pieces of your life and move on. I was lucky enough to have the army to carry me away to another place. Nothing like the gunfire of an approaching enemy to focus the mind on other things.'

'Like survival,' she said drily.

As all the shocking revelations settled in his mind, Rafe looked at Juliana with new appreciation. 'How kind and understanding you are indeed! To stand by and protect Ian to such a degree. Had the tragedy of Eric's death not intervened, you would have kept his secret, carried his burdens and allowed him to live his best, happiest life.'

'As he would have done for me as well, remember. He'd never have pushed me to become the conventional wife I could not be. We would both have been content, Ian relieved at knowing he'd done his duty, protecting the family name from disgrace and overseeing the estate until it passed to you and yours, while still being able to remain true to who he was.'

'It seems both my brother and I experienced emotional trials by fire. And you've stood by—to rescue us both.' He took her hand and kissed it. 'Shall we honour Ian by pledging a solemn vow to live our lives trying to make each other as happy as we can? As spouses, friends and lovers?'

She stared at him intently for a moment before slowly nodding. 'Very well. I pledge my solemn vow to seek your happiness as your wife, friend and lover.'

Feeling the warmth of affection for her welling up, he kissed her cheek. 'And I pledge my vow to you in return.'

After reaching up to give him a brief hug, she sat up. 'I suppose we've lazed about long enough. There must be a thousand tasks that need working on. We should get started.'

He shook his head at her. 'So industrious! But it's your first day as a married lady. I couldn't fund a holiday to London or a sojourn at a spa town, but I can at least declare this a day of leisure for you to do whatever you like.'

She gave him a provocative look. Laughing, he said, 'That, too, of course. But is there anything else?'

She tilted her head, as if considering. 'I'd like to take a long, leisurely ride about the estate, along the forest all the way to the river. I haven't been able to explore as I'd wish the last few years. My visits here were spent with Ian or visiting tenants and Mama has become more vigilant about preventing me from riding around Edgerton as I used to when we were children, when we all watched out for each other. I had Baxter pack my sketchbook when she gathered my things; I'd like to do some sketching, too.'

Before he could speak, she laughed. 'Not a very exciting prospect for a veteran soldier, used to the excitement of skirmishes in foreign lands! You see what a dull wife you've married.'

'Foreign lands are interesting, but the excitement of skirmishes is vastly overrated. I'd be happy to ride out. I've been through most of Thornthwaite, but haven't explored the woods between the two properties for years. Before you go, though, I'm famished. Shall we dress and break our fast before we order the horses?'

She smiled. 'I've an appetite to satisfy, too.'

Rafe felt a rush of heat. Did she make that double entendre intentionally? She'd been a virgin, but the love play from last night and her recent revelations showed she was no innocent. Deciding to take a chance and reply in kind, he said, 'I hope to satisfy… all your appetites.'

She gave him a roguish smile, confirming that she had intended exactly what he'd guessed. 'Then I shall be a very contented wife.'

'And I a contented husband,' he replied, feeling the happy truth of it deep in his bones. This 'convenient' marriage showed promise of being far more fulfilling that he'd ever imagined.

Strangely reluctant to leave her bed, Rafe made himself hop up, grab the banyan he'd cast onto the floor and toss it on. 'I'll leave you to Baxter's care and see you in the morning room.'

Juliana rose, naked, and walked over to embrace him. 'Thank you. For making our wedding day perfect. And our wedding night even better.'

The sight and feel of her lithe body pressed against him and the lingering kiss she gave him nearly dissuaded him from leaving after all. He had to force himself to remember that her body was still growing accustomed to the uses of passion and needed time to recover.

'It was perfect for me, too,' he told her, feeling awe and a tenderness blossom within him as he recognized the truth of that assurance.

'I'd better let you go, then.' She walked over to claim her robe, her slender hips swaying, her breasts gently bouncing, and donned the garment without haste.

Rafe marveled again at how unselfconscious she was about her body, seeming completely at ease to appear nude before him, even in the full light of day. At the same time, making no attempt to seduce or entice, as if she had no idea how powerfully her artless sensuality moved him.

Perhaps she didn't know.

That prospect was as arousing as it was surprising. Sternly he told himself he would have to wait until later to satisfy the desire she roused so readily. But his mind couldn't help sharing his body's enthusiasm about how passionately responsive his quiet little wife had turned out to be.

Chapter Six

Sketchbook stowed in her saddlebag, Juliana accepted the groom's leg up and turned her mount to join Rafe's as they set off down Thornthwaite's curving drive. Still in the glow of pleasure from last night and this morning, a swell of optimism buoyed her.

Rafe's lovemaking been even more rapturous than his kisses had led her to expect. Much as she mourned Ian, she was enormously glad now that she hadn't, all unaware, settled for a marriage that did not include passion. How tragic would it have been to have lived her whole life never experiencing such bliss!

Just as she'd hoped, the excitement of her wedding day, the camaraderie of the guests and especially the experience of lovemaking had driven paltry emotion clear out of her thoughts. There'd been only anticipation followed by a physical arousal so complete that it filled her mind and senses until she was conscious of nothing else. The unexpected, staggering intensity of release was so all-encompassing, all-consuming, she'd be unable to describe it in feeble words.

Best of all, lovemaking seemed to delight Rafe as much as it did her. After her mother's dismissive comments about her attractiveness, she was beyond thrilled to discover that he did find her desirable. That she was able to offer him a pleasure that seemed as intense as the pleasure he gave her.

Maybe they could make a success of this marriage after all.

They'd pledged to look to each other's happiness, as spouses, friends and lovers. She squelched the slash of pain at recognizing anew that Rafe would never see her as…more. But then, she'd accepted that truth from the very beginning—hadn't she?

If any tiny hope of becoming something different to him still lingered deep within her, she'd better extinguish it now. Completely. Permanently.

Being spouses, friends, lovers was blessing enough; it was foolish to yearn for more. She would concentrate instead, she told herself firmly, on enjoying the unanticipated delights of lovemaking.

The glow of new intimacy adding to the ease that, as longtime friends, they'd always felt with each other, they guided their mounts side by side with no need for chatter. Soon they'd left the carriageway and turned onto the trail that led through the woods towards the river boundary.

'Most of my memories of you growing up place you here,' Rafe said at last, smiling. 'Slipping through the trees on foot or roaming the meadows on horseback, always *searching*. What were you looking for?'

'Birds, always—the one subject that appeared frequently enough for me to sketch accurately. In the early morning or late afternoon, red squirrels among the trees—how they chase each other and chatter, if you remain silent for a while, simply watching! Pine martens as night draws near, also running among the trees. Sometimes I'd follow a badger track to its sett, hoping, if I could wait until sunset, to get a quick sketch. In the lakes or streams, there were otters. And farther on—' she gestured towards the hills rising sharply up above the nearby lake '—if the weather was fair and I could sneak away long enough, I'd climb up the fell, hoping to sight a red deer, or a magnificent peregrine falcon, diving from the heights to capture fish, so fast it's little more than a blur in the air.'

'Might we see any of those today?'

'An otter, perhaps, or at least its house by the river. At the edge of the woods, a squirrel or a hare. Birds, of course. Seeing any of the more reclusive creatures, like the pine marten or the badger, is unlikely. Once upon a time, when I was a frequent visitor, I think some of them grew…used to me. If I sat very still, they would emerge unafraid, as if they knew I meant them no harm.'

She looked at Rafe hopefully. 'Did you mean it when you said I would now be allowed to come observe the woodland creatures again? After my day's work on the estate is done, of course.'

'You may observe as much as you like. I don't mean to work you too hard, toiling away long hours to restore what deteriorated through no fault of yours.'

She sighed, still troubled by her inability to halt that decline. 'I would so much have liked to prevent that. But Sterling has been doing well as manager, don't you think? And I believe all the tenants are eager to bring Thornthwaite back to what it was.'

'In the short time since he's taken on the job, he's impressed me with his expertise and enthusiasm. The tenants all seem to like and respect him. He has the ability to engage with them, get them to say what they need to start making up for deficiencies in production without making them defensive or having them think he's criticizing for that lack of productivity.' Rafe laughed. 'I just sit on my horse, nodding agreement with whatever he says. I'm afraid, having been a soldier, I'm not much of a farmer.'

'How could you be? You never expected to inherit or become responsible for an estate like Thornthwaite. But showing interest in the tenants, as you do, and putting your support behind the projects that they and

Sterling think necessary, is as helpful to rebuilding the estate as if you were to wield a coppicing saw on some overgrown stand of willows.' She smiled. 'Though the tenants might be shocked at the lord rolling up his sleeves to harvest woodland.'

'I might be rather good at it. Shouldn't be all that different from wielding a cutlass.'

Juliana laughed as she could tell he wanted her to, enjoying the camaraderie of their exchange. Perhaps passion drained away anxiety even better than she'd hoped, encouraged by what this current ease promised about their ability to work well together going forward.

'They can tell you are as concerned about their welfare as you are about increasing the estate's production,' she continued. 'Ian had their respect, but he was always…distant. Not "lord of the manor," but not approachable, either. People could sense that agricultural matters just didn't interest him.'

'Can't expect troops to perform if they don't believe their leader is looking out for them.'

'I told you your army background would prove helpful.' Seeing an opening to satisfy her curiosity about whether—or how much—he had changed over the years, she said, 'We were so focused on the estate when you first returned, I never got around to asking what you would have done, had your duty after Ian's death not compelled you to return home.'

'Remained with the army until Napoleon was vanquished for good, which, praise God, shouldn't take much longer. If I survived that endeavour… I'm not sure what I would have done next. Seen more of world, perhaps, before returning to England to find something to occupy me. Beyond the camaraderie and the close bonds one develops, experiencing the wonders of new lands was what I most enjoyed about the army.'

'What impressed you about Portugal and Spain?'

'Overall, the land is drier, dustier than England, much warmer in summer and less green, though the flower-dotted pastures were lovely in the spring. High mountains in the north, rolling hills elsewhere cut by rivers—oh, so many times we had to ford the rivers on campaign! Rocky hilltops crowned by small villages or stone-walled convents and monasteries, where we were sometimes billeted.'

'How did you spend your days? Not the days of battle—I daresay you wouldn't wish to speak of those. But the everyday life. Letters between brothers being rather brief and perfunctory, I gleaned very little about how and what you did, all those years.'

'Most winters, we returned to Lisbon, sheltered behind Lines of Torres Vedres. Though not quite as lively as London, daily life in that city was not much different from town life anywhere. Unlike on campaign, we were billeted in comfortable buildings, with access to a wider variety of victuals. We enjoyed a full range of entertainments, from social and gaming clubs, to dances, balls, dinners. Wellington hosted and was guest of honour at quite lavish affairs, judging by the one I was privileged to attend.'

'And when you were on campaign?'

He sighed, looking thoughtful. 'Though it's often said that war is endless weeks of boredom separated by a few days of terror, I didn't find the day-to-day routine tiresome. Traveling could be long and often uncomfortable—cold, driving rain and endless mud in the winter, dust, heat and thirst in the summer. But while bivouacked or quartered in small villages, there was a variety of occupations to interest one between the marching and drilling.'

Eager to get a glimpse into this significant part of his life about which she knew so little, Juliana said, 'Such as…what?'

'Hunting, usually to scare up something to add to the often-frugal rations. But also for sport—some even brought hounds with them, though coursing after hares was the usual thing. Some racing, though the ground is often hard and stony, bad for a horse's hooves, so we limited that. Fishing in the many rivers, for trout in the spring and bass from summer through the winter. Card games of course, even amateur theatricals. There was a surprising amount of society; we were often invited to dinners and dances by the inhabitants of the towns and villages we stayed in or camped near. The people were grateful for our protection from the French, who, as they lived off the land rather than being provisioned, would descend like a hoard of Biblical locusts and demolish or carry off everything edible or useful. Wellington was scrupulous about having the army pay for whatever we took, be it cattle, chickens, bread or wine, so our residence among them was more appreciated than resented. When encamped near towns or villages, many officers were taken in by local residents, often returning to the same house several times as the army moved to and fro and becoming almost like family, though I was never so fortunate.'

'Where would you stay, then?'

'More recently, we had tents—and what a wonder the troops became at erecting them on the double, once the tent mules arrived! Earlier in the war, if we stayed in one location long enough, we'd construct huts from branches, which were better at keeping out cold and the some of the rain. In the worst case, if we arrived at our destination after dark, there was nothing for it but to wrap up in our cloaks and get what rest we could on the ground.' He chuckled. 'Though some adventurous sorts, if there were suitable trees about, would try their luck sleeping in the branches, which more often than not saw them end up on the ground.'

Juliana laughed, imagining the rude awakening and delighted with the vivid sketches he was painting of his soldier's life. 'And what would a typical day be like, if you were not on the march?'

'First, one tends to the troops, making sure they had adequate victuals, supplies and ammunition. Going to check on any who were ill or wounded. Usually there would be some sort of meeting with the staff, to advise us on pending orders and give us as much information as was available on what to expect next. Supervise drill, inspect the pickets, and finally tend to my own provisioning and mending kit, though my batman handled much of that.'

'And if you had time for any leisure?'

He gave her a rueful grin. 'You'll probably laugh, for growing up, I hardly ever had the patience to remain for long in one spot. But I came to most enjoy fishing. After the noise of camp, the cacophony of battle, I appreciated the serenity of being alone in the landscape, the only sounds the trickle of flowing water and the call of birds. One could relax in quiet contemplation or just sit and admire the often-austere beauty of the surroundings.'

'It is hard to imagine you being so still,' Juliana acknowledged.

Rafe had changed, she thought. Something she'd observed without actually making note of it when she'd first been reacquainting him with Thornthwaite after his return. Responsibility—and probably the sobering reality of possible death—had tempered the reckless impetuosity of his youth. The Rafe who'd returned was more serious, more thoughtful, more settled than the engaging but carefree young man she remembered.

The increasing depth and subtlety made his character no less attractive, alas.

'The peaceful stillness brought back vivid memories of the tranquility and beauty of Thornthwaite,' he continued quietly. 'It seemed to underscore why we'd gone over there to fight. To protect England and all she stands for.'

'My, you've grown philosophical!' she said, raising her eyebrows. 'That I would never have expected!'

'Perhaps. Maybe it's just, as one grows older, one comes to appreciate things one took for granted in one's youth.' He laughed. 'Soldiering certainly teaches one to value the simple pleasures of a soft bed with a solid, rainproof roof overhead, abundant food and clean garments. For those fortunate enough to have a home worthy of the name, one learns to appreciate one's place of birth and one's family.'

'For the most part, it sounds as if you enjoyed the wandering life,' she summed up.

'I did—though I could have done without the scorpions, snakes, ants and prowling lizards! There's satisfaction in knowing one can face fear, danger, and hardship without letting oneself or one's comrades down. In growing confident one can do one's duty, whatever it took.'

'Your closest comrades were members of your regiment, I imagine?'

'Actually, the two who ended up dearest to me were not. Their friendship was battle-born.'

'Indeed? How did that come—' Seeing a troubled look replace his smile, she broke off. Fascinated as she was with everything he was relating and much as she wanted to know *everything*, she continued, 'Forgive my curiosity! You needn't tell me if it will bring back unhappy memories.'

His expression clearing, he said, 'I'd rather not remember much of the day, but meeting Hart and Charles was a blessing. It happened outside the fortress of Badajoz.'

'During the battle?' Juliana shuddered. 'I read about the siege in the papers. A terrible ordeal, I understand.'

'It was,' he said grimly. 'Several groups of dragoons from different regiments, including mine, were detailed to cover the attack while the Forlorn Hope attempted to breech the walls. It was a slaughter, frankly, the French firing directly down at them, knocking them off their scaling ladders, throwing burning pitch into the mud-and-water-filled trenches dug beneath the walls. To say nothing of blasting away at us crouching behind whatever feeble barrier we could find, trying to give covering fire. After having several walls blown up around me, I ended up behind another one manned by two lieutenants, Hart Edmenton of the 1st

Royals and Charles Marsden of Dunbar's Dragoons. For the whole of that endless, bloody day, we covered for each other. We all knew, when it was finally over, that we each owed our survival to the others. There beneath the shattered walls of Badajoz, we pledged to be lifelong friends. And so we will be.'

Truly a trial by fire, she thought, fiercely grateful for the soldiers who'd ensured Rafe's survival. 'Are they both still with the army?'

'No. As I think I mentioned, Hart Edmenton was also brought back to England, the reason for his re-call even more unexpected than mine. His father, the younger son of a duke estranged from his family, married the daughter of Scottish gentry and settled in Scot-land. The old duke died several years ago and last year, the current duke, his grandson and Hart's cousin, also died, leaving only a small daughter. Hart was the near-est male heir.'

Rafe laughed. 'Any normal man, being notified he'd unexpectedly inherited such a position, would have been thrilled—but not Hart. Loyal Scot to his soul, he was horrified to discover he was to become a Sas-senach duke! Of course, Charles and I teased him un-mercifully about being forced to return home, tied to shouldering the heavy responsibilities of managing a great estate, while when the time came, *we* would leave the army carefree and unencumbered, able to go adventuring.' He shook his head ruefully. 'I expect to receive some unmerciful teasing in return when I next go to London, when Hart will undoubtedly tweak me about now being tied to managing an estate, too.'

Suddenly realizing the inevitability of his going to London cast a small dark cloud over her current contentment. 'I suppose you will have to go to London at some point, if only to attend Parliament.'

'I hope you're not recalling your mother's remark—which was as inaccurate as it was cruel. I'll be pleased to bring you with me when I go and know you'll be a credit to me and Thornthwaite. Hart is certain to like you and I think you will like him and wife, Clare. She was the widow of a simple soldier who followed the drum, not some pampered high-born damsel living in London, tended by servants, the most taxing part of her day deciding which gowns to wear.'

'Much as I would enjoy meeting your friends, I would rather remain here,' Juliana said frankly. 'I've little taste for mingling in Society and hardly needed my mother's comments to know I was fortunate to avoid a Season, which would certainly have been a disaster.'

'I can't agree,' Rafe said. 'You're no longer an untried girl, nor would you need to worry about winning anyone's approval. As my countess, you occupy a secure position no one can threaten.'

'Perhaps,' she said dubiously. 'But I'd rather remain at Thornthwaite.'

Rafe frowned, looking a bit annoyed. 'You'd still rather believe your mother's assessment than my assurances? Even though I am convinced, especially with my friends, that you would be welcomed, just being yourself?'

Juliana found she didn't appreciate having the former soldier exercise his commanding nature on a matter she still found painful. 'I hope you don't intend to dictate to me—as my mother did.'

She regretted the words immediately, for Rafe drew himself up stiffly. 'I should hope you would believe there is no comparison.'

'You're right—and I apologize,' she said at once, wanting to remove the stony look from Rafe's face and restore the camaraderie they'd been enjoying. 'You've given me only encouragement. I shouldn't have snapped back. It's just...the whole idea of London and Society is...difficult for me. Will you not press me about it, please?'

To her relief, he relaxed and gave her a smile. 'I won't tease you about it,' he agreed. 'But that doesn't change my opinion.'

A warning that he intended to bring this up later? Being 'herself' might serve with his friends, who apparently were not so conventional, either. But Society certainly was.

She had few illusions about how well she'd be received in London. The last thing she wanted was to endure a Season of subtle slights and snide disparagement, reviving all-too-vivid memories of the miserable years spent under her mother's thumb.

Nor would she want to prove an impediment to Rafe as he assumed his new role. She might be an ideal partner in restoring Thornthwaite, but she had none of the skills necessary to be the sort of Society hostess who would prove an asset to a new earl.

Still not wanting to spoil what had been such a pleasant outing, she let the matter drop, returning instead to one other consideration that had troubled her.

'So you did not resent—too much—being pulled from duty before your soldier's task was completed?' she asked, almost holding her breath over the answer. Their chances of a successful union would be vastly better if he held no lingering bitterness over being forced to return to England.

Rafe shook his head. 'Though I like to feel I did my part, Wellington is growing ever closer to beating Boney anyway. I might have gone adventuring with Charles, but being abroad, for all that I enjoyed the experience, taught me how strong the pull of home is. I would always have returned eventually, though I'm not sure what I would have done; Thornthwaite could only have one master. Buy a piece of unentailed land from Ian, perhaps, and breed horses. I've always loved them, but when the steed one rides often makes the difference between death and survival on the battlefield, one's appreciation for the animal increases exponentially.'

'Fell ponies and Suffolk Punch thrive here. Would you be interested in draft horses?'

'Perhaps. With so many of the sheep farms on high, craggy land that makes carriage travel difficult, there's still much demand for the ponies to transport wool. I might also try Friesians. Several of the dragoons rode them; they've been used as war horses since medieval times. Beautiful as they are, though, I'd rather raise them for riding or harness, not for battle. But before exploring any other ventures, I need to rebuild the traditional sources of Thornthwaite's income—sheep, cattle and wood products.'

By now, following the meandering trail she'd chosen, they'd come out at the clearing bordering the small river that separated Thornthwaite land from her father's estate at Edgerton. Pulling up his mount, Rafe turned to her with a smile. 'Of course you would lead us here. What fond memories I have of this spot.'

'If you don't mind, I'd like to stop, let the horses rest and do some sketching.'

Rafe scanned the surroundings. 'You think there will be birds to sketch?'

'No diving peregrines, but robins, nuthatches, jays or perhaps a grey wagtail might come for a drink. I had Cook pack some cider, bread and cheese for us.'

She couldn't help giving him a beguiling look. 'In case one's…appetite stirred again.'

To her delight, heat flared in his eyes. 'Don't tempt me.'

'I will later, if I can.'

'Oh, you can. I'll look forward to it.'

He came over to help her dismount, and though she was perfectly capable of doing so unaided, she let him, revelling in his touch as his fingers lingered on her sides, stroking gently. She was tempted to try tempting him there and then… But though he knew her to be unconventional, he'd probably be shocked if she tried to lure him into intimacy here, out in the open. He seemed pleased with her so far. Not wanting to jeopardize that approval, she restrained her instincts.

Instead, she unpacked the victuals while he spread out a blanket. After they devoured the small repast, chatting about the tenants and the work they'd begin the following day, Juliana pulled out her sketchbook. 'There's a warbler on the willow over there,' she said, pointing. 'I'm going to do a quick rendering.'

'Please do,' he replied, gesturing towards the bird.

Though she was at first intently conscious of him watching her, the imperative to capture an image before her subject flew off soon had her wholly absorbed in her task.

Laying down her pencil a short time later, pleased to have got a rough sketch done before the bird's departure, she couldn't restrain a smile of delight. 'Thank you! I can't express how wonderful it is to know I shall be able to sketch openly, without having to hide away! The only "art" allowed me at Edgerton for some time now has been painting insipid flowers on those detestable china plates.'

'May I see?'

'If you wish,' she said, suddenly self-conscious again as she somewhat reluctantly handed over the sketchbook.

Rafe studied the current sketch. 'How well you captured his appearance in such a short time!' Instead of returning the book, however, he began to flip through the pages while she watched him uncomfortably.

After a moment, he gazed back at her, looking struck. 'I'm quite impressed! I knew you to be accomplished, but these are…extraordinary!' Flipping back several pages, he pointed to her rendering of a red squirrel. 'See how he looks out from the paper inquiringly! I almost expect him to leap over and seize a bit of cheese from my hand! It's a wonderfully faithful rendering.'

Relieved and gratified that he approved, she said, 'It's easy to render faithfully something you love.'

'As you obviously love all these creatures.' Flipping again through the book, he said, 'A red deer, a falcon…and this?'

'A grebe.' She named off others as he turned the

pages and pointed, then identified the flowers and grasses she'd also sketched.

'You certainly squeezed in as many images as the pages could hold. I wish you had spaced the drawings out more, so one could cut out individual sketches and frame them.'

'It would have been better...but it's the only sketchbook I have. I purchased it when we were in London for Aggie's Season, earning the funds by doing little chores for her, as she'd been given an allowance and I had no money. I didn't have enough to buy another, so I've been careful to conserve the space.'

Hart looked affronted. 'Your parents would begrudge you the cost of a sketchbook? I should think they would be proud of your ability!'

'Oh, if I'd wanted to sketch or paint "womanly" subjects, they might have been. But they didn't have much use for red squirrels and lesser grebes.'

'How short-sighted! Your technique is unusual, too. Such...swirls of energy in the background—the gathering storm on the lake behind the tern! It reminds me of the painter J. M. W. Turner. I viewed his *Fishermen at Sea* at one of the exhibitions in London—it had the same dark, brooding atmosphere, with the moon in the distance, as in your sketch. Have you seen any of his work?'

'No. I was able to slip away to the British Museum—what an excellent collection of animals and sea creatures they possess. But no gallery trips.'

'We shall have to rectify that! I must take you to the next exhibition at the Royal Academy. Perhaps Turner will have some new paintings on display.'

Touching the sketchbook with almost reverence, he said, 'I wish you could have traveled to the Peninsula! You would have loved discovering the birds, vegetation and animals of that region.'

'I'm sure I would have. Though I've no ambition to travel so far, I have dreamed of someday visiting other regions of England to observe and sketch the living creatures there. Perhaps I may, someday.'

'After we have Thornthwaite restored, I'd like to accompany you.'

He liked her drawings—and was interested in supporting her while she wandered to do more? After being criticized by her family for so many years for her inclinations, a swell of gratitude at his honest appreciation moved her almost to tears. 'I would like that, too,' she whispered, emotion clogging her throat.

Handing her back the sketchbook, Rafe gazed up at the sky. 'Shadows are lengthening. We'd better head back.'

Loath as she was to end what had become an enchanting interlude, she realized it was getting late, with duties awaiting them both at Thorne Hall. 'Yes. Thank you for today. For letting me become reacquainted with a place I've loved so much and haven't been able to visit in a long time.'

'We reacquainted me, too. We must ride together often.'

'I'd like that, too.'

Buoyed by their renewed rapport, Juliana let Rafe help her remount, his lingering caress of her side while doing so reminding her that he'd said he'd welcome her luring him to an interlude of pleasure later. The very idea incited a tingling sensation at her center.

It appeared that Rafe would remain the good friend he'd been in her youth, tolerant and supportive of her oddities—though the matter of accompanying him to London could remain a sticking point He might be a soldier used to giving commands, but she wouldn't be commanded into doing something she so disliked. Surely she'd be able to eventually convince him her presence there was unnecessary.

She would have to keep submerged the strong feelings for him he'd made more than clear he would neither appreciate nor want to reciprocate, even if he could. But with a powerful mutual passion to underlie and deepen their friendship, she was cautiously hopeful that the desperation that led her to accept his offer might not end in disaster after all.

Chapter Seven

Several hours later, Rafe sat at his desk in the library, reviewing the latest estate figures Sterling had submitted. He intended to spend as much cash as he dared to buy additional sheep and cattle from some of the neighbouring farms to rebuild their dwindled stock, herds that the former manager hadn't bothered to replenish after the inevitable losses. The estate manager was hopeful that the lambing season, now just beginning, would produce a good supply of newborns. Their own stock, plus what Rafe hoped to procure, would allow a consistent increase in the estate's wool production, production that had sharply declined in the previous two years.

A light knock at the door interrupting his concentration, he looked up to see Juliana in the doorway. Memories of their congenial ride—and the rapturous night preceding it—brought a smile to his face. 'Please, come in.'

'If I'm not interrupting…'

'The figures will keep,' he said, motioning her to approach. 'How have you spent the afternoon since our return?'

'Being a good housewife,' she said with a grin. 'Making sure Jane, who's assumed most of the cooking duties under Mrs Henderson's supervision, will produce something edible for your dinner, checking on general household supplies, which are at low levels, but will do for the present. I've yet to do a thorough inventory of linens, plate, china, cutlery and kitchen equipment, though I can tell you the wine cellar is mostly empty.'

'Young Taylor's fingerprints again,' Rafe said with a grimace. 'My father used to keep some prime vintages.'

'Well, the local brewers do produce superior ale, a suitable beverage for an English nobleman,' she pointed out as she walked over.

'I may need a large mug tonight to recover from the shock of the wine cellar depredations.' Noting that she'd halted a step away, he said, 'You needn't keep your distance.'

He beckoned her closer, his body already stirring at her nearness.

He rose, and she stepped obligingly into his embrace. After giving her a soft kiss—and having to fight the urge to deepen it, he reluctantly let her go, reclaiming his seat in the desk chair before he was tempted to lure her to the sofa by the fire.

She reached out to him, then hesitated. 'Am I permitted to touch you…as much as I please? When no one is around to observe, of course.'

'Absolutely. I welcome your touch.'

'Then I can do…this?' Leaning down, she brushed her lips against the back of his neck, just above his neckcloth.

Arousal spiraling through him, he sucked in a breath, savoring the sensation of her warm breath and moist mouth playing over his bare skin.

'You may,' he said when, alas, she straightened. Fired by her efforts, he said, 'But you must understand, *that* inspires me to do *this.*'

He reached up to run his fingers over her breasts, thrilled to feel the nipples harden through the fine linen layers of her chemise and gown.

Sighing, she arched her neck up and leaned into his caressing fingers. After a few delicious moments, he made himself stop, trying to curb his increasing ardor despite the arousing effect of her soft panting breaths and the gaze from her increasingly passion-glazed eyes.

'Then you must realise, *that* inspires me to do…*this,*' she whispered, reaching down to stroke the hardness tenting his trouser front.

Rafe groaned as a blast of sensation hardened him

further. His brain totally focused on the response produced by her massaging fingers, it took a moment before he was able to reply, 'Then I can only do *this*.'

Gently he pulled her closer, moving his legs apart so he could fit her body against his throbbing cock.

She shuddered against him, giving a little gasp of pleasure. 'Which…inspires me…to do…*this*,' she whispered roughly as she dragged up her skirts with one hand while with the other, struggled to pluck open the buttons of his straining trouser flap.

He held his breath until, her efforts succeeding, his cock sprang free. He gasped again as she pressed him against her, naked skin to naked skin.

Speechless now, his mind blank of anything but the imperative to pleasure, he leaned backward in his chair and drew her closer, urging her body onto his.

Innocence transformed into enticement, she chuckled low in her throat. 'Not yet,' she murmured, moving away.

Before he could utter an inarticulate protest, she stepped closer again, encasing him between her thighs and moving slowly up and down to rub the head of his erection against her moist center. Then she stepped closer still, for long, exquisite moments advancing and retreating, sliding him just barely inside her passage, then out again.

Just when he thought his heart must explode from this delicious torment, she guided him within. Yanking her skirts up to her waist, he helped her onto his lap, groaning as she wrapped her legs around him and slid him to full depth inside her. Wrapping her arms around him, she leaned her head on his chest and went completely still.

Every particle of him screamed for movement, but she put a finger to his lips. 'Just...*feel*,' she whispered.

Ah, yes, he could *feel*—the hot, wet tightness of her body enclosing him, the throbbing urgency of his cock pulsing within her, the galloping beat of his heart, hers, the rising urgency of approaching climax.

Then suddenly, as if she, too, could no longer hold herself back, she began moving. He met her movements, thrusting wildly, desperately hanging on to a sliver of control so she might reach her peak with him. When at last she cried out, her nails scratching into his coated back, he emptied himself in a surge of sensation so intense it robbed him of breath and sight.

Stars seemed to be twinkling in his head when he was finally able to take a shuddering breath, Juliana lying limp against his chest. He hugged her close, kissing the top of her damp head, utterly spent.

Disjointed thoughts sparked and skittered through his mind, while from deep within awe and a profound tenderness welled up. His mind finally coalesced around the realization of what an amazement his wife was turning out to be, possessed of a strong and completely natural eroticism he'd never suspected. Unselfconscious to be naked before him in their chamber, seeming to have no reservations about pleasuring him in the middle of the afternoon in his own library, she was Rousseau's child of nature, reacting not with artifice or determination to seduce, but from the depths of her unique and sensual being.

He'd expected a competent helpmate. An engaging friend. He hadn't imagined possessing a siren.

He would never have wished for his brother's death. But he was finding himself unexpectedly grateful for the tragic circumstances that had gifted him this most surprising bride. One who could amuse him, pleasure him—but as a *friend*, one who would never, as Thalia had, evoke the fierce emotions that had once torn his heart asunder.

Though she wasn't proving entirely amenable, he thought, recalling her strong objection to his urging her to accompany him to London. Despite her immediate apology, having her compare him to her detested mother still rankled. But, he reassured himself, her sharp response simply represented how much she dreaded being on display to Society. He'd have to give her more encouragement—surely she valued his opinion more than her mother's.

If she continued to be intransigent, in the end, he could go to London without her, especially if Hart were in town to host him. He would miss her—especially given the delightful surprise of their physical compatibility—but friends didn't need to live in one other's pockets.

But that was a matter for another day. For now, he would enjoy their partnership at Thornthwaite.

She must have dozed, Juliana thought muzzily as she drifted to consciousness sometime later to find herself, skirts still ruched up to her waist, perched on Rafe's lap.

Marveling at the intensity of the release they'd just shared, she reached up to brush back the damp hair shadowing his forehead.

Just as she'd dreamed of doing so many times, years ago when she was a starstruck girl.

It felt just as wonderful as she'd imagined. A wave of emotion overwhelmed her, bringing tears to her eyes and closing her throat.

Oh, this would never do. Struggling to suppress it, she sat up straight and kissed Rafe on the forehead. *Think only of the pleasure you can give and take*, she reminded herself sternly.

When Rafe opened his eyes, looking as content as she still felt, she said, 'You truly will permit me to do…that? I haven't displeased you with my…forwardness?' she added, voicing a sudden doubt.

'On the contrary! You have pleased me very much—as you are surely aware.' He shook his head wonderingly. 'My shy, quiet, retiring little Mouse. I would never have imagined.'

'I was never truly shy,' she replied, relieved. 'And only quiet and retiring so as to draw as little notice as possible to behaviour that was likely to get me reprimanded.'

He chuckled. 'You'll get no reproof from me for this behaviour.'

She smiled, glad that he was still accepting and approving. If he truly liked her sensual overtures, she would allow her imagination full rein. Back in the dim past, she'd dreamed of being able to touch him without restriction, without restraint.

Now, with his permission, she could indulge herself. She intended to take full advantage.

Acting upon the sensual inspiration of the moment would help her restrain any further undesirable outbreaks of emotion.

Along with concentration on work, of which there was much to be done.

'Much as I delight in my current position, there is dinner and housework to supervise,' she said, regretfully disentangling herself from him and rearranging her crumpled skirts. Catching sight of herself in the pier-glass mirror over the sideboard, she chuckled.

'I'd better go repair myself first. With my hair coming down and my skirts all creased, Baxter will think I fell backwards through a hedgerow.'

Her experienced maid would probably know exactly what her charge had been up to—and would approve. Her former nursemaid was delighted that the odd child she'd mentored and protected from a disapproving family had found a husband who seemed to appreciate her. She'd already begun dropping none-too-subtle hints as she helped tidy her mistress after her wedding night that she hoped Juliana's marital activities would soon produce a new child for Thorne Hall's nursery.

Another wave of warmth went through her, one Juliana allowed herself to fully indulge. She might have to guard her mind and heart against Rafe. But a child she'd be free to love with all the passionate abandon she desired.

What a miracle it would be, she thought as she bid her husband good day and meandered up to her chamber. A part of Rafe she could openly cherish forever. She'd be able to transfer all the pent-up emotion she'd bottled up years ago when she learned he'd fallen in love with Thalia and lavish it on Rafe's child. Her child. Their child.

A child to love would change their whole relationship, eliminating the hovering risk of an emotional lapse and giving her an acceptable outlet for her emotional passion while it cemented her place in Rafe's life and her position at Thornthwaite as mother to the heir.

Having a child to safeguard would give her an even

better reason to remain in the country, far from the foul air and congestion of the City. Allowing her to avoid London and the disapproval of a Society led by matrons like her mother.

She hugged herself, wondering if even now, Rafe's seed might be growing within her. It couldn't happen soon enough.

Chapter Eight

A week later, Rafe mounted his gelding, waiting while the groom handed Juliana up onto her mare. 'We're to ride the western forest today?' she asked as they set their horses to a trot down the carriageway.

'Yes. Sterling and I have done a fairly comprehensive review of the cattle and sheep farms, but I've yet to inspect the woodlands—which we put off as unlike livestock, they didn't require immediate tending and weren't going anywhere. Sterling wants me to inspect the willow stand and review the blocks of oak and ash for pollarding. He said, you having accompanied him several times during Ian's stewardship, you would know where to take me.'

Rafe gave her a rueful glance. 'Not that I know much about either process. Forest management is another of those tasks in which, not being raised to be the heir, I received no training. And I don't think my army experience will be of much use here.'

'Frankly, you probably have as much expertise as

Ian had. As you know, he had little interest in farming and never concerned himself with the day-to-day work of the estate, even before he fell ill. Which was one of the reasons Young Taylor was able to get away with what he did.'

Rafe sighed. 'I expect you meant that to be encouraging.'

'You may not know forestry, but the mastery of detail you described that a good officer must possess— seeing to your men, their supplies, their health—will stand you in good stead here.'

'Now that is encouraging.' Feeling the truth of his words as he spoke them, he continued. 'That's why I like having you ride out with me. You always make me feel better about my ability to learn all that's required to manage Thornthwaite.'

And he did like having her ride out with him. Partly because the tenants, aware of how she'd attempted to help them during the dark days of Ian's illness and Young Taylor's mismanagement, received him more warmly with her beside him than they did if he were accompanied just by the estate manager. Not only did she buoy him up, but while overseeing the estate for Ian, she'd applied the keen powers of observation that allowed her to capture the essence of animals and birds she drew to learning the duties and needs of the estate's various enterprises. She might not have the breadth of knowledge Sterling possessed, but she knew the basic tasks that must be performed far better than he did. Best of all, she seemed to sense when to offer a word of advice or encouragement, when to remain silent, to always ensure he appeared the master of Thornthwaite, she just an assistant.

She assisted him so well, in fact, that it had taken him these last several weeks to realize just how much she'd helped ease the burden of responsibility he'd half dreaded assuming. Assistance for which he was profoundly grateful.

He smiled to himself. He suspected his clever wife could run the estate all on her own as well or better than he would.

Of course, the fact that she continued to delight him in bed played no small part in his satisfaction with life in general. She seemed never too weary, no matter how long the workday, to respond to his caresses, to caress him in turn, her clever hands and mouth finding his body's most sensitive, responsive spots and stimulating them to bring him to a shattering climax. After a month of marriage, the excitement of their intimacy had not dimmed.

He'd never been promiscuous, but he'd had a modicum of sexual experience. Intimate comfort was not much available on campaign, as he didn't fancy availing himself of any of the 'ladies' always attached to the van of the army. Perhaps his body had built up a deficit of lovemaking, because he went to his chamber every night already aroused and eager. He simply couldn't get enough of his bewitching bride.

His intriguing wife, who could go from boldly exploring his body with hands and lips in the darkness of their bedchamber, to meeting him over the breakfast table or accompanying him on rides like this with perfect friendliness, displaying not a hint of coyness or suggestion, never attempting—as had been his experience with other women—to use her sensual power to gain rewards or favour. As if her character possessed two sides, one a seductress, one a companion and sister, with her able to easily switch from one to the other.

To crown all that, she was a *friend* who would never threaten his heart.

On this fair spring day, with his charming, helpful bride at his side as he explored another vital facet of Thornthwaite's production, he meant to enjoy every minute of it.

'Did you not love to roam through the coppiced woodland as a child?' Juliana asked, recalling him from his musings.

Rafe cast his memory back and found it hazy. 'I suppose I did. Mainly I remember riding or creeping through the woodland, playing Robin of Sherwood Forest or soldiers with Cary Smith. Sometimes, little devil that I was, waiting in the hut by the river to ambush Ian when he sneaked out to find a quiet spot to read.'

'You would also accompany me to the forest when I managed to get away. As I recall, you found it amusing to watch me curl myself into a ball behind a fallen tree or crouch under a shelter of leafy branches to lie in wait for the bird or animal I wanted to observe.' She chuckled. 'You'd watch for a bit, anyway, before you grew too bored and ran off.'

'I always came back to check on you!' he protested.

'So you did. I was ever so grateful. My governess would never have allowed me out of sight if you hadn't assured Mama you would make sure I came to no harm. You were the only one who, if not quite understanding it, still indulged my keenness for observing the natural world.'

'I found your unusual interest amusing. It did annoy me, how unkindly your family treated you, just because you'd rather roam the lake, rivers, and forest than sit in the drawing room, doing needlework or practicing deportment. I could well understand your eagerness to avoid that! Another reason I enjoyed escorting you about, as having given my pledge to your mother to keep you safe, I could convince Papa to allow me to escape our tutor and roam about far more often that I would have been permitted otherwise. It was almost torture for me to be confined indoors for any length of time.'

'Which is why you were so suited for the army.

You certainly earned my devotion with your kindness, whatever inspired it. Especially after Bixby.'

He must have looked puzzled, for she repeated, 'Bixby! The baby squirrel you helped me rescue. Surely you recall that episode.'

Memory returned in a rush. 'Ah, yes! The red squirrel that had fallen from his nest. You persuaded me to help you bring the creature back to Edgerton.'

'Not just that. Knowing he would never be permitted in the house, you helped me construct a nest for him and bribed one of the grooms to allow us to install him in a vacant stall and keep silent about his presence. Anyone else would have left the poor animal to die. You helped me save him. You were my hero that day.'

Both gratified and uncomfortable, he said, 'At the risk of lowering myself in your estimation, I must confess that I didn't do it out of altruism. More out of curiosity, to see if we could actually get away with such a prank.'

'Perhaps. But you didn't brush off my concern or belittle me for wanting to save an animal many considered just a pest.'

'Whatever happened to Bixby?'

'Once he grew big enough, I carried him in the nesting box and released him into the forest.' She smiled. 'For a while, the groom reported that a red squirrel would appear at the edge of the pasture, hop up on the fence railing and run along it, looking towards the barn before returning to the woods. I saw him once or twice myself when I came to the stables for my ride.'

'Coming back to check on you and say, "thank you"?' Rafe suggested.

'I like to think so. I hope he returned to the woods, found a mate and had babies of his own to raise.'

Rafe shook his head at her. 'You have such sympathy for the small and helpless.'

'I know what it is to be small—and virtually helpless,' she said soberly. 'Unable to control almost anything in my life.' Looking up at him, she said earnestly, 'Which is why I'm so grateful to you, for changing that. For giving me this.' She lifted a gloved hand to gesture around her. 'I only hope to give you enough help and support in return to deserve it.'

Warmth welling up, Rafe wondered again why her family did not recognize the honesty, strength and goodness in her that was so apparent to him. Why they placed so little value on that, esteeming instead Society's definition of proper maidenly deportment, which so often meant mastering every feminine tool and artifice to improve one's status and position.

If he'd not sensed it before, his time with the army had made him keenly aware that character was worth far more than birth or status. When in the throes of battle, rank and elevated family meant nothing; one could rely only on the bravery, resolve and selflessness of the soldier fighting beside one, whether he be the son of a butcher or a duke.

He might have indulged Juliana as a youth because her oddities amused him. He would protect and encourage her as a man for possessing the virtues he'd come to esteem so highly.

The path they'd been following now opened up into a large field of oaks. After inspecting the broad pollarded stumps, from which thick limbs of varying length and size rose up, they rode on through uncut forest to several fields where willows were being pollarded to provide the thin branches that would be made into the baskets and fish traps that provided another source of the estate's income.

A few hours later, having ridden through the different stands of managed woodlands, Rafe had gained a much greater appreciation for the diversity of Thornthwaite's land. Since, as a boy, he'd preferred exploring the uncut forest and following his return, had focused on sheep and cattle, much of it he'd seldom or never seen. After traversing some of the bracken-filled pastures that dotted the opening between woodlands, Juliana led him along a pathway that continued steadily uphill, until trees gave way to wiry grass pasture rising up towards the fells.

'We'll call on the sheep farmers now,' he said.

'Yes. The Russell farm is just ahead.'

* * *

A short time later, they spied Mr Russell kneeling in a meadow next to a young lamb. They admired the newcomer and its mother, and discussed the progress of the lambing season before bidding the farmer goodbye.

'We're so close here, may we continue up to the top of the fell?' Juliana asked, pointing. 'Resting there, one feels on top of the world.'

'Lead on,' Rafe said, curious to hear what comments being perched 'on top of the world' would inspire in her.

Leaving the horses grazing, they started up the hill towards the summit.

'I know you plan to purchase more sheep, to help the estate rebuild its wool production more quickly,' she said, as she picked her way around the rocks and stones. 'Will there not be a problem integrating them with the rest of the flock? After all, Herdwick stock are all hefted, trained by their mothers to graze only in their home pastures.'

'True, but if we obtain sheep from neighbouring flocks, they can continue to graze where they always have. We can paint them with the Thornthwaite smit mark, so it will be easy enough to separate them out when it is time for shearing.'

'At least adding to the cattle herds won't cause similar problems. As long are there are enough fields to graze them in.'

'I've done an extensive review of the available land with Sterling. There should be sufficient meadows for grazing, along with areas of the bracken needed to produce fodder and bedding for the barns.'

'You'll need to allow some bracken to add to the thatch when the cottage roofs are redone. To keep away evil spirits, the Celts believed.'

'We must definitely keep away the evil spirits,' he agreed with a grin. 'I need all the help I can get to make Thornthwaite a success.'

'Do you know the old Gaelic song?' When he shook his head, she continued, 'It was about a fairy who, falling in love with a mortal girl, helped her gather bracken in the fields so he might be close to her. Until her brothers, discovering the trysts, hid her away from him. Bereft, he continued to gather bracken until he dropped with fatigue, hoping he might encounter her again. *Tha mi sgith*—"I am tired," it's called.'

'Sounds dreary.'

Batting his arm reprovingly, she said, 'Sad, surely, but also beautiful. As is this!' Reaching the crest of the hill, she led him to a huge boulder. While sheltering them from the increasingly fierce wind, it allowed an expansive view across the fells and down to the lake far below.

'Remarkable, isn't it?' she breathed, a look of wonder lighting her face.

She was familiar with this place, he realized. 'Is this where you came to sketch? Where you watched the peregrine falcons dive?'

'Yes. Sometimes, remaining very still, I waited to watch the red deer approach. Despite my human scent, they seemed to accept me.'

'Just another wild creature?' he teased.

'Am I not?'

Thinking of her exuberant, untutored and unselfconscious lovemaking, he said, 'I love wild creatures.'

A shadow crossed her face. 'Do you love them?' she said, an odd note in her voice. Then, her expression clearing, she said, 'I came here not just for the creatures I might encounter. Do you not feel it, sitting here, that sense of *freedom*? Sweeping views from the fells to the lake to the fields of bracken and the woods beyond! As if one could wave a magic wand and be master of the world!'

If that was how this view made her feel, no wonder, with her family struggles, that she slipped away here as often as she could.

'Except that you truly are,' she said, turning to him before he could reply. 'Earl of Thornthwaite, master of most of what can be seen from here.'

'Which inspires not the lightness of freedom, but the burden of responsibility,' he replied wryly.

'Oh, but you mustn't see it like that. Think rather of the opportunities! To help tenants, improve the land and protect all who live upon it. Ian would have been an indifferent steward. But you, with what you've seen of the world, what your life as a soldier has taught you, will be capable of so much more. Sterling sees this, the tenants do, and I certainly believe it.'

He looked at her ardent face. Knowing she gave her honest opinion, with no thought of flattery or attempt to manipulate with praise, humbled him. 'I only hope I prove worthy of your confidence.'

'Oh, there will be mistakes and setbacks along the way, I'm sure. Nothing in life is perfect. But you have the vision, the strength and the desire to protect this. And you will.'

Despite their stone shelter, just then a particularly robust gust of wind buffeted them, making her stumble against him. He reached out to steady her…then drew her close, cradling her against his chest. 'You are so good for me,' he whispered into her hair.

Lacing her arms around his neck, she leaned up and kissed him, long and slow and deep.

His body responding instantly, he hugged her closer, his tongue teasing hers, letting her explore his mouth, nipping at her lips while he moved his hands down to cup her bottom and pull her against his burgeoning hardness.

Her wildness firing his in this wild and stormy

place, he wasn't sure how far he would have gone had not a piercing whistle penetrated the fog of desire. Breaking the kiss, he heard a loud 'halloo' before, a moment later, Sterling strode into view.

Half relieved, mostly frustrated, he gently distanced himself from Juliana and turned to greet the estate manager.

'So sorry to interrupt, my lord. Farmer Russell told me you'd climbed up here. Magnificent view, isn't it? A problem has developed on one of the farms. I'd appreciate it if you'd ride with me there, so we may settle the matter.'

'You go on,' Juliana said. 'I should get back, see to dinner and other pressing household matters.'

'I don't want you riding back alone,' he objected.

'I'll be fine. I grew up roaming these woods and fells, remember. Starlight is both sure-footed and docile; she'll not run away with me or toss me into a hedgerow. Go on now, or you'll not be back to Thorne Hall in time to dine.'

'Even Starlight might cast a shoe or stumble over rocks,' Rafe objected.

'Jemmy, Russell's lad, could take a pony and ride back with her,' Sterling said.

'I'm sure Jemmy has chores to do,' Juliana objected. 'He doesn't need to waste his time riding all the way to Thorne Hall.'

'Perhaps just to the bracken meadows, then,' Sterling suggested. 'Once off the fells, the ground isn't as rocky and treacherous.'

'Starlight and I can find our way home from there with little chance of mishap. So—to the bracken, if you insist, though it's really not necessary.'

'Very well, only to the meadows. But be careful the rest of the way! I don't want to have to go out in the dark looking for a missing wife.'

Juliana rolled her eyes at him. 'When I think of all the times I explored this land alone...'

'Only because you succeeded in sneaking out and I covered for you,' Rafe retorted.

Juliana chuckled. 'Pax! Very well, an escort to the bracken fields...my lord and master,' she added in a mock-obsequious tone, giving him an elaborate curtsey.

Rafe stifled a smile. 'Careful, or I might have to dig out your old governess's switch and apply punishment later.'

'Ooh, that sounds promising,' she murmured for his ears alone as she started back down the hill beside him.

The image her remark conjured—having her bent bare-bottomed over his knees—dried his mouth and set his body aflame, robbing him of any retort. Though he would rather kiss those soft mounds than paddle them... Might that be what she'd beguile him with tonight?

He'd dispose of whatever problem awaited him at

the farm and return as quickly as possible to make sure there was no delay in serving dinner.

And then lead her to their bedchamber for another night of sensual discovery.

Half an hour later, Juliana bid goodbye, with apologies, to young Jemmy as he left her at the closest meadow and trotted off. Though he waved off her regrets and replied with a grin that he'd rather thank her, as he didn't mind a bit exchanging his chores for a task that required no more effort than sitting a sure-footed fell pony.

She watched the little mare trot away, smiling, until a cow lowing in the pasture captured her attention.

Her smile faded as her gaze swept the field to the trees bordering its far end where, on the far side of a stone wall flourished a thick undergrowth of bracken, the new green of emerging fronds luminous against the brown of the winter-killed plants.

Cutting the bracken… She heard again in her ear the sad, lilting Gaelic tune she'd learned from one of the nursemaids as a child. Small wonder returning to her rock retreat on the heights had recalled it.

She had fled there and sung it to herself often enough in the grim, heartbroken days after learning Rafe had fallen in love with Thalia Heathcote. Her last hope, that the news might be just an exaggerated bit of her mother's London gossip, being snuffed out when he returned home, his face alight with passion and talking of nothing but his incomparable Thalia.

That confirmation of his feelings put an end once and for all to daydreams about a future with him she only then acknowledged she'd wanted more than anything. Making her realize with soul-deep despair that, as he saw Thalia as *his* one true love, he was *hers*.

She would never claim the love of the childhood friend who'd roamed the fields with her. The young man who'd indulged her and helped her hide away a red squirrel named Bixby. Who'd always made time for her, who didn't seem to find her odd or embarrassing, who never tried to coax her into behaving like a typical young lady.

That discovery left her alone, bereft, abandoned and wandering the woodlands and meadows they'd explored together like the fairy of the song, 'Tired and alone/cutting the bracken, cutting the bracken/forever cutting the bracken.'

As the deep sadness of those long-ago days welled up, she struggled to banish the emotion, force it back into the hurting place deep within into which she'd imprisoned it years ago. Her story had ended much better than that of the lovesick fairy, she reminded herself. Her lover had not been forever parted from her, but was here now, at her side.

She might not have his love, but she had his company, his kindness and his promise of fidelity. She'd discovered with him a depth of passion she'd never dreamed existed when she was indulging her girlhood dreams.

A passion in which Rafe obviously delighted as much as she did.

Forcing back the memory of love unrequited, she turned her thoughts to their interlude on the fell.

Had they not been interrupted, would Rafe have made love to her, there under the wind-driven clouds, in the shadow of her rock fortress?

Her body shivered in response at the thought.

She'd seen the passion darkening his eyes and quickening his breath. He'd desired her, she knew without doubt.

He loved 'wild creatures' he'd said, inferring that he viewed her as one. Better to lock away the hopeless dreams of youth and concentrate on tempting him with the 'wildness' he found appealing. Forget about a love he could never offer her and bind him closer instead with the passion they both shared.

Chapter Nine

On a warm, bright, sunny May noontime two weeks later, Rafe helped Juliana unpack the blanket and saddlebags at her favourite spot by the river after their morning review of the sheep farms. Lambing season was almost done; with the weather warming, the ewes with single lambs had already been allowed to return to their traditional grazing grounds high on the fells. The occasion demanded, his formerly industrious wife declared, that they take advantage of the moment and the beauty of the day and indulge themselves with some time off for a picnic.

Just the two of them, she'd said, her wide brown eyes gazing at him. Though the timbre of her voice when she'd suggested the outing this morning had not contained any undertone of sensuality, as he settled their supplies near the stream, Rafe couldn't help feeling a rise of anticipation. They were alone; the day was warm and fair, and who knew what his ingenious wife might be planning?

'We probably should have brought a pole and some lures,' she was saying as she spread out the blanket. 'You said you find fishing relaxing, and the trout should be running. I remember we caught some fine fish in years past from the bank over there, where the salmon ladders are, though it's not the right time of year for them. Still, trout makes a good meal.'

'We can bring some next time. There will be pike and perch as well as the summer advances, though more in the larger lake than here.'

'That spot by the tree was one of your favourite swimming places, too, as I recall.'

He looked up from placing the basket in surprise. 'How would you know?'

She grinned. 'I might have seen you and Ian there once or twice. Did you never sense someone watching you?'

The idea that her eyes had followed him as he frolicked, nude, with his brother, made his pulses accelerate. 'Wicked girl! Your governess would have shut you up on bread and water if she ever knew.'

Juliana only chuckled, mischief in her eyes. 'True. And Mama would have had apoplexy. Despite the evidence in the farm animals all around, she would have had me believe that men possessed nothing beneath their breeches.'

'Were you impressed to learn what was beneath my breeches?'

She gave him a look that made his breath catch. 'A wondrous introduction to what would come later. But come, let's have our luncheon.'

She took a seat, patting the blanket beside her.

He sat beside her, their shoulders touching, his body stirring in the way she always seemed to affect him. He marveled once again that he'd ever thought her shy and retiring, this creature of unconscious sensuality who lit his desire like a flame set to dry tinder.

She kept him on that sensual edge throughout their rustic meal, feeding him bits of cheese and ham, slowly licking her lips or sucking the strawberry bits from her fingers and his, her eyes on his face.

She knew what she was doing to him, he was certain, for once they'd finished the last of the bread and cheese, she murmured, 'Let me clean up the crumbs'— and leaned up to slowly lick his lips, from one corner of his mouth to the other, nuzzling and nipping at them.

He groaned, opening to her, and her tongue swept inside, exploring his mouth, laving his tongue with her own. With a growl, he pushed her back against the blankets, kissing her harder, deeper.

He burned to bury his face against her naked breasts and draw the taut pink nipples into his mouth, but she was armored in a breastplate of linen and wool, several thick layers of chemise, shirt and riding jacket. But then, still kissing him deeply, she pulled up the skirt of her habit and guided his hand past boot and knee to the softness of her upper thighs. Sliding sideways, she widened her legs and brought his hand to her hot, wet center.

His cock leapt and she gasped as he pushed one finger, two, into her tight passage, caressing in and out to the rhythm of their panting breaths, until she gripped his arms and writhed, gasping and pulsing around him.

She sagged back against the blankets, dazed for a minute while he covered her face with small, nibbling kisses. Then, reviving, she deftly plucked open the buttons of his straining trouser flap, yanked up her skirts and urged him over and into her.

Eyes closed, panting, she moved with him as he thrust deep, he holding off until the last possible moment before overwhelming passion exploded into completion.

Sated, spent, he rolled her to the side and bound her close as they both dozed into the soft twilight aftermath of passion fulfilled.

Sometime later, she woke him with a nibbling kiss to his chin. Sitting up, she lifted the heavy braid from her neck. 'My, how warm the day has become!'

He chuckled. 'I expect our…activities made some contribution to the warmth.'

'Perhaps. But I know just the remedy. It's time for a swim.'

Rafe laughed. 'It's not yet June! You'll freeze!'

'Nonsense. It will be…invigorating.'

'I don't think so.' Shaking his head, not sure whether she really meant to go through with it, he watched as she unbuttoned her jacket, pulled off the garment and tossed it onto the blanket, then unfastened her skirt and stepped out of it.

'Help me with the blouse and stays, please?' she said, turning to offer him her back. 'I can't reach all the fastening.'

Despite his recent satisfaction, his body stirred at the idea of seeing her standing naked before him, revealing the breasts he'd not been able to caress, the nipples he still burned to taste. With his avid assistance, she soon stood before him, chemise, shift, stays, habit, shoes and stockings discarded on the blanket beneath them. 'Ah, the warm sun is glorious!' she murmured, arching her head back into a sunbeam.

Sunlight painted her lithe body with gold, gleaming on the silken hair of her head, at her thighs, outlining her body in a halo of light, brightening the rose of her nipples to pink.

'Afraid to join me?' she teased.

'That sounds like a challenge,' he said on a sigh, aroused but wary.

'Surely you will rise to the occasion,' she said, dipping her gaze to his trouser front, where his member was obligingly stirring. But she stayed his hand when he attempted to loosen his neck cloth. 'Let me. But you must stand *perfectly* still.'

He tried very hard to obey that command, though it gradually grew almost impossibly difficult. Insisting he remain immobile, not touching her, she disrobed him slowly, slowly, one garment at a time, kissing and nibbling each bit of skin she revealed.

His chin and the back of his neck after she pulled off his cravat. His shoulder blades, and the outline of his ribs once she shucked off his jacket and pulled the shirt over his head. She raked her teeth gently over his nipples as she pushed down his unbuttoned trousers, then sat him back on the blanket to pull off his boots, stockings and breeches.

While he tried to sit still, his heartbeat throbbing and his breath coming in gasps, she caressed and nibbled from his toes to his knees, slowly up his thighs, until he was fully erect again, aching for release. Until at last she took him in her hands, kissing and suckling.

After lasting about as long as a callow youth with his first sweetheart, he collapsed, gasping. She reclined on her elbow beside him, stroking the damp hair off his brow until he regathered his breath and his heart stopped trying to beat itself out of his chest.

Running a finger over his lips, she said, 'My, you seem even warmer now. I think it must be time for a swim.' Laughing, she leapt up and ran to the river, leaping in with a delighted laugh.

'Come in, it's glorious!' she cried, wading out into the deeper water.

With resignation, he followed her, gasping at the cold shock of the water. 'Glorious?' he grumbled. 'More likely I'll end up with an inflammation of the lungs.'

'What, here on a balmy English day after you survived the rain and ice of Peninsula winters? Nonsense.' She slapped the water, dousing him with a blast of chilly liquid, then dived in and swam off.

With a growl, he plunged after her. Laughing, she swam away, splashing and dodging. For some minutes, they played the game of approach and escape, until at last, with a satisfied sigh, she turned over to float on her back.

He swam back to shallower water and stood a moment, admiring the vision of her naked form half revealed, half submerged. Her breasts bobbing above the surface, the cold making her nipples peak as if in the throes of pleasure…the round of her belly and knees breaking the surface, sinking under.

Swimming over, she drew him back into waist-deep water, wrapped her legs around his torso, her arms around his neck and, suspended by the buoyancy of the water, fitted him inside her. 'Just let me float,' she murmured.

And so he braced himself against the current and let the water move them. Their shoulders and torsos sun-warmed, their legs and hips submerged, the water lifted her against him, pushed and pulled him within her to its own rhythm, slow, languid, sensuous, like nothing he'd ever experienced.

Despite the cold, the softness of her bottom under his hands, the taste of her nipples he leaned down to suckle, had his erection strengthening until he once again filled her. Moving with, against the water, he thrust harder, faster, until they both reached a shuddering climax.

Legs trembling, he pushed them into deeper water, needing its support to avoid falling over. Smiling languidly, she leaned up and kissed him.

He pulled her close, sensation still sparking and fizzling along his nerves, like the last gasps of a nearly spent Congreve rocket. His brain, at first numb with sensation, slowly filled with a sense of awe and wordless wonder.

When his legs could function again, he lifted her and walked them into the shallows, then sat with her on his lap, her head resting against his chest while a dove cooed in the shadows, siskins warbled, the afternoon sun warmed his back and water lapped gently around them.

Finally, with a sigh, she lifted her head. 'I suppose we must go back now. Duties await.'

He shook his head at her. 'I can't call you "Mouse"

after this. No, you're a water sprite sent to enchant me. A true naiad.'

She angled her head. 'Naiad?'

'In Greek mythology, naiads were nymphs sent to guard the springs. Beautiful, light-hearted, kind. As you are.'

She nodded. 'I feel so ignorant! Mama never let us learn anything beyond needlework, dancing, a little music and how to manage a household. If it weren't necessary to know a modicum of mathematics to do that, I wouldn't even know my sums. I so envy the education you had at university!' She made as if to continue, then hesitated.

'What is it?'

'Well, I couldn't help noticing what an excellent library Thorne Hall possesses. I've always felt...cheated, that I never had the opportunity to learn more. Would it be possible, once I've finished my household duties, for me to...study some of the books there?'

'Of course. They are *your* books now, too, you know.'

She gave him a brilliant smile that made him feel guilty for not previously offering a permission she seemed to have been waiting for. 'Not that I'm not grateful for what you've already allowed me to learn here at Thornthwaite.'

He moved against her. 'I love what you've been

learning. And what you've been teaching me, like today.'

She chuckled. 'I want to learn everything. Everything that gives you pleasure.'

'You're an excellent pupil. Though I believe your instincts are better than any tutoring.'

'You would encourage me to…continue following my instincts?'

'With all my heart.'

'You are certain? I was… I was afraid I might have shocked you.'

Rafe sighed. 'Oh, please, continue shocking me.'

She gave him another kiss. 'Then I will.'

Gradually, as his thoughts slowly broke free from the fog of desire, with a niggle of discomfort, Rafe marveled at how freely they'd frolicked beside and in the river. Not that he expected someone to discover them. It was still too cool for local farm lads to venture here, seeking relief from afternoon heat. This stretch of the stream was bordered by woodland and a few open glades; there were no meadows nearby to feed cattle that needed human tending and Herdwick sheep, trained to their traditional high meadows, would never stray this far, requiring a shepherd to come in search of them. But…to make love openly, in the woodland, for anyone to see if someone *had* stumbled upon them…

Juliana appeared not to entertain any such concern.

She rose calmly and walked back to the jumbled as-sortment of clothes they'd left on the blanket with no haste, seeming perfectly at ease. After he followed her over, she gave him a gentle kiss before she helped him back into his garments while he assisted her, but there were no teasing aftertouches to underline her sensual power over him.

She'd turned from siren back into assistant as if the change were completely natural, exhibiting no awk-wardness at all in making the transition.

Indeed, already her attention had turned to mus-ing about the possibilities for dinner and wondering whether the skill of their apprentice cook might ex-tend to preparing a meat pie with roasted vegetables.

While Rafe wondered when his wife might sud-denly turn temptress again. After their activities at the stream, he wasn't sure he'd be man enough to respond if she did try to lure him into a tryst in one of the for-est glades they passed on the way back to Thorne Hall, or in a conveniently empty stall in the hay barn. But tonight in the privacy of their bedchamber...

As he helped her remount, she gave him a luminous smile. 'I hope our interlude relaxed and refreshed you. It certainly did me.'

'I'm so relaxed I may doze off and fall out of the saddle,' he retorted only half joking as he swung into the saddle.

She chuckled. 'I'll chatter to you, then, to make sure

you stay awake. After your legendary performance at the stream, you are due some rest.'

'A performance nowhere as legendary as yours.'

She made a wry face. 'If I confess something, will you not take me to task?'

His curiosity piqued, Rafe had no idea what might be coming next. 'That's hard to promise, but as I've never yet known you to do something I would find worthy of chastisement, I suppose I can.'

'Those years ago, when as a young girl I watched you swimming with your friends while I observed un-seen… I imagined doing what we did today. Not the fulfillment part, of course—I had no inkling yet that such a thing was possible. I envisioned just…having you all to myself, being able to touch and caress you with the river as my assistant. Using the assets of the natural world to enhance and extend my embrace.'

Once again, she'd surprised him. 'How old were you then?'

'Fourteen, fifteen, perhaps. Old enough to have… urges and desires that were quite strong, though I didn't understand them at the time.'

'You've always been a child of nature,' he said, mar-velling anew at this further testament to how deeply sensuality was embedded in her nature. How could he have been ignorant of that for so long, thinking her a meek and girlish innocent?

'I suppose I am. I imagined us splashing and playing like otters, even dozing as we drifted along, hands clasped together. They do, you know—otters. Though they usually return to their dens or caves for sleeping, I've seen them floating along, a mother on her back with her baby on her belly, or two adults, clasping each other with their paws so they could move together as they napped. Keeping each other close, as you held me close in the shallows today. And then, in the deeper water…' She sighed. 'It was even more wondrous than I'd imagined.'

She looked over to smile at him. 'Perhaps you are a child of nature, too, and are only just realizing it.'

His brain stretched to try to accommodate that totally unexpected possibility. Did he, frolicking naked in forest glades, possess a hitherto hidden and more deep-seated sensuality?

Before today, he certainly would never have predicted he'd become an avid participant in an interlude like the one just passed. But for the still-simmering nerves in his sated body, he found it hard to believe the tryst had actually happened, that he'd not just awoken from some wondrous erotic dream.

Even in his army days, he'd not looked favourably on soldiers coupling with their partners out of doors. Not that he was shocked by it; such things happened regularly when soldiers were on campaign, bedding down in tents or wrapped in blankets on the ground. Even when billeted in buildings, stables, or the huts they constructed, true privacy was limited, but those with wives or temporary women were unwilling to refrain from claiming the comfort they offered.

To be truthful, he'd always found it coarse and a bit distasteful. But what had happened today at the river had been...magical.

She spoke of learning from him, but he was learning, too, from his ever-surprising wife. Learning to appreciate sensuality as natural, beautiful, somehow... pure. Unsullied by a man's lust or a woman's attempt to use a man's desire to twist him to her will. An exchange of pleasure for pleasure, each partner intent only on fulfilling the other.

Teaching him to appreciate simple things of nature he'd looked at but not truly seen. The wonder of pollarded trees, where a single oak might provide everything from bedding to fodder to roof thatch to the decking for a warship and do so for hundreds of years. The tree serving its master as faithfully as a hound, but for much longer.

Showing in her drawings how charming was the smile on the face of a Herdwick lamb. How mischievous the expression of a red squirrel, how majestic the dive of a peregrine falcon.

She seemed to go through life as if she were picking a bouquet of wildflowers. Unlike the large blooms cultivated in a garden, each flower was often small and delicate. But massed together, they created a mosaic of stunning beauty.

And she offered them to him, almost every day, some new, perfect collage of unexpected insight or ordinary but extraordinary beauty.

He'd thought he was rescuing her when he proposed this marriage of convenience, that they would have an amicable union based on friendship and shared history. He was beginning to think that she, if not rescuing him, was certainly changing him, broadening and deepening his understanding as she dazzled him with sensuality and gradually opened his eyes to a surrounding world that he'd never fully appreciated.

Like Turner, whose unique paintings revealed the wild natural beauty within the objects and events he painted, while other artists merely captured the outward image of them.

His chest expanded with a depth of emotion—until abruptly, with a little pang of alarm, he caught himself. Yes, the unexpected complexity he'd discovered in Juliana…intrigued him, but he mustn't let his feelings get too carried away. They'd established this marriage on a bedrock of friendship. An…*expanding* of his affection was harmless enough, he supposed, but friendship only is what their relationship must remain.

'You're quiet,' Juliana observed. 'Not falling asleep, are you?'

'No. Just…reflecting. I thought we might take a tour

of the library tomorrow,' he said, steering himself back to safe and prosaic ground.

Excitement lit her face. 'Tour the library? That would be wonderful. Are you certain you'll have time?'

'I'll make sure of it. What do you want to learn from there?'

'Oh, everything!'

Rafe laughed, charmed by a display of enthusiasm other females would probably reserve for the prospect of buying gowns or attending balls. Certainly her sister, Aggie, would never have seen exploring a library as a treat.

'There's a bit of everything in there. Papa was a great collector, as was his father before him, so you'll find a good selection—literature, translations, natural history, botanical texts. If I'm recalling aright, there's an edition of Bewick's *A History of British Birds*. Wonderful illustrations, which I think you will find inspiring.'

'I shall work all the harder tonight and tomorrow morning to finish my tasks, so I have time to study any books you allow me to take away. I should particularly like to read any that will instruct me to better assist you in managing Thornthwaite.'

'Learning is valuable for its own sake, whether the knowledge you acquire is practical or not. Particularly if what you learn about gives you pleasure.' He paused, feeling the truth of it. 'As it delights me to offer what gives you pleasure.'

She looked up, a wisp of a smile on her lips. 'As you well know, it delights me to do the same.'

'Then how can we not get on well together?'

'Indeed we shall,' she confirmed, urging her mare to pick up the pace as they reached the carriageway leading to Thorne Hall, set like a jewel on the verdant crest of the hill beyond them.

He would indeed be delighted to open her to the possibility of formal study she'd apparently always craved to have. A fitting response to the insight she was giving him into the natural world that was her domain.

They were partners, just as he'd hoped. Partners, lovers and warmly intimate *friends*.

Chapter Ten

The next afternoon, Juliana hurried to the library, anxious to begin the exploration Rafe had promised.

Her heart full, she allowed herself to feel a moment of pure happiness. Her instincts had turned out to be correct; Rafe's years with the army had not substantially changed the young man she'd grown up admiring, though he was definitely more commanding. She thought uneasily of their dispute over the eventual trip to London, a matter of contention he had not addressed again and that she'd carefully avoided bringing up. Pushing aside that worry, she reminded herself that, commanding as he might be, soldiering had not coarsened him or ground out of him the consideration he had always shown to those around him.

Rather, as he'd told her, his experiences with the hardships and horror of war had made him more appreciative of the blessing of living in England and his good fortune in owning productive land he could manage in peace. Having seen the devastation wrought in other lands made him more determined to master his responsibilities and ensure this estate provided a good living for his family and for the farmers, crofters and sheep-herders who worked on it.

Now, he was going to give her access to the world of learning for which she'd always yearned. He had given her so much, it would be foolish to pine to possess a heart that was no longer his to give. She must keep firmly buried any fantasy of openly loving him or having him love her in return.

His friendship and esteem would be enough. And if she could give him a son, she would possess virtually everything she'd ever wished for and never believed she might have.

Compared to what she'd feared would be her destiny, buried at Aggie's estate as a drudge attending upon her children, it would be churlish to long for more.

She'd just reached the door to the library when she heard footsteps behind her. She permitted herself one last swell of happiness before she reined in the emotion, damping it down before it could threaten her resolve.

Instead, she focused on the physical sensations tingling through her as her husband approached. When he reached her, she leaned up to give him a lingering kiss. He responded instantly, pulling her closer. When, after a few delicious minutes, he ended the embrace, she traced his lips with her tongue, banking the desire coursing through her for later.

He groaned, touching her wet mouth with a fingertip as he as released her. 'No more of that now, or I'll forget my promise and carry you away to our chamber.'

'You may carry me away after dinner with my blessing.'

'I must force myself to wait then.' He swept a hand towards the bookshelves. 'Shall we go in? Where would you like to start?'

She walked in on his arm, a thrill running through her as she surveyed the large room walled with bookshelves reaching up to the high ceiling. 'Section by section?' Spreading her arms wide, she twirled in a circle. 'It's a place of wonders! What a marvelous gift you are allowing me to unwrap!'

Halting to see him grinning at her, she said, 'You may find my enthusiasm amusing, but you can't imagine the euphoria of being given access to what, for your whole life, has been denied you. How could you? Allowed to attend school and university, able to study the whole realm of knowledge for as long as you wished, limited only by the time available and the depth of your interest. Then able to travel abroad and experience other lands, languages and cultures! While I, like most women, have been restricted to hearth and home, free only to roam the nearby woods and fells, with even that freedom limited to such moments as I could borrow or steal.'

His smile fading, he said, 'You're right. Though when exams by the masters loomed, the "gift" of study sometimes seemed more a burden, and battle is an experience perhaps more horrifying than broadening, I can't imagine what it would be like to have my movements and possibilities severely limited.' He shook his head at her. 'Though I doubt there are many women who view their position in life as "restricted".'

'Perhaps not. Having *been* restricted, I've not had the opportunity to meet many females outside my own family. One of the few, my London friend, the late Lady Fallsham, certainly chafed at the limitations placed upon females. But enough of that. Show me the books. I cannot wait to get started!'

'Let us begin, then. My father, like his father before him, had broad and eclectic tastes, but was rather haphazard about shelving his collections. Ian did us a service by organizing the books by subject, recording them in a ledger and grouping them on the shelves. Shall we start with literature?'

'Yes. Perhaps something about naiads?'

Rafe chuckled. 'That might be difficult unless you managed to learn Greek.'

She gave an exasperated huff. 'I've a smattering of French and Italian, no more.'

'I admit, my Greek is rudimentary as well. Only

those at university who were looking to take holy orders were thoroughly schooled in it. Fortunately, although Papa obtained Greek originals, we have both William Cowper and Alexander Pope's English translations of Homer's *Iliad*, Pope's version of *The Odyssey* and several volumes of John Dryden's translations of Greek stories by Horace, Juvenal, Ovid and Theocritus. In the latter's works you'll find stories about your water nymphs.'

For the next forty minutes, Rafe led her to several groups of shelves. After selecting Pope's *Iliad* and Dryden's tales by Theocritus, they continued to the area housing Scott's epic tales of the Scottish Highlands and Ann Radcliffe's *Mysteries of Udolpho*. Juliana added to the stack several volumes by contemporary poets Cowper, Blake, Shelley and a Lake District neighbour, Wordsworth. Rafe ended their tour of literature by offering her Byron's *Childe Harold's Pilgrimage*, a poet and a work so notorious even Juliana had heard of it.

She tucked the volume under her arm with a mischievous chuckle. 'I remember Aggie and her friends discussing Byron in hushed tones. Mama would suffer palpitations if she knew I'd even touched a work by the man.'

'To finish up, let me show you our small collection of volumes that deal with the natural world. A first edition as well as reprints of Hill's *The Gardener's*

Labyrinth, which gives advice on the timing of cultivation and about the medicinal benefits of plants, herbs and flowers. I think you'll appreciate the excellent illustrations.'

He opened the volume, showing her a drawing of a gardener hard at work in a formal flower border. Instantly eager to study the artist's sketch for techniques she might incorporate into her own work, she said, 'Oh, yes, I must have that one!'

'Not much has been published about mammals, but we have Edward Donovan's volumes on birds, insects and fish,' Rafe continued, moving down the bookshelf. 'And here are several I think you will particularly like: George Edwards's *Natural History of Uncommon Birds* and, best of all, Bewick's *History of British Birds*, the work I told you about. Bewick bears closer inspection.'

Pulling out the two-volume set, he led her to the sofa before the fireplace. 'Bewick not only created marvelous woodcuts that faithfully represented the birds, he also ended each section with little illustrations of everyday life that I think you'll find especially interesting and amusing.'

'Show me!' Juliana said, even more intrigued by this description than by his praise of Hill's illustrations.

Rafe seated himself beside her and opened the first book. 'At first, it seems to be just a sketch of a commonplace activity, a woman hanging out washing. But look more closely, and you'll notice in the foreground a chicken walking over one of the freshly laundered shirts, leaving muddy claw prints behind.'

He started to flip the page, but she halted him, wanting to study the woodcut more closely. 'Marvelous! Show me more.'

'How about this one,' he said, flipping a few pages farther. 'A fine image of the yellow wagtail, but in the distance, a man plowing. Or this—a hunter retrieving from the water the duck he's downed. Or this one—boys sailing their boats on a river.'

'They are all wonderful!' she breathed, as impressed as she was excited to study them more closely. 'Let me take the Bewick volumes, too.'

The sudden thought occurring, she said, 'You said that literature and book collecting were Ian's great loves. But you must have spent a great deal of time browsing the collection, to know it as well as you do.'

Rafe's face colored. 'Humbling as it is to confess to one so eager for learning, I was never much of a scholar. Well, you'll remember how ready I always was to escape my tutor and go off adventuring in the woods! However, knowing I would be bringing you here, I did a quick review of the ledgers Ian compiled detailing the collection's contents, so I might point out the volumes I thought would be of most interest to you.'

He'd taken the time and trouble to research the collection—for her. Touched, she said, 'That was so kind. Thank you.'

He looked as if he might say something...tender in return? But even as her heart quickened with hope, he gave her a jaunty grin. 'You've accumulated quite a stack! Perhaps I erred bringing you here. You may become so lost in study, you will forget about me entirely.'

Squelching an irrational disappointment, she said, 'I won't neglect to finish my duties before doing any reading, I promise. And I could never forget about you. Oh, Rafe, this—' she gestured to the books they'd selected, almost too overcome with gratitude and wonder to speak '—all of them are so amazing! *You* are amazing. And kind. And indulgent, to allow me time to read and study. I imagine few husbands would even understand a wife's zeal to study, much less encourage it. How can I thank you enough?'

He smiled down at her, his expression once again tender. 'I love to see you happy. You are, aren't you? I know you had...reservations about marrying me.'

'I am happy. How could I not be?' she replied, ruthlessly suppressing the little niggle of sadness that 'kind' was the warmest emotion she could hope for from him.

'If I'd known you were going to be this excited about the library, I should have introduced you to it much sooner.'

'I shall try to show my appreciation…in every way I can,' she promised, leaning up to give him a kiss.

In every way he valued, anyway. With her lips, her hands and her body.

Not, never, with her heart.

He stilled, letting her direct the kiss, opening his mouth to the caress of her tongue, lifting his chin to the nip of her teeth against his neck. 'This, and more,' she whispered.

'I shall very much look forward to it.'

The mantel clock struck, and he straightened. 'Back to tedious reality,' he said with a sigh. 'I must hasten to the stables if I'm not to be late meeting Sterling at the Crandall farm.'

'Go, then. I promise not to be lured into reading before I make sure dinner will be ready and the mending and cleaning of the unoccupied bedrooms progressing as planned.'

'I'll have a footman carry the books up to your chamber. Where I'm sure I will find you later, oblivious to the world.'

'Never oblivious to you.' Which, alas, was becoming all too true for her peace of mind.

'I must run.' He jumped up, then leaned down to give her nose a quick kiss before striding out.

Hugging the Bewick to her chest, Juliana watched him go. How could she even think of being disappointed, when she had *this*—her gaze swept over the selected volumes again. All this, her work at Thorn-thwaite, and Rafe in her bed.

No, she had no reason to repine, she told herself firmly.

A week later, Juliana rode out with a groom to meet Rafe, who'd gone with Sterling earlier to meet some tenants in one of the willow woods. All the trees had been coppiced in late spring, but it was time to thin the new shoots so they would have light and space to grow properly for the next year's harvest. She'd persuaded him that after he finished inspecting the work, he should join her for a picnic and some fishing, the activity he'd told her had become a favourite during his time with the army, but which during the busy spring season he'd not yet taken time to do.

Unfortunately, she thought with a sigh, it would be *only* a picnic and fishing. On Sterling's recommendation, Rafe had had the field on the far side of the swimming spot cleared to allow grass to grow to provide pasturage for the additional cows he'd purchased. Though it was unlikely any farm boys would come through the field during the afternoon, it was still possible. As uninhibited as her husband had been in trysting with her in the river, she didn't think she could lure him to it again if there was the least chance they might be observed.

They could have a long private chat, though. She'd

become increasingly mindful of the clock ticking off the days in her head; soon, with the crops in and spring chores completed, there'd be no further excuse to delay having him go to London to attend Parliament. Though they'd not yet discussed the matter since that first, sharp exchange, she knew soon he'd be likely press her again to accompany him.

Much as she still disliked the prospect, she had to admit her opposition was wavering. Still, the idyll they'd been enjoying in the country, most often just the two of them for breakfasts and dinners, with long rides in between to view farms or fields, when she'd had him all to herself to talk with, tease…and seduce, would almost certainly cease if she did go with him to London.

At the very least, he would leave her to attend Parliament. Doubtless he would also encounter friends from university or the army, like his soldiering compatriot, the Duke of Fenniston. He'd want to spend time with them at their clubs and other venues like Tattersalls where such men gathered. Then there would be balls, musical evenings, and other sorts of social events like the ones that had filled Aggie's Season, during which she would see little of him. During which she would fade into the walls with the bluestockings and dowagers, the elegant Society matrons giving her patronizing smiles while whispering behind her back about how regrettable it was the new earl had wed so unprepossessing a countess.

The prospect sent her spirits spiraling lower.

Taking a deep breath, she shook off the dismal reflections. She'd wouldn't allow worry about London to spoil the time they would have together today. When one isn't sure what the future holds, one must enjoy every second of the here and now.

The sound of chopping mingled with male voices and laughter as they approached the willow wood. In the distance, she spied about a dozen men engaged in cutting away some of the shoots sprouting from the recently coppiced willows, most of the men stripped to the waist against the warmth of the late May sun.

One of them was her husband.

Having signalled her horse to halt, Juliana froze, the breath catching in her throat.

Warmth filled her as she gazed at the hard, lithe body she knew so well. His booted feet planted wide to maintain his balance, his bare shoulders glistening in the sun, his muscled arms rippled as he bent and straightened, bent and straightened, his knife flashing as he cut off a stem at its base, then rose in a swift motion to toss the cuttings into the stack beside him before bending down again.

His eyes focused on his work, Rafe didn't notice her approach, so she was able to watch him for some minutes. Desire spiraled in her belly, intensifying her regret that there could be no tryst at the swimming site. Perhaps they might pass a more private grove on ride back…

He looked up then, spied her and smiled. Handing his knife to one of the other workers, he walked over to greet her.

'You see, I'm earning my leisure this afternoon.'

Pulling her mind from its sensual haze, she said, 'You're sure you haven't done this before? You seem… quite skilled.'

'As I suspected, my years wielding a sword have proven useful after all. Chopping down with a knife isn't nearly as tiring as slashing with a heavy saber. Let me grab my shirt and jacket, and we can be off.'

'Don't put on your shirt on my behalf,' she murmured, giving his torso a lingering glance that should leave him no doubt about her appreciation of his body—or her desire to see more.

His eyes darkened, as if he knew she was thinking of trysting. 'I suppose the field north of the bend in the river is fully cut, Sterling?' he asked, turning back to the working party.

'Aye, m'lord. The men finished it just last week. With the land more open to the sun, we should get a good new growth of grass. We've already pastured some cows on it,' he replied before pacing off to answer a question from one of the workmen.

'More's the pity,' Rafe murmured, turning back towards Juliana. 'I suppose it will have to be fishing after all. Just fishing.'

'We'll share a meal, too. Jane has become rather proficient at putting together cold ham, cheese, bread and ale.'

He scanned her body with a hot glance. 'You know what I'd rather have for lunch…'

The heat spiraling within her intensified. She would have to look very carefully at the groves they passed riding home. Trying to put that imagining out of mind, she said, 'None of that until later, naughty man.'

'Later I should like to be very naughty.'

'Ooh, is that a promise?' she teased.

'Count on it.' Turning towards Sterling, he called out, 'Will the men finish up the coppicing soon?'

'In about an hour,' the supervisor said, walking back to them. 'But you've done your part, though you had no need to! Good luck with fishing.'

'I like to be useful. I like to know how to do the work of the people who work for me. As I always did in the army.'

'Which made you a fine officer, I'm sure,' Sterling said. 'Enjoy your afternoon, my lord, my lady.' With a bow, he walked off to rejoin the workers.

To Juliana's disappointment—once they reached the river, she could have at least played her fingers over his bare back and stomach and tracked the soft hair down his chest until it disappeared in his breeches—

Rafe tossed his shirt over his head and shrugged back into his jacket.

'Ready, my sweet?'

'More than ready.' Like a glutton about to be offered a sumptuous meal, she intended to devour every morsel of time alone with him, all too aware of how soon such private afternoons would end.

After giving the groom who'd accompanied her leave to return to the stables, Rafe mounted his gelding and set off with her.

'Did you gather as many branches as Sterling hoped?' she asked as the horses trotted along.

'Yes, we made a fine haul. Sterling will parcel them out to the farms at the eastern edge of Thornthwaite and to the cottages below the sheep crofts. There's little growing there from which they can fashion thatch of their own.'

She sighed. 'I am sorry Sterling chose to cut the woods by the river.'

He turned to grin at her. 'Thereby limiting our activities?'

'There will be no swimming together naked, alas. Though you look warm enough to enjoy a dip in the river. You could swim by yourself, if you like. While I sit on the bank and...admire.'

'I'm afraid you've spoiled me for...swimming without you. Well, the loss for me is a gain for Thornthwaite. The former wood will support another field of grass for cattle and the one adjacent will increase our yields of bracken, once it has time to grow. You're no longer cutting the bracken alone, you know.'

A shock of surprise and alarm zinged through her. Surely he couldn't have guessed at the despair she'd once felt over knowing he would never love her?

Surely she'd done an adequate job of covering the emotions she still couldn't quite suppress with a protective barrier of sensual distraction.

And surely, she thought with a pang of mingled hope and sadness, his comment couldn't indicate that he might be developing stronger emotions for her, the fairy lord having won back his lover—could it? 'I asked Old Mrs Morse about the tune when Sterling and I came to check her cottage,' he continued, apparently interpreting the shock she hadn't been able to hide as surprise that he knew the song. 'I had her sing it for me. You're right; it's sad but lovely. You're not just my naiad, you're my fairy sprite, and I intend never to lose you.'

Might she really be touching his heart? Not daring to believe that, she forced the idea away as she dashed a glitter of foolish tears from her eyes. 'I do promise never to drown—or blind—you.'

'I am relieved,' he said with a chuckle. 'Then I am safe, at least as long as I don't go pining after another.'

By now they'd reached the clearing by the river. The site was peaceful and lovely, gilded with afternoon sun and warmed with the soft green of newly emerging leaves and ferns. Bird calls echoed by the lowing of cattle grazing in a recently cleared field beyond serenaded them as Juliana unpacked the blanket and supplies while Rafe set his fishing gear near the bank.

'Will you fish with me?' he asked as he helped her spread the blanket against the broad trunk of a tree near river's edge, where they could watch the water swirling in eddies and listen to the soft rush of the stream.

She shook her head. 'I brought Pope's *Iliad* to entertain me while you pursue your hobby. I hope fishing here will prove as tranquil as the sessions you remember from the Peninsula. There should be wildflowers in the new meadow next spring, too, along with bracken. Not the same as the ones in Portugal, but lovely. Bluebells, like the ones that lined the path into the woods this spring.'

'There were daffodils, too, in the sunnier spots by the bank.'

'How accurately Wordsworth captured the spell they cast! "For oft when on my couch I lie/In vacant or in pensive mood/They flash upon the inward eye/Which is the bliss of solitude/And then my heart with pleasure fills/And dances with the daffodils,"' she quoted. 'I may be sitting on a blanket rather than a couch, but my heart still dances, remembering them. What a graceful way with words the poet has, painting so vivid a picture with his verses.'

'You have a way with your sketches, recreating scenes just as vividly. I'm pleased that you are enjoying your studies, but you must continue with your drawing, too.'

He touched a finger to the tip of her nose, his gaze unexpectedly tender.

She shrugged and looked away, warmed by but still uncomfortable at his praise. She shouldn't gaze too long into his ardent eyes, lest her guard slip and she began to delude herself that he cared for her more than he did. 'I may have to content myself with reading; I've already filled just about every available space in my sketchbook.'

'We shall have to do something about that.'

'First, we must do something about your victuals. After cutting branches all morning, you must be starving.' She gestured to the blanket where the food had been set out.

'With you, I'm always starving,' he said, as he lowered himself to the ground.

She felt the always-simmering arousal intensify—and was grateful to move away from emotion onto safer ground. After glancing over at the field and noting its sole bovine occupants were paying them no heed, she dropped down beside him.

'We shouldn't swim, alas. But I might be able to satisfy that hunger…another way.'

Reaching up, she urged him to recline against the tree trunk, then kissed him. As they tangled tongues, the kiss becoming deeper and more urgent, she moved her hands down to his trouser flap, plucked open the buttons and reached within to fondle him.

He groaned, the warm flesh hardening under her fingers. 'Ah, this could be wonderful. But…unfulfilling for you.'

'Not necessarily.' Lifting her skirts, she straddled him, and after settling the concealing fabric around them, guided him inside her.

As she leaned down to kiss him again, he tugged open the buttons of her riding jacket and slipped his hands in to caress her breasts. As she wore beneath it only a fine muslin blouse and a thin chemise, having left off her stays, she felt his cock jerk within her as he realized how little barred them from his touch. Urging her back, he leaned down to suckle her nipples through the fine barrier of cloth.

She gasped, feeling him fill her as sensation sparked from her breasts to her center. As the tension mounted, she pulled his chin up and wrapped her arms around him, kissing him urgently as they moved together, harder, faster, until they both reach a shattering climax.

After an intensity of bliss that robbed her of breath, she slumped against his chest, boneless. Breathing heavily, he clasped her against him. After long, languid motionless moments, he stirred, kissing her hair and her cheek.

He tilted up her chin and shook his head at her. 'You never fail to amaze me.'

Emotion still suspended in the aftermath of completion, she said, 'I continue to try. But now you truly are in need of sustenance.'

She eased away from him and after refreshing herself in the river, returned to see he had portioned out the food. Silent in the companionable aftermath of completion, they fed each other bites interspersed with little kisses. The food consumed, she sent him off to fish and took out her book.

Much as she was enjoying the *Iliad*, the words danced away from her on the page like those drifting daffodils. She turned to watch Rafe, admiring his skill and the economy of motion as he cast his line, pulled it in, cast it again.

For a few brief moments, she allowed a depth of emotion to well up. She would indulge herself this once, for liberation from forever keeping a guard over her emotions might be at hand. She wasn't certain yet, but she suspected she might be with child.

She'd been so busy with estate matters and preoccupied by Rafe, she'd only just realized she'd not had her courses in two months. And her body had started to feel...strange.

Ah, that it might be so! To have a child, Rafe's child, on whom she could redirect every bit of emotion her overfull heart kept trying to produce. Whether a hoped-for heir or a no-less-cherished daughter, a child would allow her to release all the pent-up love she'd hoarded for years.

Rafe would dote on his child, too. Love came in different forms; despite what he'd felt for the lady he'd lost years ago, there remained a deep well of emotion he could lavish on a son. She felt sure he would embrace fatherhood as passionately as she looked forward to being a mother.

Sharing a child would enrich and deepen the bond between them. Even if he never felt for her more than affection and friendship.

Chapter Eleven

In the late afternoon a week later, Rafe headed for the library. By now, his industrious wife had likely finished her day's tasks, and if so, he would probably find her there. She'd brought the books of poetry up to her chamber and often read to him in the languid aftermath of lovemaking, but she preferred to study the illustrated botanicals in the library, where she might leave the book open on the desk with room enough for her sketchbook beside it, where she added small drawings to its crowded pages.

With a sigh, he slowed his steps. She seemed so happy with her books, her duties, and their life in general. There was even a new glow about her these last weeks which reassured him that she was not regretting her decision to wed him.

All factors that made him reluctant to have this upcoming discussion with her. But with the estate's limited spring planting finished, the lambing season ended, the new calves delivered and the forest maintenance tasks accomplished, it was time to plan that trip to London.

He'd tried on several occasions since their one sharp exchange to introduce the matter in a more congenial manner—with no success. She'd either tried to distract him by introducing some other 'important' topic, or softly begged that they forego discussing it at the moment.

He shook his head, sighing. For an instant, he felt a modicum of sympathy for her overbearing mother, who had tried without success to push or pummel her into becoming the sort of well-brought-up maiden that lady believed she needed to be. Quiet Juliana might be, but she could be quite unmovable when she chose.

It still stung that she seemed to place more value in her mother's disparagement than in his reassurances.

But then, her mother had had years to instill those doubts. He must do his best to counter them—and he needed to succeed at that *now*.

For though initially he'd thought he might just as well go to London alone, over the last few weeks, he'd discovered he enjoyed the daily company of his wife a good bit more than he'd expected. He really would prefer to have her remain at his side—his best friend, helpmate and marvelous lover—in the City as she had been here at Thornthwaite.

Compelling her to discuss the matter would be hard enough and persuading her even more difficult. Ignored by her father, so often having her appearance and abilities denigrated by her mother and sister, she was, he knew, convinced she could only be a burden to him in London.

He was just as convinced she would not. After all, he had no interest in mingling with the shallower members of Society whose chief interests were food, parties, jewels, clothing and gossip.

He was eager to see Hart Edmenton again, to have Juliana meet him and his wife Claire, whom he admired—and had once seriously considered courting. He recalled with a grin that it was his tentative pursuit of the lady that shocked his friend into ceasing to overlook the treasure at his side. The widowed sister of the previous duchess, Claire had acquainted Hart with the ducal estate and its duties when he first returned from the army after unexpectedly inheriting the title.

At the time, Hart had been holding out for a Grand Passion like the one his own parents shared. Having suffered a Grand Passion himself, Rafe had strongly advised his compatriot to seek instead a Grand Friendship.

A Grand Passion. That surprisingly sharp ache stabbed again at his ribs. Absently, he rubbed a hand there to soothe it. He'd worked so hard to suppress any thought of Thalia, he'd almost convinced himself that he'd successfully buried for good the misery of losing her. But apparently, like a crack plastered over, the fault still lurked beneath the outward concealment.

Firmly he suppressed both the ache and the memories.

As he'd assured Hart, courtesy, respect and affection provided a far better foundation for long-lasting happiness in marriage. The kind of friendship, respect and affection borne of shared interests and common endeavours he shared with his Juliana.

Then he recalled that, to his and Hart's surprise, Claire ended up becoming Hart's Grand Passion.

He pushed the disconcerting thought aside. What more bliss could he wish for? He had a highly competent wife with whom he shared a warm affection and a powerful sensual connection that kept him permanently simmering on the edge of arousal, no matter how often—and it was very often—his enterprising wife satisfied him.

Why would he ever want to complicate that with the drama and misery of Grand Passion? He wouldn't, he told himself firmly. Nor would he want his dear Juliana to suffer from it. She'd been sensible enough not to have fallen for Ian. If he prided himself that she cared a bit more deeply for him than she had for his brother, he'd still not want her to care *too* much more. So much that it destroyed the easy companionship and friendship they shared.

An uncomfortable niggle that was something like

doubt nipped at him, but he pushed that away, too. Enough dawdling; time to face the task at hand.

Rafe walked to the open library door a moment later and paused. Juliana was indeed seated at the desk, her gaze moving back and forth from the illustration in the book open before her—one of Bewick's, he noted— to her sketchpad. Smiling, he watched as she carefully sketched away, probably copying some figure that had caught her eye or creating a different image inspired by it.

He wondered how he'd ever thought her meek and childlike. True, her figure wasn't voluptuous, but it was well-rounded, with firm breasts, wide hips, slender hands, and a lush mouth. For a moment, he was distracted by memories of what she could do with those hands, that mouth, those legs wrapped around him…

Pulling himself back from the sensual heat she seemed to always arouse in him, he reminded himself he was equally taken by her great, expressive brown eyes, so alive with intelligence, curiosity and concern. How her keen observation and unique way of looking at the world continually surprised him with new insight, or some fresh vision of something he thought he knew but then realized he'd never really *seen*.

Then there was that still-mystifying, ever-compelling, chameleon-like ability to switch in an instant from enticing siren to helpful assistant.

He shook his head. He truly was one lucky man.

She looked up then and smiled. 'Repairs completed on the roof thatching?'

'Yes, we finished up today. I rode out to the south farms with Sterling, then inspected the repairs to the stone fences on the fells that were damaged by winter frost. Now that the sheep have gone back up to graze, it was the last spring task we needed to accomplish to bring all the work on the estate up to date.'

Her smile faded. 'You'll be needing to leave for London, then.'

'Yes. Parliament is already in session; I don't want to delay much longer to answer the writ and claim my place. I'm anxious to hear the progress of the army; Napoleon abdicated last month and will be exiled to Elba, the newspapers say, but I don't know anything about what will happen to the different units. They'll get the latest news sooner in London.'

'Are you concerned about your friend, Lieutenant Marsden?'

'Yes. One benefit of being still with the army; one can keep better tabs on one's friends, even if one's units don't take part in the same campaigns. Charles is not much of a correspondent, it turns out.'

'Surely you would have heard something, if anything had happened to him.'

'Not necessarily. He has little family—an orphan, he was brought up by a childless couple who would

serve as his next of kin, should ill befall him. If anything did happen, Hart, with his contacts at Horse
Guards, would be more likely than me to hear of it.
As you know, I've been very anxious to see Hart and
have you meet him and Claire. No, please!' he urged
as she opened her lips, doubtless to forestall him. 'I
know the matter distresses you, but we must talk about
it. It's quite important to me.'

She stilled and looked at him warily. 'Are you going
to harangue me until I agree to accompany you?'

'No. I apologize if it seemed I was "haranguing"
you when I mentioned this before. I can't undo in a
few weeks the negative view of your abilities instilled
in you by years of your mother's reproofs. All I can
ask is that you give some weight to my opinion, which
contradicts hers in several important particulars. Will
you listen?'

She looked unhappy, but at least she didn't object—
or flee the room. 'Very well, I'll listen.'

'I want you to meet the people who matter to me,
and have them meet you. And though I hope, finding yourself welcomed and accepted by them, that
you will feel more confident about venturing out into
Society, you may participate in the Season only as
much—or as little—as you choose. Whatever events
you approve, we'll attend together. Not everyone in
Society is like your mother and sister, overly concerned about rank and fashion. There are intelligent,

thoughtful females, too. Lady Fenniston is one, certainly. Wasn't your friend, Lady Fellsham, one as well?'

'Yes,' she affirmed reluctantly.

'We'll only go to entertainments given and attended by sensible people, friends or associates connected with Parliament or the army. Neither your mother nor your sister will be in Town, so you needn't fear their scrutiny. We can visit the theater. Ride in Hyde Park in the early morning, which while it isn't wild like your beloved Lake District, is pretty enough. You can return to the British Museum as often as you like and do more sketching.'

Moving to stand beside the desk, he gestured to her sketchbook. 'Your work is really very good, you know. As far as I'm aware, no one has yet published sketches of British mammals. You ought to put together a collection—"Animals of the Lake District," you could call it. Begin with your sketches of the Herdwick lambs, the red squirrel, the deer, the peregrine falcon and go on from there. You've completely filled your sketchbook; once in London, we can get you more materials.'

She smiled. 'I don't know about gowns and furbelows, but I would love a new sketchbook.'

Rafe shook his head fondly. 'Other husbands worry about their wives spending hundreds of pounds on jewels and finery. My wife wants a few shillings for a sketchbook. But there is one final, most important reason for you to accompany me.'

He paused, waiting until she looked up at him inquiringly. 'I find I've grown quite fond of having you near me—friend, wife and lover. I find I don't like the prospect of being without you for several weeks or months.'

'*Fond* of having me near you?' she repeated.

'Excessively fond,' he elaborated. 'I should miss you very much if you chose to remain at Thornthwaite. I hope you're not going to wound me by saying you would not miss *me*,' he added, initially teasing, but suddenly feeling almost…uncertain about the answer. She was so capable, so self-contained—would she miss him?

After a short pause, during which his wordless alarm intensified, she said, 'You may rest easy; I *would* miss you, terribly.'

He felt a flood of relief whose strength he didn't wish to examine.

'Then won't you, dear wife, agree to accompany me to London? You did pledge to do what you could to make me happy, you'll remember.'

She sighed. 'So I did. I admit, I'm…not quite as opposed to going to London as I was. I… I truly would miss you a great deal if we were apart. But aside from your close friends, who will accept me for their love of you, I still doubt I will be well received by the rest of Society. However, if it is so important to you, I… I will endeavour to endure the trip.'

'Excellent!' Rafe replied, not bothering to hide his sense of relief this time.

'I do fear that with your duties in Parliament and catching up with your friends, I won't see much of you. Here at Thornthwaite, I've got rather used to spending time with you every day.'

Feeling pleased, he pulled her to her feet and gave her a hug. 'Don't worry about that,' he soothed, leading her to a seat on the sofa. 'I doubt you'll see me much less than you do here, as I'm often out with Sterling much of the day. We will have social engagements, it's true, but we should have dinner and the evenings together most every day, I would think. And every night.'

'Unless you dine at a club and remain there late, catching up or playing cards with your army or university friends.'

He shrugged. 'I'd rather meet them during the day and save my evenings for my wife. Though I imagine you'll want some time to yourself. I doubt you'd want me to live in your pocket. After all, how much of me do you want to see?'

As she gazed up at him, he suddenly realized from her intent expression the double meaning of his words. As always, the sexual innuendo sparked in his ever-eager body an immediate stir of response.

'Well, there is one part I'm particularly fond of.'

His breath caught and he felt himself harden. 'Is there, now?'

'Oh, yes. A part I am always thrilled to see…and appreciate.' Once again turning to seductress, she gave him a wicked smile and slowly licked her lips, leaving them plump and sheened with moisture.

'A part that, in London, I shall probably not be able to see and appreciate in your library in daylight. So I should make the most of my opportunities here.'

Then, her eyes never leaving his, she dropped to her knees and with excruciating slowness, undid one by one the buttons of his trouser flap.

At the first touch of her lips, his brain shut down, pure sensation taking over as he arched back on the couch and gave himself over to pleasure.

Sometime later, back in her own chamber, Juliana regarded her image in the pier-glass. 'What have you agreed to, little fool?' she asked her reflection with a sigh.

No going back on her word now. And perhaps London wouldn't be the disaster she feared. She was reasonably sure Rafe's friends would be kind. And if he truly wouldn't push her to attend any events whose high-born Society guests would make her inadequate and unwanted, maybe the social engagements at which they did appear wouldn't be overly trying.

She might have continued to refuse…if only she hadn't known in her bones that she would miss him terribly if she held firm and remained at Thornthwaite. If only she hadn't dreaded that, if she gave up the daily contact that had drawn them closer, when he returned, she might never recapture it.

He'd become 'fond' of her company, he'd said, she recalled, feeling again the sharp ache of longing for some deeper feeling from him, an ache she didn't seem able to completely suppress.

Well then, if 'friends' was all she could hope for, they would be the dearest ones, she told herself stoutly. Fortunately, as the episode in the library just demonstrated, Rafe still responded eagerly to her sensual advances.

She meant to use every tactic she possessed to hold on to every bit of closeness—even if it meant venturing to London.

Chapter Twelve

Two weeks later, Rafe escorted a nervous Juliana up the steps of the Duke of Fenniston's imposing London townhouse in Jermyn Street.

'I thought Thornthwaite House was large,' she mumbled. 'This is a great hulk.'

'It should be. Hart is a duke, I'm only an earl,' Rafe said, giving her an amused look. 'Surely you've entered some grand edifices when in London.'

'Not really. On my only sojourn, I wasn't "out", you'll remember. The few members of Society I encountered I met at home, in the townhouse Father rented for the Season, my family not being sufficiently wealthy—or important—enough to own a house in town. It was comfortable, but certainly not imposing. I never returned to London, since, as you know, after Ian and I agreed to marry, it wasn't thought necessary to present me officially. Not doing so saved my family a great deal of blunt, which Carlisle was already spending freely and saved Mama palpitations from wondering how my odd behaviour might embarrass her in front of Society. Anyway, I was perfectly agreeable to remaining at Edgerton.'

Rafe frowned, as if about to comment that he saw that as yet another slight visited upon her by her family. But before he could say anything, the door opened and the butler bowed them in. The interior was just as opulent and ornate as one would suspect from the exterior: marble floors, elaborate plaster decoration on the walls, an elegant crystal chandelier swaying above her head.

As they turned over her cloak and Rafe's hat and cane, a tall, regal woman emerged from the room off the entryway. 'Thank you, Tompkins, I'll take over now.'

'As you wish, Your Grace. Shall I have tea sent in?'

'Yes, and notify the Duke his guests have arrived.'

Juliana looked up in some trepidation. Her hostess, nearly as tall as Rafe, towered over her by almost a head. Though the rest of her appearance was not alarming. Unlike the ostentatious surroundings, the lady was simply dressed, her lustrous dark hair arranged in an uncomplicated style, her gown, though fashionable and of obviously expensive material, plain, unadorned by lace or embroidery, and she wore a single strand of pearls.

While Juliana was inspecting her, the Duchess turned to her husband. 'Lieutenant Tynesley! How good it is to see you! Hart has been impatiently await-ing your visit. Though I should properly call you Lord Thornthwaite now.'

She turned startlingly blue eyes on Juliana and held out her hand with a smile. 'You must be Lady Thornth-waite. I'm so pleased to meet you! Not knowing when you might arrive, Hart is finishing up some estate business in the library, but he will be down directly. We are both delighted to welcome you to London. Do come in,' she urged, waving them into the parlour from which she had emerged and seeing them seated on the sofa before the hearth.

'Have you settled in yet?'

'Not quite,' Rafe answered when it became obvi-ous Juliana was not going to. 'We only arrived night before last. Yesterday we were buried in a flurry of unpacking.'

'You're to be introduced in the Lords shortly, I ex-pect.'

'Yes. I'm dreading the elaborate ceremony almost as much as Hart tells me he did his presentation. The Black Rod, the King of Arms, sponsors fore and aft in full regalia, bowing to this and that! Though I suppose I must get used to calling Hart "Fenniston".'

'As I must get used to calling you "Thornthwaite",' a deep voice said from the threshold.

Rafe jumped up and strode over to embrace the tall, dark-haired man who'd just entered. As they backed to arms' length, looking each other over, the Duke laughed. 'Quite a change in circumstance from our days on campaign, isn't it?' he said, gesturing to the ornate room around them.

'Are you accustomed to it yet?'

The Duke made a wry grimace. 'Not really. Though my charming wife has done all she can to make it easier. Now, you must introduce me to *your* charming wife.'

Waving Juliana to keep her seat, the Duke walked over to kiss his wife on the cheek. Juliana couldn't help noticing the warmth in his eyes as he looked at the Duchess…and the corresponding joy in hers as she leaned up into his kiss.

They are in love, she thought with a pang, trying not to feel envious.

'Darling,' Rafe said, interrupting her melancholy, 'May I present my dear friend, the Duke of Fenniston? My wife, Lady Thornthwaite.'

As the Duke turned to her, despite his gesture meant to set her at ease, Juliana rose and made him a deep curtsey. 'A pleasure to meet you, Duke.'

He gave a deprecating wave of the hand. 'Please, don't call me that. I have to tolerate it from outsiders, but not from the wife of my best friend. If you can't bring yourself to call me "Lieutenant," at least call me only "Fenniston."' He made a face. 'I'd still rather be "Edmenton", but there you have it.'

'I see you're not much more reconciled to the title than you were when you first learned it had landed upon you,' Rafe said.

The Duke shrugged. 'There was no choice but to accept it, and duty is duty, so I'm doing my best. Thank Heaven, I have Claire to help make it tolerable.'

'Any chance that among ourselves, we might be just "Hart", "Claire", "Juliana" and "Rafe"?' her husband asked. 'I'm not as resistant to catching a title as you were, but I still think of my father whenever someone says "Thornthwaite."'

The Duchess gave him a conspiratorial glance. 'I don't see why not, when it's just us. Hart still chokes over the "Duke" title and when someone calls "Duchess", I look around to discover who they are greeting.' She turned to Juliana. 'Being addressed by title is quite an uncomfortable leap for a girl who grew up simple "Miss Turnville" and spent several years as a lowly lieutenant's wife, following the drum through the mud and heat of Portugal.'

'Say, now, we lieutenants were not "lowly,"' her husband objected.

'Valiant, the backbone of the army, but not numbered among the lofty, except for those on Wellington's personal staff,' the Duchess amended.

'That's better,' the Duke allowed. 'And yes, let it be "Hart" and "Claire", "Rafe and Juliana." If your lady will permit.'

'I must, before my husband argues for even greater informality and gifts you my childhood nickname,' Juliana said wryly. 'Mouse,' she added at their inquiring looks.

'Mouse?' Claire echoed. 'Either he was a great jester as a youth, or you've changed markedly! "Juliana" is much more fitting.'

'That's settled, then,' Duke said.

'You must stay and dine with us tonight,' the Duchess—Claire—said. 'Especially since your own establishment is not sorted out yet.'

'It certainly isn't,' Hart said. 'To my knowledge, Ian never opened up the townhouse after he inherited and the neglect shows. Nor have we a proper cook— a long story I won't bore you with now. Our current cook, Jane, still very much a beginner, was awed almost to tears by the set-up at Thornthwaite House on Upper Brook Street,which apparently my mother modernized before her death. In addition to which, we'd need an army to clean the whole place properly.' He sighed. 'It might have been easier to rent rooms, but I didn't want to spend the blunt to do that now—but you don't need to hear about that, either. We'd love to stay for dinner, wouldn't we, Juliana?'

'That would be very kind,' she said, halfway between comforted by the obvious friendliness of Hart's former army mate and his wife and a lingering anxiety about dining with a duke and duchess.

'Before we go any farther, you must have the latest news about the army. Have you heard from Charles?'

'You know Napoleon abdicated in April?' At Rafe's nod, he continued, 'The former emperor arrived in Elba last month. Our army units are just now return-ing. Charles was slightly wounded at the final battle of Toulouse but should be coming back to England soon. Last I heard from him, he was going to rejoin his unit at Calais; Horse Guards tells me they are to set sail for England in July.'

'Praise the Lord! Then it's over at last?'

'One hopes so. The luminaries are going to gather this fall in Vienna to carve up the spoils.' He laughed. 'It will be quite an act of diplomacy to keep all the players happy. Russia and Austria want back the lands Napoleon conquered, with Italy returning to the Haps-burg fold. And nobody's worried about poor little Poland, who was promised its independence by Na-poleon.'

'Now, I know you two old soldiers want to talk about the army and exchange war stories. Why don't you re-pair to the library and find some brandy while we la-dies chat over tea. If that's agreeable to you, Juliana?'

Juliana felt a little dismayed at losing the reinforce-ment of Rafe's presence, but she had been anticipat-ing talking with this former lieutenant's wife about following the drum—the main reason she had been cautiously looking forward to meeting the Duchess when she was not eager to meet anyone else in London. She was still hungry to learn anything and everything about Rafe, anything and everything that could help her bind them close enough that he would continue to want her daily company. Surely, this lady who had experienced life with the army could broaden her knowledge about this significant period of his life.

Besides, the Duchess had thus far been nothing but kind and welcoming, as understanding and non-judgemental as Rafe had promised she would be. Though sitting beside this elegant, accomplished woman, she felt all too much like the 'Mouse' Rafe used to call her. Even as little as she followed fashion, it was obvious that her braided coiffure looked like a schoolgirl's and her gown was out of style as well as rather worn.

Hart dropped a kiss on his wife's head as he and Rafe rose. 'We won't bore you with soldier talk, then. But we won't abandon you for too long.'

Rafe gave Juliana a wink before he strolled out with his friend.

'Now, we may be comfortable,' the Duchess said.

Juliana wasn't so sure about that, but gamely launched into the topic that most interested her. 'If it's not too impertinent, I would like to talk with you, Duch—Claire—about your time with the army. Rafe told me some of his adventures while on campaign, but I'm sure he exaggerated the delights and minimized the discomforts. We've been friends since we were children, but I know very little about what his life was like during his army years. I'd like to know what it was truly like to live on campaign. I must add, I admire you so much for having gone with your husband and endured what must have been at best a difficult existence.'

'Difficult at times, yes. But also interesting, rewarding, even exciting. But in return, you must tell me all about yourself as well.'

Juliana made a minimizing gesture with her hand. 'There's not much to tell. Before moving to Thorne Hall, I lived my whole life at Edgerton Manor, west of Carlisle in the Lake District. Except for a few months in London when my older sister was presented.'

Claire shook her head. 'There's much more than that, I know. Rafe has written to Hart about you. I must say, you've made him very happy.'

A little shock of mingled delight and disbelief went through her. 'Why do you say that?'

'I can see it, just looking at him. He's relaxed, his eyes bright with hope and purpose, his manner carefree. I was halfway expecting him to be tense, weary, and obviously worn down by the burden of his inheritance. Unlike my husband's property, which had been smoothly run, he'd written to Hart that the estate was in a shambles. He said you had been an immense help in sorting out what needed to be done. Obviously you have been.'

Juliana flushed, pleased that Rafe had complimented her to his friend, embarrassed by feeling she didn't deserve such high praise. 'I hope I have been. I'm nowhere near as expert at running an estate as you are; I understand you managed Steynling Cross almost single-handedly before the new Duke's arrival. Rafe is making progress in bringing Thornthwaite back into fighting trim, mostly through his own efforts. I've only guided him. I spent a lot of time around the estate while I was engaged to his brother, especially during his last illness. I had no authority to order things as I might have liked, but I did learn a lot about what needed to be done.'

The Duchess nodded. 'Both men are intelligent, capable and driven to do their duty. The soldier in them, I suppose. I imagine Rafe is taking over the reins as competently as Hart did.'

'He is doing well. He's a fast learner and much more...approachable than his late brother, who was rather distant and reserved, in addition to having little interest in the day-to-day working of the estate. The tenants appreciate seeing Rafe riding out among them every day, actively managing the land and clearly interested in their welfare.'

'Traits of a good military officer,' Claire said. 'Also like Hart. So you were engaged to Rafe's elder brother? It must have been...devastating to lose him.'

Juliana nodded, ready to offer Claire some explanation, but with no intention of confiding the whole story. 'I understand you were widowed, so you know what it's like.'

'True. But I had years to recover before I eventually fell in love with Hart. Were you…agreeable to marrying Rafe? Of course, Hart believes him a paragon and thinks any female must be thrilled to become his wife. I hope you weren't…obligated into it.'

'Not at all.' Which wasn't exactly the truth but she wasn't prepared to disclose everything about their complicated arrangement, either. 'As I mentioned, we've been friends since childhood. We're…comfortable with each other.'

She nodded. 'Rafe always insisted friendship formed the best basis for marriage. Although it's quite obvious you share more.'

Not being good at deception, she had meant to curtail any further discussion of her feelings for Rafe, but at that, she found herself blurting, 'What do you mean?'

Claire laughed. 'Sparks fly when your husband looks at you, my dear. Which is a very good thing.'

Surprised and somewhat embarrassed that their physical attraction might be so obvious, she said weakly, 'We are good together—in that way.'

'It's a true bonus in a marriage.'

After replying with a noncommittal murmur, she

said, 'Won't you tell me what it was like following the drum? I want to hear everything!'

'Very well. But only if you agree to tell me all about yourself afterwards.'

'A rather unequal bargain, as I promise you, there's not much to tell. But please, begin!'

'My, how to start? First of all, being allowed to accompany one's husband happens by chance, no matter how desperately a wife might want to go. Officers may bring their wives, but must provide for them. Each unit of soldiers is allowed only a fixed number of wives to accompany it, the names drawn by lot. It results in quite a heartbreaking scene at the dock when the soldiers embark!'

'Was the sea journey difficult?'

Claire nodded. 'The transports were crowded. Fortunately, I'm a good sailor, but not all wives fared as well. Marches were difficult, there's no denying. Fierce sun and rocky, dusty roads in summer that only donkeys could tolerate—no fancy steeds for we women! Hot as summer could be, winter was worse; rain that turned such tracks as passed for roads into slicks of mud, freezing wind that could cover everything, from your tent to the blanket under which you slept, with a glaze of ice. But there was entertainment and enjoyment, too. The friendship and hospitality of the Portuguese, even in the smallest village, was famed. Winter quarters in Lisbon were often quite merry, with dances, parties, dinners and fetes to make one forget the travails of the march. And the men were almost uniformly chivalrous and helpful. Yes, it was difficult…but I wouldn't have missed it for the world. But that's more than enough about me! Now, tell me about you. Rafe says you are quite the naturalist, knowledgeable about all about the birds, animals and even the fish in the Lake District area.'

'I'm no expert,' she protested. 'I've just always enjoyed tracking, observing, and sketching them. To be honest, I'm much more at ease with creatures of nature than with the human of the species. I'm hopeless at clever drawing room conversation. When I was in London with my sister during her Season, Mama ended up forbidding me to speak when we entertained, as I asked too many questions and apparently made my impatience too apparent if I received a lackwit response. Or challenged the accuracy of some gentleman's boast. Nor did I ever master the art of flirting. Fortunately, I didn't have to. When my elder sister, whom our parents initially intended for Ian, received an offer from the son of a marquess, both Ian and I were content for me to replace her.'

Claire looked like she wanted to question the depth of Juliana's 'contentment' but after a moment, said instead, 'You helped with Thornthwaite while you were engaged to Rafe's elder brother, you said?'

'Yes. Even before the…illness that incapacitated

him later, like his father, Ian was more interested in literature, poetry and painting and left estate management to his manager. Which was fine while the original manager worked at Thornthwaite, but the man who took over when he retired was…venal. I'm certain he was embezzling estate funds, though it could never be proven. Certainly he never invested anything back into the estate. I witnessed what was going on, tried to help as much as I could, but as we were not yet wed, I had no authority to intervene.'

'A difficult situation,' Claire commented. 'Enough said about that distressing matter. What is Thornthwaite like?'

'Beautiful! Much of it is forested, with some stands of trees pollarded and coppiced for wood products used on the estate or sold. Upland meadows reaching to the heights of the fells are given over to sheep—wool being another primary source of income. There are cattle, too, and a few crops, mostly corn to provide feed for the livestock. Have you ever visited the Lake District?'

'No. I understand it's magnificent country.'

'Oh, it is! Such vistas from the heights of the fells! Hills, peaks, valleys; the long blue lengths of the lakes! The crystal clear water of the rivers, teeming with fish, soared over by sea-birds, played in by otters. The meadows home to red deer, stoats, badgers, squirrels and a variety of smaller creatures, all of them endlessly fascinating.'

'Creatures you capture excellently in your drawings, Hart says.'

'I do draw them all, though I'm not so sure how excellently. How I wish I could truly capture all their wild beauty! Speaking of beauty, it's obvious looking at your appearance that my wardrobe is quite out of date. Much as I'd rather avoid it, I expect I shall have to attend a few social functions and I don't want to be an embarrassment to Rafe. May I count upon your good nature to help me shop for a few gowns that won't make Rafe blush when his wife meets his army or Parliamentary colleagues?'

'Of course! What lady could refuse a chance to shop? I can also show you to the bookstores and lending libraries and advise where you can find anything else you might need for Thornthwaite. Though I know Rafe told Hart you were observing strict economies while he works on building back up the estate's income.'

A knock sounded at the door and the butler bowed himself in. 'Excuse me for interrupting, Your Grace. Nurse says you wished to be called when the Young Master woke from his nap.'

A smile lit Claire's face. 'I did.' Turning to Juliana, she said, 'Would you like to meet one of the lights of my life?'

'Very much!'

'Do you like children?' she asked as they left the tea things and she led Juliana up the stairs towards the nursery.

'I've not been much acquainted with them. I don't much like my sister's,' she added with a grimace. 'They always seem to be either quarreling or whining.'

'All children quarrel or whine at times, but it sounds as if they are not well managed.'

'My sister gives them whatever they ask for. And scolds their Nanny if the older ones tell her she tried to discipline them.'

Claire shook her head. 'She may not keep that Nanny much longer, then.'

'I am very much looking forward to having Rafe's child—our child. In fact, I'd like to ask a few questions, if I may.'

'Of course, ask me anything. I don't claim to be an expert, but I have been a mother for some time— I have an older son, Alexander, who is four years old now and completely charming.'

Juliana smiled at the mother's obvious bias. 'I'm sure he is.'

'We often have my sister's daughter, Arabella, staying with us as well. She's almost of an age with Alex. My sister finds motherhood…fatiguing, and being recently married, wants time alone with her new husband.'

Juliana detected a slightly disapproving note. 'How…disappointing for Arabella.'

'We try to shower her with enough affection to make up for it. But Bella is a tough little thing. She'll survive having a distant mother. I did.'

Feeling a stab of empathy for the little girl, Juliana was surprised into volunteering, 'Or a disapproving one, as I did. I may know little about being a mother, but I vow that my children will know only cherishing.'

Claire squeezed her hand. 'Then you know what, in my opinion, that is the most important thing about being a mother.'

Reaching the nursery, Claire sent the nursery maid off to have tea, telling her they'd tend the child. Picking her son out of his cradle, she hugged him close before turning to Juliana.

'May I introduce you to our young viscount, Lord Edmenton,' she said, displaying the baby proudly. 'We named him Arthur Charles after Hart's father, but we call him Charlie. It may not be correct, but I can't bring myself to call a three-month-old infant "Edmenton."'

After kissing his head, she cuddled him close again, her joy in him apparent. Juliana felt a surprisingly fierce pang of longing. How she yearned to have a child of Rafe's to cherish!

'Would you like to hold him?'

'May I?'

'Of course. He's quite sturdy, he won't break.'

As his mother handed him over, Juliana gazed down at that perfect little round face, the child's dark eyes gazing up at her inquiringly. 'What a handsome little lordling you are,' she breathed. 'No wonder your Mama dotes on you.'

'We're in private now. What did you wish to ask me?'

Her need for answers prevailing over her discomfort in broaching so intimate a matter, Juliana said, 'As I mentioned, I'm not...close to my mother. My maid, Baxter, is the nearest thing I have to a female friend and confidante, but she's never had any children. I grew up in the country, so I understand what is necessary to conceive child, but...how does one know when that has happened?'

Claire gave her an inquiring look. 'Do you think you might be with child?'

'I might be. I haven't had my courses in over two months.'

'If they normally come regularly, that's a good sign. How are you feeling?'

'My appetite is good, but... I have lost my breakfast every morning for the last week or so. Which might be the result of riding in the coach, as I've seldom traveled such long distances.'

'Perhaps, though stomach distress is often an early sign. Has there been anything else?'

'Just recently my breasts seem...swollen and tender.'

'Another good sign. There's no way to be certain until you feel the child move within you, which doesn't happen until one has been *enceinte* for five months or so. But it sounds as if you might be.'

Juliana had to damp down an emotion so strong, she was almost in tears. Hardly daring to hope it might be true, she couldn't trust herself to speak.

'Would you be happy if it were true?'

'Ecstatic!' she burst out. 'Rafe and I are so...comfortable together. A child would be the final thing to make our relationship complete.'

Claire gave her an assessing look, making Juliana uncomfortably aware that she'd left out any mention of 'love' in describing their union. But refraining from commenting about that, the Duchess said instead, 'Does Rafe know?'

'Oh, no! I've no intention of saying anything yet. I might well be mistaken, and I would want to be very sure before I raise his hopes. Now that he holds the title, he is of course very concerned about having an heir. Though I'm certain he would love any child of his.'

'Then I hope your suspicions may be correct.'

'Is there...anything I should be doing? Or not doing?' She laughed. 'Which I suppose is a foolish question to ask one intrepid enough to accompany the army on campaign while *enceinte*.'

'Actually, I spent most of my pregnancy comfortably tucked away at a house in Lisbon. There's no need to wrap yourself up in cotton wool. It's fortunate the current fashion for high-waisted frocks will allow you to purchase new gowns that are loose in the bodice. If you truly are with child, you may find yourself becoming more fatigued than usual the first few months. You should rest if you are and eat sensibly.'

'Can one ride? I expect you did.'

'Indeed. If you enjoy riding, you may. Avoid galloping, though it's unlikely you could harm the child unless you took a particularly bad tumble. Continue to do all the things you enjoy.' She gave Juliana a naughty glance. 'There's no need to discontinue doing the things you enjoy with your husband, either.'

While she waited for the appearance of the little being on whom she could lavish all her love, it was a relief to know she could distract herself with passion. 'I'm very relieved to hear that,' she said, making Claire laugh.

The nursery-maid bustled back in. 'I can take over now, Your Grace.'

'I suppose you must,' Claire said, handing the child back with reluctance. 'I don't want to disturb nursery routine *too* much.'

As they walked out, Claire said, 'Why don't you rest before dinner? I'll have Mrs Reynolds ready a bedchamber for you. On another visit, I shall take you to the schoolroom to meet Alex and Arabella. They are walking in the Park now with their Nurse.'

'I should love to meet them.' And absorb as many insights about motherhood as she could gather, hoarding them up against the day when she might be able to use them with her own child.

'Do you know which entertainments you are going to attend?' Claire asked as they walked back towards the bedchambers.

'I've no idea.'

'Of course not; you've hardly unpacked yet. I'll speak with Hart before dinner and see if he knows when Rafe intends to make his entrance into the Lords. And check our own invitations, to be sure we attend the same events.'

'It would be a great comfort to attend those you will be present at.' Juliana shuddered. 'So I do not have to face the dragons of Society on my own.'

'You must remember you are the wife of an earl now; a countess is given much more leeway in her conduct than some lowly unmarried miss. Nor will Society wish to offend a Duchess by slighting her friend.' Claire made a face. 'As I can't escape the title, I might as well make use of it. You should, too.'

'It would certainly be a change not to have to worry about offending or embarrassing anyone,' she said ruefully. 'Fortunately, Mother is not in town this Season.

No matter what I did, she would find something to criticize. I'm relieved I won't have to deal with that.'

'If she is not supportive, ignore her. You're a countess now. You no longer need her approval.'

Juliana sighed. 'That's what Rafe advises. But it's still hard not to cringe when I see her coming, always ready with unfavourable comments about my conduct and appearance.'

'After our visit to my modiste, your appearance will be perfection. And a countess may conduct herself as she chooses.'

'Following animals in the park, sketchbook in hand? Studying fossils at the British Museum?' Juliana asked wryly. 'Don't worry! I will refrain from both—or at least, be careful not to be observed. At entertainments, I should be relieved to be able to follow in your train and let you do the speaking.'

'You may do so if you wish. But I hope you will soon feel confident enough to mingle on your own. In the meantime, if you just smile, nod, dance with your husband and his friends, you'll be fine.'

'I hope so.' As the Duchess led her to a chamber to rest, for the first time, Juliana felt less anxious about her upcoming time in Society. With her new friend to guide her, maybe she would weather London without committing any faux pas that could threaten the closeness with Rafe she'd developed at Thornthwaite—the closeness she would do all in her power to preserve.

Chapter Thirteen

Two nights later, anxious and wary despite Rafe's reassurances, Juliana clung to his arm as they entered the Anderson townhouse for their first social event.

'Relax!' he murmured, patting the fingers she'd locked in a death grip on his arm. 'This isn't a grand ball; just a rout; most of the guests are former army associates, along with a few of the men Hart works with in Parliament.'

'So Claire said when she took me to her modiste.'

Rafe scanned her with a glance. 'A fine session it was! You look absolutely charming, Mouse.'

His use of her old nickname—before she was to be introduced as a countess—with its reminder of their long friendship and all the ways he'd supported her in the past calmed her, as she knew he meant to. Still, she felt marginally better knowing she truly did look her best in a simple evening gown of pale green, the tiny puff sleeves threaded through with a dark green satin ribbon echoed in the satin rouleau on the bottom edge of the skirt. The low-cut bodice framed the Thornthwaite emeralds, the matching diamond-and-emerald drops at her ears testimony to a time when the estate had been thriving.

May it be an omen of the future, she thought. Taking a deep breath, she vowed not to allow her trepidation to spoil Rafe's first evening home among friends.

So she tried to bury all the doubts and still the quell of alarm that shocked through her as the butler intoned 'The Earl and Countess of Thornthwaite.' Scarcely breathing, she entered on Rafe's arm, staring straight ahead so as not to notice all the gazes that turned to inspect them as they entered the ballroom.

Their host, Colonel Anderson of the 1st Regiment of Foot Guards, having been wounded in the Pyrenees campaign, had returned in advance of the rest of his unit, which was not due back until July. Resplendent in his Guards uniform, he greeted Juliana cordially and Rafe with enthusiasm.

'So good to see you fully restored to health,' Rafe said.

'Dashed nuisance it was, having to be invalided out like that. Your husband and his calvary unit backed us on many an occasion,' he told Juliana. 'We must have a brandy later in the card room and catch up, Thornthwaite. If your lovely wife can spare you.'

'I'd never keep him from his friends. One of them

might have saved his life in battle once upon a time, a fact for which I can only be truly grateful.'

'Well-spoken,' Anderson replied. 'Though I suspect the only thing I saved him from was being fleeced by that card sharp major in the 10th corps, that night in Lisbon. You remember?'

'Oh, yes,' Rafe said with a laugh. 'A lucky escape indeed, for which I do owe you thanks.'

'We shall chat later,' Anderson told him, nodding a dismissal as the receiving line moved on.

'Card sharps in the army?' Juliana asked, amused.

Rafe gave her a rueful look. 'While in winter quarters or encamped between battles—which were often months apart—card playing is one of most common occupations, once drill and standing duty for the day completed. Some men became…quite skilled.'

'I imagine one might be "accidentally" shot while on picket duty if one became too "skilled."'

'Certainly, if he came from the ranks. If a gentleman by birth, he would have to be more cautious. Nothing would get one ostracized more quickly than to be discovered cheating at cards. Ah, there is Hart and Claire.'

Juliana felt an upswell of relief as Rafe led her over to his closest friend—and her newest one. For a good friend Claire had proved to be. She'd borne Juliana off to her favourite modiste and offered useful commentary on the gowns the proprietress presented that could be completed or altered within two days. Though initially shy at appearing in her chemise before the elegant duchess, Juliana found Claire soon set her at ease, even, to Juliana's surprise, offering compliments and exclaiming how well the high-waisted, long-columned skirts would display to advantage on her. She'd been gratified almost to tears even if she'd not fully believed her, recalling how often her mother had bemoaned her short stature and woeful lack of bosom.

The modiste, fully mindful of the benefit that would come from having her designs recommended by a duchess and worn by a countess, was all obligation. After a murmured consultation with Claire, she offered several day gowns, a walking dress and two ball gowns—procured at prices Juliana guessed were well below the lady's usual rates—along with a promise to have the first delivered the following day and the rest by the end of the week.

'Now I must introduce you to my particular friends,' Rafe said, breaking through her reverie. 'In addition to our host, I see Lieutenants Ross and Barnes and Captain Lord Cole, all of whom served in the army with us.'

'Cole, a baron, took up his position in the Lords last year, when I did,' Hart informed her. 'Shall we?'

The duke offered his wife his arm, Rafe took hers and they made a circuit of the room, Rafe introducing her to the men he'd mentioned and their wives, along with a scattering of others Hart knew from Parliament.

'You should expect to receive invitations to dance from most of those gentlemen,' Rafe warned her after their transit as he snagged her a glass of wine. 'But don't worry. You look lovely and they will find you charming.'

'I suppose they will expect me to talk with them,' she said, trying to fight off the anxiety that threatened to revive. 'I'm not sure what to say. Mama always said, "A lady allows the gentleman to direct the conversation," but I know so little of fashion or current doings in London, I'm not sure I could hold up my end of the chat.'

Rafe waved a dismissive hand. 'With army men, ask about where they were posted or interesting experiences they had while serving abroad. With the Parliamentary types, ask what bills they are currently working on. Then, you need only nod and smile.'

His advice made her feel a little better. 'That I can do, and I won't venture anything more, no matter what I think about what's been said. Mama says, "A lady never expresses an opinion, except to agree with a gentleman's."'

'I'm sorry being in London seems to have recalled your store of motherly admonitions,' Rafe said acerbically. 'I had hoped you'd left all that claptrap behind with her at Edgerton.'

'London does bring it all back,' she admitted.

He squeezed her hand. 'Just remember that, in almost all cases, your mother has been wrong in virtually everything she's ever said to you since childhood. Don't let her disparagement spoil what could be an enjoyable evening.'

Juliana took a deep breath. 'I'll try not to.'

Though she wasn't able to banish all her trepidation, as the various new acquaintances sought her out, Juliana found to her relief that Rafe had been right. Her dance partners, many still in uniform, were all easy to talk with, some openly admiring, though she still lacked the knack of responding to flirtation. By midevening, she felt confident enough to send Rafe off to the card room to catch up with their host.

Even better, while standing beside the Duchess, she needed only to follow her friend's lead, nodding, curtseying or smiling to all those who came to greet the new countess.

'How do you do this so well?' Juliana murmured after Claire smoothly deflected the too-forward advances of an obviously inebriated young lord.

'I weathered two Seasons before I was wed. In my first, I was accorded a good deal of attention by the late Duke of Fenniston, Hart's cousin. Having not yet inherited, he was still Viscount Edmenton then. When a lady is noticed by a future duke, other gentlemen follow. Some of them as ill-behaved as that young man.'

'The duke ultimately chose another?'

Claire smiled faintly. 'In my second Season, my younger sister Liliana was presented. Edmenton took one look at her—to be fair, she was the acclaimed Diamond of her debut year, her hand sought by many competing gentlemen—and turned his attention there. I drifted into the company of Alexander Hambledon, a family friend since childhood.'

'Like Rafe and I.'

'Yes. There was…rather more to it, but I'll not go into it at a rout.'

Noting her faint look of sadness, Juliana cried, 'I'm sorry to be so inquisitive! I didn't mean to bring up… unhappy memories.'

Claire touched her hand. 'Don't distress yourself. As it turns out, the late duke was not worthy of the regard I had for him. I did grow to love Alexander. Not with the rapture I feel for Hart—' she looked fondly in the direction of the card room into which their husbands had disappeared '—but in a warm, comforting, gentle way.'

'Did you fall in love the moment you saw Hart?'

Claire laughed. 'Oh, no! We were quite wary of each other at first. Indeed, he tricked me into thinking he was a rude Scot with no knowledge of how to behave as a gentleman! Though to be fair, that was what the former duke had led me to expect. I quickly learned otherwise, but it took time for the two of us to learn to…appreciate each other.'

The Duchess had come to feel a 'warm, comfortable' love for her childhood-friend husband after having been in love with another? Juliana felt a faint stirring of hope. Maybe, after a time, Rafe might develop the same sort of love for her?

'Time spent in Society, especially when I'd drawn attention by being favoured by the Viscount, taught me how to deal with overbearing matrons and impertinent gentlemen,' Claire continued. 'Then, as Father was a diplomat, I attended some of my parents' political dinners, where I could observe how the powerful and famous behave and copy their manners.'

'You observed well!' Juliana noted. 'You appear very "regal."'

Claire smiled wryly. 'Father was only an "honourable", the younger son of an earl; if I were not imperious, the Society dragons would skewer me for having wed a duke, attaining a rank well above my station. So I nod and offer a slight smile. It also helps if you can perfect a slightly bored expression that says you consider this-or-that one's approach only a bit short of presumptuous. Save your honest smiles and compliments for your friends, of course.'

Juliana shook her head. 'I'll settle for nodding and smiling. I'm not sure I could perfect any sort of expression.'

'Except delight, when you see Rafe approaching.'

Her eyes widening in alarm, Juliana scrambled for something clever to reply, and failed.

Claire patted her hand again. 'You care deeply for him, but don't worry, I won't say anything, not even to Hart. I know Rafe insists that the best marriage is a union of friends. But he cares deeply for you, too, even if hasn't quite realized it yet.'

It was an appealing thought, though Juliana wasn't sure it represented anything more than kind encouragement. But…maybe she could hope?

That in itself was a development welcome enough for her to be thankful after all that they had attended the rout.

In the afternoon a week later, Hart returned from a morning away and found his wife, as he anticipated, sitting at the desk in the library. He was looking forward to spending a few hours alone with her; the business of getting ready to enter Parliament and the distraction of encountering former friends and associates had occupied more time than he had anticipated.

He found he missed his wife's company. To say nothing of trysting in unusual places. Though, he acknowledged with a sigh, there was little chance of finding anywhere to indulge in one of those interludes in overcrowded London.

'Did your errands go well?' she asked, smiling and closing her book.

'Yes,' he said, crossing the room to kiss her cheek. 'I met with Hart and several others to discuss my introduction to the Lords. Then went to Ede & Ravenscroft to be measured for the presentation robe. It's crimson, trimmed with fur, very exquisite. I think you'd like it.'

'I'll look forward to seeing it. When do you expect to be presented?'

'Probably next week.'

She sighed. 'Then you'll be gone more often, attending sessions?'

'Some afternoons and evenings. Parliament tends to begin late and end late, so we might have mornings together. But I hope we'll have more time than we have since first arriving, when I've often been detained at the clubs or social events by running into friends from the army and university. I think by now I've caught up with everyone I wish to see; mere acquaintances who want to hang on the sleeve of a new earl, ones who paid me little attention when I was expected to remain simply "Mr Tynesley", are not worth my breath. You are still reading *The Iliad*, I see. Are you enjoying it?'

'Yes, though it is a very *manly* account. Women seem to feature only as sources of trouble—Helen, for all her beauty, inspires a kidnapping that causes a war. Cassandra's only use is to predict disaster. Then there's Achilles, who must choose between one of two rewards, either "glory" or "home"; if he stays to fight, he will die, but create a legend that will last for all time; if he returns home, he'll have the joy of family and children, but his name will be lost to history. Is that hope of immortal fame what inspires men to join the army?'

Surprised by the direction of her thoughts, he considered the question. 'Some dream of glory on the battlefield, I suppose. Many go to fulfill their duty to king and country, to defend England and their loved ones. Common soldiers may have different reasons. For the poor, life in England, whether working the fields or in factories, is often hard. Taking the king's shilling gives those men a certain freedom, transporting them to new, exciting lands with the possibility of spoils.'

'For all his ditherings, I like Achilles. It doesn't hurt that his mother Thetis is a sea goddess.'

'Naiads again?' he said, laughing. 'I should have known that would appeal to you. I'm glad I found you here, for I have something for you. I meant to obtain it much sooner—my only excuse for my tardiness is my being dragged to all those meetings, consultations, and long sojourns at the club.'

Lifting up the package he'd been holding behind his back, he handed it to her, excited to see her response.

'How kind! I've received few enough gifts in my life, I shall appreciate it, whatever it may be.' After placing the package on the desk, she carefully untied the string and unwrapped it, to reveal a large, leather-bound sketchbook.

'It's lovely!' she said on a gasp, her eyes lighting as she fingered the thick drawing paper within. 'It's much finer than the one I bought years ago. Thank you!'

Delighted to have pleased her, Hart said, 'I noted you've hardly done any sketching since we arrived in London, even with Bewick's *History of English Birds* to inspire you. I figured you must have completely run out of space in your old book. Now, you have all the room you like to begin again. I obtained a fresh supply of pencils and charcoal, too.'

'I shall have to begin again immediately! There isn't much choice of wild animals in London to inspire, but there will always be birds in the garden.'

'We might be able to do better than that. I thought, to repay your patience with my frequent absences, we could go to the British Museum this afternoon. I recall you telling me you'd found a number of examples there to inspire you on your last visit to London.'

'Are you sure you can spare the time?' When he nodded, she said excitedly, 'I'd love it! Shall we go now?'

'As soon as possible. I understand it closes by four, so we should leave at once.'

'Just let me fetch my bonnet and spencer.'

He shook his head, looking at her fondly. 'Any other female would protest she must change her morning gown for an afternoon or walking dress—and take an hour in the process.'

She frowned at him. 'I'll be wearing the spencer. What difference does it matter what sort of gown I'm wearing under it?'

'Just my point. Go, go. I'll be waiting.'

'I shall be back in a trice.'

She gave him a quick kiss on the cheek as she passed him. Hearing her rapid footsteps mounting the stairs, he shook his head again.

His unique, ever-surprising wife. Another female would have taken him to task for abandoning her so often these first weeks, when she had few friends to occupy her. Claire and Hart had been solid supports, but Hart still shouldered the task of supervising estate business along with his Parliamentary duties, while Claire was occupied with a new baby, two other children and supervising the large ducal household.

Considering again how he'd found her alone in the library, Rafe frowned. As he'd predicted, Juliana had been well-received by Society, but having been so isolated in her youth, she had a natural reserve and didn't make friends easily. She endured calls from those eager to meet the new countess, receiving guests politely but giving no encouragement for them to linger and become better acquainted. Used to being solitary and, frankly, not sharing many interests in common with most females, who filled the calls with discussions of fashion, household events and gossip, though she had attended all the evening events Claire had recommended, she had not yet found a larger circle of ladies with whom to spend time while he was occupied with his obligations.

He would have to pay her more attention himself. He didn't want her to be lonely and unhappy.

By the time he reached that conclusion, Juliana was rushing back into the library, her cheeks flushed with excitement. 'I'd been planning to go to the museum soon myself. But it will be so much more enjoyable to have you accompany me.'

'I want to share the things that interest you. I bought you several sketchbooks, by the way; so don't worry about running out of space. That is by way of apology for my neglect, in addition to which, I promise we shall ride together at least three mornings a week. Would that make you happy?'

She nodded, her cheeks pinking. 'You've no need to apologize. I'd be delighted to spend more time with you, but I'm realistic. You are an earl who will soon take up your duties in Parliament. You also have a circle of friends from the army and university with whom you wish to spend time and conduct discussions not in female company. I would never wish to hamper you from doing any of that.'

'I also appreciate my wife's company. And I don't wish you to spend so much time alone.'

'I'm quite able to amuse myself; I have since childhood, as you know. I can't pretend I don't prefer my fields, woods and fells to London, but I mean to make the most of the opportunities here. Walk in the parks with Baxter to attend me, ride with a groom in the early morning. I do find the varied architecture interesting; in the absence of animals, I shall make use of the new sketchbook to record some of the buildings I find of interest. Westminster Abbey, for example, has marvelous animal carvings, from gargoyles to griffins. Our household is small, but it still requires some management. And I have my reading.'

Rafe felt another stab of remorse at hearing her detail how she spent her time alone or among servants. 'I promise to do better.'

She smiled. 'As long as we have our *nights*, I shall be content.'

Ah, the nights. To his delight, neither the sensual pleasure his inventive wife provided, nor her eager desire for physical encounters had decreased since their arrival in London, even if their activities had been confined to the bedchamber.

There was something to be said about soft beds and silken coverlets.

He was still smiling at those images when the butler approached. 'A note has just come for you, my lord,' he said, bowing as he presented the missive on a silver tray.

Curious, Rafe broke the seal. As he quickly scanned the contents, his smile faded, an amorphous pain he couldn't put a name to and a sense of foreboding settling in his gut.

'What is it? What's happened?' Juliana asked urgently.

Irritated that his unguarded reaction would make it impossible to avoid answering, he felt forced to tell her the truth. 'It's from Hart. He wanted to warn me that…that Earl and Lady Altorn have just arrived in town. The earl's wife is the former Thalia Heathcote.'

He watched with deepening self-annoyance as Juliana's eager expression faded to a look of concern. 'I see. Will that present a…difficulty for you?'

'Nothing I can't handle if the need arises,' he replied, trying to imbue his voice with a breezy confidence. 'You mustn't be anxious. As a duke's heir, Altorn will be escorting his wife to the sorts of Society entertainments we avoid, so it's quite possible we'll not encounter them at all. If we should chance to meet, I'll acknowledge Lady Altorn—it would be rude to ignore her—but I'll not need to be more than polite.'

'I should hate to think seeing her would be…wounding for you.'

As she glanced away, not meeting his gaze, he tipped up her chin so she had to look at him. 'Thalia is a part of my past, Juliana,' he said urgently. 'A heartache I got over long ago. You and I together are both present and future for me. You mustn't doubt that for a moment. Promise me?'

She gave him a tentative nod.

'Then show me your lovely smile, and let's go enjoy our outing.'

As he escorted her down the entry stairs and summoned a hackney to carry them to Great Russell Street, he told himself he would take his own advice to heart and dismiss any further thought of Lady Altorn.

By the time a short while later, when Rafe handed his wife down in front of Montague House, Juliana seemed to have recovered her customary calm. He intended to devote every effort to making sure she forgot about the unsettling news and thoroughly enjoyed their visit together.

Concentrating on pleasing her would help him forget it, too.

'At the risk of appearing a bumpkin, I've never been to the museum,' Rafe admitted as they approached the handsome domed façade

'It's not where I would expect the energetic outdoorsman you have always been to spend any time, so I'll not hold it against you.'

As they walked inside, she said, 'Have you any interest in Greek and Roman antiquities? Most of the ground floor is occupied by the extensive library, but they do have Sir William Hamilton's collection of vases and sculpture along with Egyptian antiquities, including the Rosetta Stone.'

'Ah, yes, even I know about that—the key to deciphering hieroglyphics. Brought back by our stalwart troops after they defeated Napoleon at the Battle of the Nile. Some military men are interested in culture, redeeming the army's reputation from dolts like me. Viewing the sculpture would be interesting, but I'd prefer to see what most interests you.'

'That would be the natural history collection on the second floor.'

'Lead on.'

Rafe followed her upstairs, where she led him into the first of a series of galleries. 'My friend, Lady Fallsham, introduced me to this. She was the friend of a friend who came to dine with the family after Aggie was engaged and ended up talking with me. When she asked me about making my debut the following year, I thought to put her off by confessing I preferred remaining in the country, observing and drawing plants and animals, to mingling in Society. To my surprise, she avowed her own interest—and invited me to accompany her here.'

'That was kind of her—and clever, too. I'll wager she was even more surprised to discover how excellent your drawings are.'

'She knew the Sloan collection so well, she was able to guide me to the parts of it she thought I'd most enjoy. The large array of plants, some of which I sketched with her. And yes,' she added with a faint blush, 'she did admire my work. My favourite exhibits are here. The birds.'

Juliana led him into another room, where a wide variety of bird species were featured, some by their nests, some posed on branches. 'Especially these—the ibis, from Egypt. And this little jewel—a hummingbird, from America. How I should love to see one in the wild someday! Is it not a wonder?'

Rafe was pleased to note that, surrounded by creatures she loved, she seemed to have wholly forgotten the news about Thalia. He would relax and simply enjoy watching her, her face radiant as she gestured towards the tiny bird. He was touched that she would share it with him, this creature from another world she admired so much. And once again amazed, that she treasured this brilliant, glittering collection of feathers that way other women would treasure the sparkle of a diamond or the faceted face of an emerald.

'Do you mind if I take time to sketch it?'

'Of course not. That's why I gave you the sketchbook and invited you to come here.'

'I won't take long.'

While she sketched, Rafe roamed through the room with the birds and then several other adjacent rooms, inspecting the vast collection of shells, coral, fossils and plant specimens. From time to time, he glanced back, to see her so totally absorbed in her work, he suspected she'd forgotten his presence.

Perhaps he would try to take her to the Americas one day. He knew she would thrill to such an adventure, while he could enjoy her awe and wonder at the plants and animals they would see and treasure the drawings she would make.

At length, she finished the sketch and looked up at him. 'Thank you for bringing me. Coming here reminds me that I had a letter from Mrs Earnshaw, Lady Fallsham's cousin who lived with her. She wrote that she regretted I wasn't able to join them before her ladyship's death but invited me to visit whenever I could and stay as long as I liked, sketching the birds and animals of the region. I don't think I'll ever get to the Americas—' she gestured towards the hummingbird '—but I should like to visit Cornwall.'

'They have the red deer, otters and the badgers I'm so fond of,' she continued, her eyes bright with enthusiasm. 'Hares, foxes and wild ponies. Birds of prey like the kestrel, osprey and falcon. Being right on the ocean, there are even more water birds than we have at the lakes, a whole variety of geese, ducks and swans.'

She smiled, gazing off into the distance. 'She described their great cliffs overlooking the sea, sheltered caves near the beach…'

'Smugglers' lairs, I'll bet. Cornish smuggling was famous.'

'Perhaps. I can imagine settling in sheltering rocks above the beach to sketch sea-birds, or perching atop cliffs, like on the heights of the fell, wind whipping my hair and trying to tear the pencil from my fingers, the waves crashing below. The vista even vaster than that atop the fells! Truly one could see forever, nothing but ocean all the way to the Americas. Besides the sea-side, there'd be hills, valleys, woods and meadows to wander, looking for hares, foxes, deer or wild ponies.'

'When this session of the Lords ends, after I check on the estate, maybe I could take you there. I won't be needed to supervise at Thornthwaite until harvest. I'd like to see Cornwall myself.'

'Truly?' she said, gazing up at him, those dark eyes excited but wary, cutting him again with the reminder of how little encouragement she'd been given to pursue what interested her.

'Truly,' he confirmed, determined to do all he could to make up for that lack. She demanded so little of him, it inspired him to want to offer *more*.

Being well away from London, with no chance of encountering someone he'd just as soon not meet, would be another advantage of the trip.

He looked over her shoulder at the sketch. 'How well you've captured the little bird!' he exclaimed, impressed anew by her skilful rendition. 'Your drawing looks more alive than the actual specimen. You really should consider creating a book of your drawings. If such likenesses need to be engravings, we could inquire about having you take lessons from one of the instructors at the Royal Academy. I wager you'd prefer that to receiving Society ladies for tea or promenading in the Park.'

'I should love it!' she cried. 'But not until later, when the estate is in better form. Mama was forever bemoaning not being about to spend every Season in London, residing in the city being so expensive. I hope we can return to Thornthwaite as soon as your duties in the Lords are completed.'

'I should like that, too.'

'The museum closes soon. We must leave.'

Glancing at his pocket watch, he discovered she was correct. He helped her stow away her sketchbook and pencils, sorry to end this private excursion and resolved to have more of them. Together they descended the stairs and walked back into the courtyard where she waited while he summoned a hackney.

Riding back, she leaned on his shoulder while he held her hand. A sense of satisfaction suffused him that he'd succeeded in dispelling her alarm and making her happy, as he had vowed to do.

In return, she'd once again given him a deeper look into the wonders of the world as she saw it, the beauty in the everyday, the majesty in a whirl of iridescent feathers. Enriching his life, as she enlightened it.

Cornwall was farther away, but Thornthwaite would

serve, too, to distance him from any ghosts from the past that might cause him disquiet. A place where he and Juliana could preserve and deepen the quiet camaraderie they'd shared today, a sense of well-being underlaid by a strong sensual bond.

How thankful he was to have ended up with a wife who inspired him with only stable, calming, quiet emotions, feelings that would never threaten to plunge him again into a chaos of anguish.

Chapter Fourteen

A few days later, Rafe was able to follow through on his resolve to seek out more excursions to delight his wife. As she reclined in his arms in bed after their early-morning lovemaking, he said, 'Would you like to visit the Summer Exhibition at the Royal Academy? It won't present an opportunity to sketch, but you could study the landscapes, which will almost certainly include some drawings of animals.'

He was rewarded by her immediate flare of interest. 'I would love to! Will you obtain tickets?'

'I already have. We can go today, if you like.'

'How thoughtful of you! I'll be ready in a trice! Thank you!' She gave him a long, lingering kiss that made him question whether she needed to leave the bedchamber just yet.

'I think we'll have time to breakfast first,' he called after her as she rushed to her dressing room, amused at her eagerness. What a clever devil he was, he thought as he rose and threw on his banyan. To spark such an enthusiastic response, most husbands would have to expend a great deal of blunt on fine jewels or a costly gown. All he'd needed was the shilling price of an entry ticket to the Royal Academy.

An hour later, after taking a hackney to Somerset House, they entered the building with a flurry of other early visitors.

Looking through the catalogue, Rafe found the work for which he'd been looking. 'J. M. W. Turner, the artist of whom your work reminds me, submitted only one painting for this show, *Dido and Aeneas*. Shall we find that first?'

'Let's do. I'm curious to see which artist I remind you of—though I can't imagine my simple offerings resemble those of a craftsman as renowned as Turner! Aeneas…he's featured in *The Iliad*,' she commented as he guided her to the appropriate gallery.

'Yes. One of the Trojans, Hercules's friend, who survived Troy and, legend says, went on to found Rome. On the way, after being shipwrecked in Carthage, he fell in love with its queen, Dido.'

'If he went on to found Rome, I assume that relationship didn't end well.'

'No. Though it's written that they were very much in love, when he left to fulfill his destiny, she killed herself. But this painting, the catalogue says, represents the early, idyllic days of their association, before duty prompted him to leave and break her heart.'

'Much better to illustrate happiness than the misery of being broken-hearted,' she said, such emphasis in her voice that he gave her a searching glance.

Had she been broken-hearted at some point? He knew she hadn't felt more than fondness for his brother. He'd first suspected her 'other plans' for escaping her family were woven around the interest of some astute gentleman, but she'd insisted that becoming a companion to Lady Fallsham had been her only outlet.

If so, how could she have experienced heartbreak? Disappointment and sadness at her ill-treatment by her family, but true heartbreak was reserved for the loss of one's dearest love. Something, he thought as he suppressed another sharp pang, about which he knew all too much.

Had she met some unknown young man and lost her heart?

Though he couldn't see how or when that might have happened. But if it had, he felt a wave of compassion for her. He of all people knew how devastating such a loss could be. How long and difficult it was to claw one's way back to any semblance of enjoying life.

But under the sympathy lurked another less noble emotion…surely not *jealousy*? That she had cared so much for another man that she would see his loss as heartbreak?

Watching her smiling as she gazed at the works they passed, he told himself he was being ridiculous. Cloistered away at Edgerton Manor, she'd had virtually no chance to meet an eligible gentleman with whom she could fall in love.

Unless it had occurred during her sojourn in London during her sister's come-out? Had she fallen for one of Aggie's suitors, and as a younger daughter not yet out, not even had a chance to win his affections?

A fierce sense of possessiveness succeeded his speculation. Despite the odd tone in her voice, with its stark edge of sorrow, it was highly unlikely she'd been speaking from personal experience. For which he was glad and relieved. He wouldn't wish her to suffer as he had. And he was *very* glad—ignoble as that feeling might be—that another man had not claimed her before he could.

Shaking his mind free of such useless speculation, he escorted her into the room where the Turner painting was displayed, where a number of visitors clustered to view the work,

The painting was calm, majestic, dominated by a grand sky, with clouds at the top of the canvas looking like a flight of birds. The human figures, the titular focus of the work, were dwarfed by the natural world surrounding them…trees, hills, that enormous sky. To him, they looked…insignificant, despite being grand figures of ancient literature. His eye was drawn instead to the trees on the hills behind them, reaching out over the river as if they wished to embrace each other from their opposite shores—perhaps meant to symbolize the star-crossed lovers?

'May we linger a moment, so I might study the brush-work and technique?'

'Take as long as you like.'

She had her sketchbook deployed before he finished speaking. Rafe watched her as she stood, rapt, her gaze darting around the canvas. He could almost *feel* her brain noting the shades of color, the luminosity of the sky, the hues of the shadowed hills and limpid water.

'It's very *grand*,' she said eventually. 'Do you truly think my work resembles this?'

'Not in grandeur. But in its emphasis on the natural world and its wildness. Like those clouds in the mid-ground, reaching up like fingers trying to grab the clouds above them, which are fleeing like birds at the top of the canvas.'

'Another hint of the sad end of the love affair, Dido reaching out for departing Aeneas?'

'Perhaps. Like your sketch of the diving peregrine falcon, its swiftness and speed emphasized by the wild flurry of cloud behind him—all violent, feral motion. Shall we look at some other works?' Rafe asked.

At her nod, they wandered through the spaces, stopping to view several paintings by the eminent portraitist Thomas Lawrence.

She stopped to study each, saying 'I've not done much portraiture. Maybe I will give it a try. But not formal portraits like these; like with my animal studies, I'd rather attempt to capture my subject in a natural pose. Perhaps I could do some sketches of Hart and Claire's children. As I once told you, I only make likenesses of something or someone I care deeply about. The Duke and Duchess have been so kind and supportive, especially Claire.'

They moved on to study some of Constable's landscapes, then to discover the work of several lady artists. Juliana particularly admired the room hung with drawings, exclaiming over Miss Whitworth's *Butterflies from Nature*, chuckling at Miss Maynard's *A Fly* and closely studying the *Fish* by Miss Roberts.

They ended their tour in the Council Room, which was hung with works for which the artists had been elected as Members of the Royal Academy. As they paused beneath Turner's *View of Dolbadern Castle*, Rafe said curiously 'What do you think of this one?'

'Though the verse under the painting refers to the imprisoned Owen of Wales, the figure, so tiny at the bottom of the painting, seems unimportant. It's the vast sky, with the castle tower silhouetted against it, that captures one's attention.'

'The boiling clouds behind the castle a metaphor for the prisoner's despair, perhaps?'

She shook her head. 'Perhaps. One great difference

in my work; I wish to capture the essence of the subject. If I were drawing an imprisoned prince in despair, I should focus on him, rather than the sky and clouds. That said, I prefer sky, clouds and creatures of nature to grand allegorical schemes. I suppose those are the sorts of pictures collectors wish to buy, else the prominent painters wouldn't produce so many of them. Well, I suspect by now you are more than ready to take your leave.'

Much as he was admiring the artwork and enjoyed watching Juliana's delighted absorption, he couldn't help but admit she was correct. 'Shall we treat ourselves to tea at Gunter's? Perhaps accompanied by a pineapple ice, their specialty, to counteract the heat of the day. Then I have a suggestion about how we might finish off the afternoon.'

She raised her eyebrows. 'Really? At Gunter's? Do the plane trees in the square offer that much concealment?'

'No erotic interludes, minx. Not at Gunter's, at any rate. Come, let's get that tea. I'll tell you my idea while you devour your ice.'

Half an hour later, they were seated in the tearoom, their treats on the table before them. 'Once we've refreshed ourselves, I propose we go to Turner's Gallery,' Rafe said. 'You may have noted Turner showed only one painting at the Exhibition this year. He's well enough known now that he prefers to keep much of his work at his own gallery and sell directly from there. In addition, he keeps several pieces on display that are personal favourites he doesn't wish to sell—*Frosty Morning* and one of his signature pieces, *Hannibal Crossing the Alps*.

Juliana looked up at him curiously. 'First the tour of the Royal Academy, then Turner's Gallery? I had no idea you were so knowledgeable about art.'

Rafe grinned. 'I might try to brag about having hidden depths, but in honesty, I must confess that while at the club last week, I bent the ear of one of my Oxford classmates, Charles Leiminster. Art has been Chuffy's passion since university, and he *is* quite knowledgeable. It required only a few questions to set him off spouting a flood of information of which I probably recall less than half. I did try to memorize as much as possible about Turner, thinking you would appreciate his style.'

She paused, spoon of ice halfway to her lips, studying him wonderingly. 'You went to so much trouble—for me?'

Rafe shrugged. 'Knowing how reluctant you were initially to come to the City, I want to make sure you enjoy it as much as possible. Before we return to Thornthwaite, I want to give you every opportunity to take advantage of what the London art world offers. To inspire you to expand and continue your own work, here and when we return.'

To his alarm, her eyes filled with tears. Before he could say anything, she touched his arm, dashing away the tears with her other hand. 'I don't mean to turn into a watering pot. But…most of my life, what I love to do, the things that are important to me, have been criticized or at least discouraged. Your support means more than you could know.'

'It's about time you were encouraged,' he said bitingly. 'Even were you not as talented as you are. I find it something close to criminal that your parents were so disobliging.'

'I can only thank you again. But…are you sure you've not had enough art for one day?'

'I can handle a bit more. With me about to make my entry into Parliament, soon my daytime hours may not be my own. I won't have to attend all the debates, of course—few members do—but since I am just beginning, I should be present rather faithfully for at least a few weeks. So I may not have another opportunity to escort you.'

'Then if you are sure you truly haven't already had a surfeit of artwork, I should love to go,'

After finishing their treats, they embarked in another hackney to Turner's Gallery on Harley Street. Excited to view so many works in the artist's distinctive style, Juliana immediately gravitated to the sketches and landscapes of ordinary people, preferring those to grand 'historical' paintings so beloved of critics and collectors.

Drifting from one to the next, she stopped short with a gasp before his *Distant View of Plymouth*, in which the artist's usual brown-hued canvas featured instead a sea of vivid blue with fields of bright green and gold.

It seemed the perfect moment for Rafe to achieve his primary purpose in bringing her here. 'I wish I had pockets deep enough to purchase a painting for you, but I don't—for now. Fortunately, there is another option.'

As he led her across the gallery, he said, 'For several years now, Turner has created mezzotints and engravings of his watercolors. The prints, unlike his paintings, are quite affordable. I should like you to choose one, to keep as inspiration and a memento of our London sojourn.'

Stopping before a display that featured an assortment of the prints, Rafe waited while Juliana leafed reverently through the collection. At length, she pulled out a view of the Yorkshire coast, with fisherman trying to put out their boat across the pounding surf in a squall while sea-birds struggled against the wind. Then she found a more pastoral one of a flock of sheep on a hillside, their shepherd lounging in their midst.

'I can't decide,' she said, looking up at him. 'The

Yorkshire coast is so wild and free, but the flock of sheep makes me think of home.'

'Take them both.' When she began to protest, he said, 'Don't be silly. The two together cost less than one fancy gown. And, I think, would be much more prized by you.'

Once again, her eyes sheened with tears. 'They would. Are you sure I may have both?'

She looked so sweetly awed and grateful, something twisted in his chest, filling him with an aching tenderness. He'd almost pulled her close in a hug when a shock of warning stilled him. *Step back and calm down,* a little voice insisted. No need to become so... emotional.

'You shouldn't indulge me so—but I can't resist. Oh, yes, let me have them both!'

Purchases made and wrapped for the transit home, she took his arm, still gazing at him wonderingly as they walked out to call a hackney. 'I shall treasure this day forever.'

'I'm glad. I wanted you to have a treat before I'm forced to abandon you for the joys of attending Parliament.'

For a moment, she looked...shaken. Then, rallying with a smile, she said, 'With these to inspire me—' she nodding to the packaged prints '—I shall put my time alone to good use. I shall also be thinking of something particularly special to do for you to show my appreciation.' She caressed with her fingertips the arm under her hand.

He grinned, his simmering senses immediately firing at her touch. 'I like the sound of that. A shame we are promised to the Arlingtons for dinner tonight.'

'But we're not obligated to go to the rout afterwards, are we?'

'Since it should be the usual crush, I doubt our absence would be noted.'

'Then let's return to the house after dinner. And I will endeavour to do my utmost to please you as much as you have pleased me today.'

'I shall look forward to it,' Rafe said, his body already throbbing in readiness. 'You should learn to etch, so you might create prints like these for your drawings,' he said, needing to distract himself from his sensual urgings.

'But why would I have need of more than one copy of a drawing? Unless I wished to sell some?' She giggled. 'Mama would be horrified by the very idea of my offering prints of my birds and animals for sale. My subject matter was one of her most frequent criticisms. "A lady confines herself to genteel projects, like needlework or watercolors of garden flowers." She thought my work "harsh" and "brutal."'

'And I thought we'd agreed to dispense with recalling any of your mother's erroneous aphorisms on the proper behaviour of a gentlewoman.'

She sighed. 'It's hard to erase them all from my brain, repetition having etched them so deeply.'

'You must continue to excise them,' he said, rubbing her forehead as if to start the elimination process. 'Replace them with more suitable Rafe Tynesley ones. Such as "A lady should use her skill to fashion unique creations as she envisions them."'

She shook her head. 'Mama would most certainly never agree with that! You may regret this excursion. I'm excited to pull out my sketch-pad and begin some new drawings at once.'

'You should. Here's another Rafe Tynesley saying: "Talent should not be wasted." The housekeeper can supervise the household; you have a rare skill not possessed by anyone else. You must use it.'

Once within the hackney, Juliana leaned up to give him a long, slow kiss, teasing his tongue, nibbling his lips while slipping her hand beneath his coat. 'Until tonight,' she promised.

By the time they reached Thornthwaite House, Rafe's aroused senses were urging him to find some excuse to cancel their dinner engagement. But the group gathered around the table was to be a small one, he knew, and his university friend would miss them if they failed to appear.

So after guiding his wife up the entry stairs, he reluctantly released her, determined to head to the library to console himself with a drink and allow her to take her precious engravings up to her room to study, as he knew she was anxious to do.

'I'll expect to see dividends on that investment in the form of the many drawings and sketches it inspires in you,' he said, as she handed her cloak to the butler and prepared to mount the stairs.

'With these and my new sketchbooks? Oh, there will be! I promise!' She gave him a saucy smile. 'And you know I keep my promises. Until…later.'

'Minx,' Rafe said with a groan, feeling his body harden again. But anticipation would make the reward all the sweeter later, when he had her all to himself tonight in their bedchamber.

Resigned to the wait, he walked into the library and poured two fingers of port into a glass, pleased and gratified by the results of their outing. He'd meant the day almost entirely for Juliana's pleasure, but he'd enjoyed viewing the artwork more than he'd anticipated. More than that, he felt a deep sense of satisfaction that bordered on joy to see her so pleased and excited and know that excitement had come from his efforts. He truly wanted to encourage her to do more work of her own, talented as she was.

He might not be able to cancel out the years of disparagement and criticism she'd suffered, but he could prove that, with him, she would receive only support and appreciation. He was excited to see where, finally given the opportunity, her interest and talent would take her next.

Anticipation filled him, knowing he would be there to observe and support her as she took him with her down ever-new pathways of exploration and discovery. Life would never become dull or routine with Juliana beside him.

Or soul-crushing. Faint unease stirred again. They'd attended several entertainments now without encountering the Earl of Altorn or his wife. He couldn't help hoping they would finish their time in London without such a meeting. He'd didn't fear that he'd be vulnerable to Thalia again, but he'd spent too much time and heartache burying his emotions to want to experience anything that would remind him of that unhappy time.

Once again, he congratulated himself for having been wise enough to wed instead a friend and lover like Juliana.

Chapter Fifteen

A few days later, wrapped in a thick robe, Juliana reclined in a chair near the hearth in their bedchamber, enjoying the warmth of the fire as she read *The Iliad* and waited for Rafe to return from his evening engagement. With his introduction to the Lords taking place tomorrow, she'd been happy to send him off to meet Hart and some Parliamentary colleagues to verbally rehearse the ceremony and give him a summary of the bills under consideration that he would hear discussed after he took his seat.

At least she could feel *safe*, knowing he would be with his male colleagues. Not at some entertainment where he might encounter Thalia.

Her initial alarm had eased somewhat, as they had attended a number of parties since Hart's warning without crossing paths with the Earl of Altorn or his wife. She hoped that would remain the case for the remainder of their time in London.

It wasn't that she didn't trust Rafe's vehement assurance that he no longer felt anything for his one-time love. It's just that she suspected one never *completely* recovered from such a loss. She knew she would never get over losing Rafe, should he suddenly depart from her life.

She hated the idea that seeing the woman might revive his pain.

And she couldn't quite squelch the fear, despite his assurance, that seeing Thalia again might somehow weaken the bond they'd built.

She shook her head as if doing so could dislodge the disturbing thought. Better to concentrate on what she could do to *strengthen* that bond…what she planned to surprise Rafe with tonight.

The presentation robe he'd picked up that day hung behind the open door to his dressing room, its red wool splendour reflected in the glow of the fire. And despite Rafe complaining about its high cost, it *was* splendid—that long sweep of crimson wool with its three gold-laced bars of fur on the right side indicating his rank of earl, its white silk lining, its black silk ribbon ties.

She wished she might be able to help him into it when he departed for the Lords tomorrow, but unfortunately, he wouldn't don the robe until just before the ceremony. Which is why she'd planned for a special ceremony of their own tonight.

She recalled again the magical day he'd given her

at the Royal Academy exhibition and then the visit to Turner's Gallery. The incalculably precious gift of the Turner etchings he'd allowed her to purchase, which she'd already spent several hours studying and making copies of in her sketchbook. This had already fired her mind with ideas about the drawings she would make of her favourite subjects once they returned to Thornthwaite—the squirrels, the sea-birds, the otters. Another sketch, more wild and free against the soaring clouds, of the falcon in a dive.

She'd do some portraits, too, She had always drawn what she most loved...which was why the sketchbook now included several studies of Rafe.

She wasn't yet satisfied with any of them. Perhaps she never would be with any she made of him. How could she ever adequately capture his warmth, his kindness? The way a mere glance from him could light her senses on fire?

Fortunately, as she wasn't ready to show him any of her portrait attempts, she didn't need a live model. She need only close her eyes to recall every dear feature of his face, every bold line of his body, while the echo of his voice, his laugh, filled her ears.

As she hoped, she thought, touching the slight round of her stomach, his child would soon be filling her belly.

She had picked up her book again, determined to while away what might be a number of hours before he returned—who knew how long his colleagues would keep him to 'rehearse'—when she heard the sound of his footsteps approaching.

Pushing away any disturbing thoughts, she let delight and a wave of sensual awareness wash through her. The best part of the day was about to begin.

Spying her in the chair, he paused on the threshold. 'Juliana! I thought you would be long asleep by now.'

'I'm too excited about your presentation tomorrow to sleep,' she said, walking over to embrace him. 'I'm glad your friends didn't keep you too late. You shall want to look alert and interested when you take your seat.'

He leaned down to nuzzle the bare skin at her neck. 'Unless my wife keeps me up late. Which will make it worth arriving tired and muzzy.'

'Well...maybe not too late.' Detaching herself, she walked over to pour him a glass of wine and bring it back to the table beside the bed.

As was usual of late, they dispensed with their valet and maid in the evenings, enjoying the process of disrobing each other. He stilled while she pulled off his coat, untied his cravat, then knelt to pull down his evening trousers and slide off and remove them and his socks and shoes. As he stepped out of them, clad now in his long shirt, she waved him to the bed.

'Make yourself comfortable while I put these away.'

'Leave them on the chair. Haverton can deal with

them tomorrow. If I must have a valet, I can at least give him something to do.'

'He'll need to brush the coat and shine the shoes, which should be sufficient employment.'

Though it wasn't concern for the valet that led her to whisk the garments into the dressing room. Once inside, she dropped her own dressing gown onto the floor and carefully donned the heavy Parliamentary robe.

Tying the silk ribbons in front to hold it in place, she walked back into the bedchamber, her short stature increasing the length of the train sweeping behind her. Stopping by the bed, she said, 'The material is so glorious, I couldn't resist. Indeed, it's quite a shame you must wear garments beneath it. So you cannot feel…this.'

Parting the robe so he could see she was naked beneath it, she rubbed the lining against her chest. 'Silk…it feels so sensuous against the skin. But not as delightful as this.'

Pulling the robe father apart, she clutched the front and rubbed the band of fur over her breast, leaning her head back to enjoy the delicate softness of the fur against her nipple.

'It's a travesty to deprive the senses of this. Or this,' she continued, rubbing the fur down her belly, to the junction of her thighs. 'Softness without…increasing the desire for hardness within.'

She looked back to see Rafe watching her, wine glass abandoned, his eyes smoldering, his rigid arms clutching the coverlet. Robe trailing behind her, she walked to the bed, urging him to stand up so she might pull the shirt over his head.

She scanned his now-naked body with a hungry glance, halting her gaze at his erect manhood. 'Ah, that is as delicious as the feel of this robe. Shall I show you?'

She pulled him closer, wrapped the robe around them both and leaned up to kiss him.

After a shocked moment, he seized her, binding her close, kissing her hard and deep, his tongue scouring hers as he reached down to cup her naked bottom and tumble them back onto the bed.

Sometime later, sated, she nestled at his side, for long moments lost in bliss. At length, she opened her eyes to see him gazing at her, a bemused expression on his face.

'I suspect, should the law ever learn of it, we might be prosecuted for that bit of sacrilege against the Crown,' he said, pointing to the robe lying crumpled on the floor. 'A symbol of British power yielded to the superior force of my wife's sensuality.'

'No one need ever know. I won't tell if you won't.'

Chuckling, Rafe shook his head. 'You've complicated it, you know. I'll never be able to don that ceremonial robe again without thinking of you, naked, under it.'

'Have I spoiled your image of it?' she asked, concerned. 'That was certainly not my intent.'

'Oh, no. The image I have now is far better. But it's going to be hard to keep a fatuous smile off my face during what should be a solemn ceremony.'

She gave him a saucy grin. 'I like to imagine you distracted into thinking of me in solemn places.'

Rafe sighed. 'You are incorrigible, minx. Siren. Nymph. But I wouldn't have you be any other way.'

'You wouldn't?'

He shook his head. 'You bedevil, beguile and delight me, my treasure.'

At that description, her heart beat faster again. 'Am I your treasure?'

'Absolutely. In every way.'

She felt a rush of anticipation. Might he now feel it, say it? That he didn't just esteem her, he felt a warmth of love for her? So she might make a measured, restricted vow of tender devotion in return?

But instead of speaking further, after placing a kiss on her cheek, he closed his eyes and lay back. Within a few moments, he was deeply asleep.

Juliana pushed back a feeling of disappointment. With his gaze so loving and gentle, he'd seemed close, oh so close, to making her a declaration.

Surely it wasn't just a case of her wishing and *hop-*

ing it might be so. She felt certain Rafe was edging closer to realizing, like Claire had with her first husband, that he had gone beyond mere affection to truly loving her.

Not with a Grand Passion—there'd be no chance of that. But feeling more than just warmth and deep regard.

She could settle for a tender, gentle love. She would still have to limit her own feelings and keep leashed the all-consuming passion he would not want. But a gentle love would be close, much closer, to something she'd never imagined he could offer her.

The night after Rafe's presentation they were to attend a grand ball. Juliana had progressed to the point that, if she didn't look forward to an event attended by all the most influential members of Parliament and the *ton*, she at least wasn't dreading it. Rafe would probably not be able to spend much time by her side, but by now, she knew several of his army and university colleagues and their wives, enough to feel comfortable chatting and dancing with them. And Hart and Claire would be there to support her.

Wearing the most elaborate of her new gowns, Baxter having taken special care to arrange her hair in a more sophisticated style, she felt she looked her best as she descended the stairs to meet Rafe, who awaited her in the entry, resplendent in his black evening attire.

How handsome and commanding he looked, she thought, her heart swelling with pride and affection. A momentary shiver went through her, the thought that she must be living a dream, that she couldn't truly have wed this man.

'I feel like Cinderella going to the ball with a handsome prince,' she told him as he took her hand to lead her to the waiting carriage.

He laughed. 'Just remember you will not be turning into a ragged waif at midnight. Nor are you permitted to run off and abandon me. I'll need an excuse to escape the card room or avoid being pulled into a long rehashing of what was discussed at today's Parliamentary session.'

'I'm pleased to be your excuse,' she said, as he handed her in.

'What you promise me for later is far more alluring than any drink or chat I could be offered at a ball,' he murmured as he took his seat beside her. After the footman closed the door, he kissed her cheek as he slipped a hand beneath her cloak to run his fingers slowly over her breast.

She sighed, leaning into his touch. 'Must we stay until midnight?'

'Perhaps not. Until the first supper is served, at any rate. The Rousleys' balls are always a grand crush. Most of the others will dance, drink and play cards until dawn, but I think we can steal away.'

'I'll hold you to that.'

A short time later, they joined the slow procession of elegantly garbed guests making their way upstairs to the ballroom. After passing through the receiving line, they eased into the crowded ballroom where, as Juliana expected, Rafe was soon surrounded by government colleagues congratulating him on his entrance into the Lords. He was able to procure her a glass of wine and turn her over to one of his army friends before the political gentlemen bore him off, with a promise to return to claim her for the dancing.

Juliana chatted idly with several of the other guests, glancing frequently over to the ballroom entrance—and was finally rewarded by the sight of Claire and Hart, greeting their hostess. She was about to be gauche enough to wave at her, when Claire, scanning the room, saw her and smiled.

Juliana uttered a sigh of relief as her friends approached. 'Rafe carried off by the gentlemen of the Lords?' Hart asked. 'I was afraid he might be. Nothing so appealing to a long-time member as bending the ear of a newcomer. I'll let Claire keep you company and go in search. I promise to rescue him in time for the dancing.'

'He did promise to return by then.'

'I'll make sure he does.' Giving Claire a kiss on the cheek, he walked off through the crowd.

Claire pulled out her fan and plied it. 'I don't know

why hostesses seem to delight in inviting far too many people to balls like this. The room is stifling already, and the ball's hardly begun.'

'I suppose she doesn't want to leave out anyone and run the risk of offending someone.'

'Perhaps. It's even worse when the ball is given by someone with government connections. One must include all one's own supporters and a fair number of the opposition. As well as, of course, those who are socially prominent or come from important families.' She shook her head. 'Give me a small rout-party or musical evening any day.'

'Or a nice, companionable dinner,' Juliana agreed.

Snagging a glass of wine from a passing waiter, Claire said, 'Shall we look for a quiet place out of this crush? We can chat until the dancing begins.'

'You don't want to circulate and speak to the other guests? I wouldn't hold you back if you wish to socialize. I can find a quiet spot on my own.'

'No, I shall have to play "Duchess" at some point this evening, but I'd rather put it off until later.'

'Then I'd be happy to join you.'

They made their way across the crowded ballroom, Claire doing her best 'Imperious Duchess' imitation, nodding royally to those who greeted her but allowing no one to detain her.

Having discovered an anteroom occupied by only a quietly chatting foursome, Claire led Juliana to the sofa in front of the hearth in which a cozy fire burned. Seating herself, she took a long sip of her wine. 'What a gauntlet,' she said with a sigh. 'But we should have a half hour or so to have a quiet chat. How was the Royal Academy Exhibition? I should think you very much enjoyed it.'

'Wonderful! I'm not sure what I was expecting, but there was such a great variety of art. Everything from paintings to drawings to sketches to architectural drawings to sculpture. Some works by artists so famous, even I had heard of them. Other works by ones I've never heard of. Even works by ladies! Including some marvelous drawings.' She laughed. 'Fish. Butterflies. Even a housefly. Probably not drawings others would find remarkable.'

'I'm so glad you found works you could admire.'

'Oh, so many! I could have lingered for days, studying technique. As it was, we spent far more time there than I intended. Rafe was so kind, never complaining a bit, though I'm sure he was longing to leave far sooner than I. So kind, in fact, that after having a break for tea at Gunters, he took me to Turner's Gallery—and let me purchase two wonderful engravings.'

'My, that was indulgent.' Claire gave her a naughty glance. 'I hope he was suitably rewarded for his gallantry.'

Juliana felt her cheeks pink. 'I gave it my best efforts.'

'Ah, I hear the orchestra tuning up. We'd better return to the ballroom so our errant husbands can find us for a dance.'

They deposited their glasses and made their way through the crush back to the ballroom. Claire, with the advantage of height, was able to spot Hart almost immediately and wave him over. He nodded, then made a motion towards an anteroom.

'He's going to rescue Rafe and escort him to the ballroom,' she interpreted. 'I expect they should return in time for the first dance.'

Rafe did return to claim her, squeezing her hand and giving her a smile so tender and admiring, she felt a wave of emotion she made no attempt to quell. How could a look be more loving? Surely it wasn't just her imagination that he was regarding her with more warmth.

'Have I told you how lovely you look tonight?' he asked as he led her to take their place in the line. 'I'm the envy of half the men in the ballroom. And if the gentlemen knew your sterling character, I'd be the envy of them all.'

It was nonsense, of course; there were several dozen females in attendance who were vastly more beautiful, but tonight Juliana didn't intend to worry about truth. If her handsome husband wanted to compliment and flirt with her, she intended to just enjoy it.

'It's more likely that I would be locked in the Ladies' Retiring Room by females wanting to steal you away, the new earl and newest member of the House of Lords.'

'Then we shall agree we are both very lucky. Luckier than I ever expected to be.' He gave her another smile of bone-melting tenderness before bowing, as the figure of the dance was about to begin.

Her heart soaring like a butterfly in a sunbeam, Juliana enjoyed the dance as never before, and the next, a waltz, even more. Rafe whirled her around the room, holding her scandalously close and murmuring outrageously naughty suggestions in her ear as to how they might utilize the couch in the anteroom, the table in the refreshment room, or the benches on the moonlit terrace outside the ballroom.

'Seriously, though, you enchant me, you know that, my Mouse? My naiad and nymph. I can't imagine how I managed before I brought you into my life.'

Smiling, she reveled in the feel of his arms surrounding her. She felt valued and cherished as never before, almost fizzy with wine and happiness. When the waltz ended, he led her into the refreshment room, refusing to let any of the other guests waylay him, responding to greetings and invitations to tarry with a smile and a shake of his head. Reaching the table full of delicacies, he filled a plate for her and whisked her into a quiet corner, where he fed her tidbits, promising later, when they were finally alone, he would pay homage to her in other, more intimate ways.

But he was an earl, and he did have social duties, which inevitably made their claim on him. Ceding when one of his Parliamentary sponsors begged him to attend him, he walked her back to Claire, before, with a wry grin, going off with Hart to some consultation.

'We got a few dances, anyway,' Claire observed as the men walked away.

'Shall we have any others?'

'Probably. But in the meantime, we should punish them for their desertion by dancing with every gentleman who asks us.'

Juliana imagined Claire would have no lack of partners, but was surprised to discover she was sought-after as well. The positive effect of having the friendship of a Duchess and an earl who seemed to dote on you.

Did he dote on her? Was he finally, finally about to cross the line from friendship into love?

Had his attentions tonight not been ardent enough, whether or not he ever voiced feelings she yearned for him to express? Putting a halt on her fervent imagining, she told herself not to hope for anything more.

Feeling suddenly fatigued, she refused her next partner and made her way to the chairs at the edge of the ballroom, where after the next dance, Claire joined her.

As they chatted, a group of late-arriving guests entered the ballroom, one of them a tall, graceful lady who was one of most beautiful women Juliana had ever seen. Curious, she leaned over to ask Claire who it was.

'The Countess of Altorn. She married a duke's heir somewhat older than herself. Now that she's delivered him an heir and a spare, they usually go their separate ways, I'm told.'

A chill settled in the pit of Juliana's stomach. 'Th-that's the Countess of Alcorn?' she stuttered.

'Yes. Have you met her?'

From Claire's disinterested tone, Juliana surmised that Hart's wife was not aware of Rafe's previous attachment. 'Not yet,' she said faintly.

At that moment, Juliana spied Rafe walking back into the room. Before she could signal to him, the group around the beautiful newcomer laughed, drawing his attention.

He stopped short in mid-stride, freezing in place.

As he stood staring at Lady Altorn, the shock on his face turned to an expression of such anguish, Juliana felt as if she'd been punched in the stomach.

Nausea welling up, she stood abruptly. 'Suddenly I feel so warm! No, don't get up. I must… I must get some air!'

Stumbling in her haste, Juliana wove her way past the mingling guests until she reached the doors leading on to the terrace. Bursting outside, she searched for the stairs into the garden, running down them not a moment too soon before she found a shadowed spot behind some shrubbery and leaned over, retching.

Chapter Sixteen

Halfway across the ballroom floor, Rafe stood frozen, his gaze locked on the lady at the center of a group of laughing guests. *Thalia*, his shocked brain whispered.

Despite his resolve to meet this moment calmly, long-buried memories burst through the wall he'd erected to contain them.

That same beautiful face upturned to him, laughing, as he partnered her in a waltz at the Collington ball, where they'd first met.

Thalia, laughing as they sneaked away from a garden party into the friendly shrubbery, where she'd allowed him their first kiss.

Thalia, a tremulous smile on her face when he gathered the courage to ask whether she thought she might want to be with him for a lifetime.

Her white, unsmiling face as she delivered the horrible, crushing, at-that-moment incomprehensible news after he'd returned from a brief sojourn at Thornthwaite that her parents would be announcing her engagement to Lord Altorn. A duke's wealthy heir, whose offer in her family's eyes was a triumph far superior to winning the hand of an earl's landless younger son who would have to make his own way in the world.

The sense of disbelief followed by the stark horror of knowing he would never be permitted to see her alone, dance with her, kiss her again, had sent him into a dark hole of despair from which it took him months of service in the army to gradually recover, far away in the Peninsula where there was no chance of seeing her at a ball, watching her on the arm of her fiancé, reading about her nuptials at St. Mark's, just off Hanover Square.

No, no, he would *not* revisit this, he told himself, struggling to subdue the turbulent emotions. Having spent so much agony and effort into burying all these memories and his hopeless love, he would not, would *not*, allow them to ravage him again.

He knew the moment she saw *him*, recognition in her eyes like a stab to the heart. And then realized, while he stood there frozen, she was approaching.

With an iron discipline honed on the battlefield, he clawed his mind from the memories, willed his pulse to steady and readied himself to greet her.

She halted beside him, smiling up at him with the sweet expression that sent the acid roiling through his gut again. 'Rafe! Though it's Thornthwaite now, isn't it? Congratulations on assuming the title. You'll be a credit to it, I know. It's so good to see you!'

He scrabbled for a response, coming up with just, 'You are as beautiful as ever, Lady Altorn.'

Her smile dimmed a little at that, but she continued, 'I followed your career in the army, you know. How grateful and relieved I always was when your name didn't appear on any of the injury lists after the battles! How pleased I was to learn you'd inherited, an event I knew would pull you out of the army and away from danger.'

Her violet eyes looked up at him entreatingly. A deep, unusual shade of violet, those large, lustrous eyes were one of the first things he'd noted after being at first captivated by her overall beauty—the graceful figure, generous breasts, porcelain skin, perfect oval face, straight little nose and rosebud lips…that he would *not* remember kissing.

Wrenching his mind free again, he said, 'It's been… a long time. How have you been?'

'Well enough, I suppose. I have two sons now, a four-year-old and a two-year-old, scamps both, and the despair of their nanny. With them growing up, I'm left with more time on my hands. Lord Altorn has… other interests.'

Rafe thought four and two were still too young to be considered 'growing up', but he didn't know much about how children were handled in the ducal household where she still resided with her husband. Probably aristocratic mothers at that level were tripping over servants and left with little to do. Her delicate reference to her husband's 'other interests' and the fact that he apparently had not accompanied her to the ball tonight hinted that, having done her duty to provide him with heirs, she'd been set aside while he pursued feminine comfort elsewhere.

Anger at the unfairness of it all added to the chaotic mix of emotions seeing her again had stirred up.

She was still gazing at him, expecting some response. 'My congratulations on your sons. They must be a comfort to you.'

Preliminary notes were sounding from the orchestra, indicating the next dance set would be forming. 'Shall we stroll for a bit?' she asked. 'I'd like to catch up, and one can't do that during a pattern dance.'

Still feeling flayed inside, he had no desire to extend the torment by remaining in her presence. But short of causing a scene by bolting across the ballroom, he had little choice but to offer her his arm and stroll off down the corridor towards the refreshment room. With the dance beginning, the room was relatively deserted. After he'd fetched her a glass of wine, she waved him to a seat in one of two chairs drawn close together by one of the windows, where they could talk undisturbed.

'I'd been hoping, once I heard you'd become the

earl, that you might return to London,' she said, after sipping at her wine. 'Congratulations as well on taking your seat in the Lords. Will you be remaining for the rest of the Season?'

Although details about Parliament were printed in the papers, she must have been following news of him to know so much about him. Rafe wasn't sure whether to be gratified or even angrier. 'Only for a month or so, most likely, unless some important bill is under consideration. My late brother had been ill for some time before his death and the estate was left in a rather... precarious position. There's still much work to be done there, so I don't mean to tarry long in London.'

'I'm sure you will soon put it to rights. If only you had inherited sooner...'

He gave her a sharp glance as another blast of acid scoured his gut.

'You wouldn't be in the position of having to restore it,' she added.

He made no comment to that. Taking a deep breath, she looked up and said softly, 'My...interests have never changed, despite what my family obliged me to do. I hope...you don't hold against me what I couldn't prevent.'

His anger melted away. This was the apology he'd never received the awful day she woodenly informed him about her upcoming engagement and told him she couldn't see him again. Even though he'd believed at the time, still believed, she wouldn't have jilted him willingly, she'd never so plainly stated that.

Perhaps she'd been as devasted as he was, only able to get through that last interview by stating the bald facts, her heart breaking as his was.

That didn't make this meeting any easier.

'Of course not,' he replied, only at the last moment refraining from the idiocy of taking her hand.

She gave him a tremulous smile. 'I'm relieved to hear it. Very relieved! And I hope, now that you are in London, we might…see more of each other.'

Thankfully, for Rafe had no idea how to politely respond to that, a gentleman approached them eagerly. 'Lady Altorn! Fortner told me you were here! What a lucky chance! You must come dance a waltz with me. You did promise me one, you know, at the Manningtons' ball last week. You'll release her, won't you, Thornthwaite? Not fair to monopolize the most beautiful woman at the ball.'

He murmured assent, which was superfluous, as the gentleman—Randolph, he vaguely recalled—had already claimed the lady's hand to urge her to her feet.

'We shall talk again later, I hope,' Lady Altorn said, giving him as she left on Randolph's arm another of the sweet smiles he remembered with such bittersweet pain.

Conflicting thoughts ricocheting about his head like a rack of billiard balls just broken by the cue, Rafe stood up as well. His pulse still unsteady, he stumbled away, unsure what to do next. Unsure what to think or feel.

He *was* sure he couldn't make idle social chat or become embroiled in any Parliamentary discussions. Turning from the ballroom, he walked swiftly away, relieved when his instincts proved correct and he found the library, thankfully unoccupied.

He stood by the window overlooking the garden, trying to settle his pulse and calm the thoughts still whirling about in his head.

Well, he'd not done such a fine job of finessing that encounter, he thought acidly. Despite believing he'd been prepared, he'd been almost paralyzed by a violent maelstrom of emotions.

It was just that…to survive, he'd put her firmly out of his heart and mind, any thought of her entombed behind a door he'd slammed shut and intended never to walk through again. Until she spotted him across the ballroom and hurried over, wrenching it open.

He felt…raw, as if some essential part of him had been ripped apart.

He had put her out of his heart, hadn't he?

He'd buried the feelings, certainly. But in the aftermath of the shock of seeing her, he felt…unsettled, the long-suppressed hurt, anger and pain sending him so off balance he didn't know what he felt.

Having been shaken to the core, it would be impossible to act naturally with Juliana tonight, to tease her and whisper naughty words and make love to her. He'd have to plead fatigue or find some excuse to spend the night on his own—and work hard to make it believable.

Not for the world would he want to hurt her.

He spent another half an hour hidden away, trying to regather his composure so he might return to the ballroom and act normally enough that she wouldn't suspect something was wrong.

Once he'd regathered himself enough to mention the meeting, he'd have to be able to discuss his former love casually, as someone from his distant past who no longer affected him.

He was nowhere close to being able to do that tonight. Not with his far-too-perspicacious wife.

At length, he felt he had himself well enough under control to return to the ballroom. Pacing in, he scanned it quickly, relieved to see that it appeared Lady Altorn was no longer in attendance.

Had she come purposefully only to see him?

Thrusting out of mind the implications of that possibility, he looked around for Juliana. As he prepared to seek her out, he only then realized that he would probably need some excuse to explain his long absence.

He hadn't yet figured out what to say when Claire and Hart discovered him. 'There you are at last,' Claire said. 'Where did you disappear to?'

'Winston and Claiburn asked some probing questions about one of the bills under consideration. As they might come to a vote soon, I slipped off to the library to think about them. Too noisy to think here.'

Hart raised his eyebrows, but didn't challenge what he knew his friend probably thought a dubious excuse. Fortunately, Claire didn't know enough about the current events in Parliament to be equally skeptical.

'Where is Juliana? Has some impetuous swain whisked her away to the refreshment room?' he asked before Claire could make further uncomfortable inquiries.

'Would serve you right if one had,' she replied tartly. 'I'd been looking for you. Juliana was feeling ill. I tried to get her to wait until I located you, but she felt she must leave at once.'

Rafe felt a pang of alarm. 'Nothing serious, I hope!'

'Probably nothing out of the usual. I offered to accompany her home, but the most she would allow was for Hart to find her a hackney.'

'I'll leave at once,' Rafe said, worried and wondering. Juliana was never ill. From childhood, she'd been able to tromp the woods and fields in all weathers, never seeming to contract so much as a cold.

Had someone been unkind to her, embarrassed her, or prompted her to do or say something she would feel might prove embarrassing to him? In such a case, she would have wanted to remove herself from the scene immediately.

'I should hope so,' Claire said, her expression still reproving.

'I'll see you both soon, I imagine,' he said, giving Claire a quick bow and pacing off to bid his hostess goodnight.

There would be nothing she could have done that he would find distressing, but he knew, thanks to her detestable mother, she was much more sensitive about how her behaviour was perceived than he was.

Surely he could pull himself together enough to discover what had happened and reassure her, if she did feel she'd committed some faux pas.

Or make sure Baxter was taking good care of her, if she truly felt ill.

Worry might be a good thing, he thought ruefully as he tripped down the stairs, grabbed his coat, hat and cane and took one of the waiting hackneys. Concern for Juliana would distract him from his upset over Thalia.

A short time later, Rafe hurried up the stairs at Thornthwaite House. Pausing outside the door to their bedchamber, he listened, but heard no sound from within.

Opening the door silently, he saw by the dim light of the banked fire that Juliana was already sleeping.

Relief on several levels swept through him. She looked peaceful, not tossing and turning, so if she had felt ill, she must be better. And if there were some matter to discuss, it could wait until morning, as he had no intention of rousing her.

By morning, he'd have himself back under control and be able to act normally.

With that cheering thought, he tiptoed into the bed-chamber, doffed his garments, and climbed into bed beside his sleeping wife.

Eyes closed tight, Juliana pretended to be slumbering as she heard Rafe enter the bedroom, tiptoe in and disrobe, then lie down beside her. After a few minutes, his deep, even breathing indicated he'd fallen asleep.

She lay awake, staring at the ceiling, the searing image of Rafe staring at his lost love replaying over and over in her mind.

He'd claimed that, while he'd been devastated by the affair, he'd long ago moved on. Moved on to marry her, his good friend and lover.

But had he?

The anguish she'd witnessed argued otherwise.

But if he hadn't—what did she mean to do about it?

A part of her wanted to flee back to Thornthwaite and avoid broaching a subject that couldn't help but be painful to them both. But precisely because it was so painful, if they were to recapture their previous easy camaraderie, it would have to be resolved. One way or another. Running away wouldn't solve anything.

But how even to begin? She might confess that she'd seen him—what? That she'd observed him staring at the lady? That she thought he'd worn an expression of anguish? But claiming that might make him feel she was accusing him of some kind of wrongdoing, putting him on the defensive or even leading him to shut down the conversation before it had truly begun.

Perhaps it *was* just surprise, and she was overreacting.

But a moment's reflection, replaying that hideous scene again in her mind, argued that she was deluding herself if she tried to dismiss his reaction as mere surprise. She ought not to take him to task for the emotion she'd read on his face, but she knew she'd not misinterpreted what she'd seen.

Raw, naked pain. Grief and longing.

Well, what could she expect him to feel? Thalia Heathcote had been his Grand Passion, the agony of losing her the reason he'd become convinced that a marriage was better made between friends. To avoid the highs and lows of extreme emotion, he said. But she knew it was to avoid ever again caring so deeply that the loss of that person could devastate.

She, more than anyone, ought to know one never 'recovered' from such emotion. The only alternative was to bury it, as he had. As she'd tried to do.

Had he effectively banished it? Had the misery she'd witnessed been the last, final death throes of his one-time passion? Or had Thalia's sudden reappearance revived all the love he'd once felt? And if it had…what was *he* going to do about it?

He wouldn't leave her to pursue the lady; he had too much sense of his duty to the estate and too much honour to abandon her. Besides, however unsatisfying her marriage had become, Lady Altorn was unlikely to want to forfeit her position in Society or be forever barred from seeing her children by running away with her former love.

There were other arrangements that could, and in the aristocratic world, often were made to accommodate two married people who wished to spend time together. She felt nauseated again just thinking of it.

Would Rafe contemplate establishing an illicit relationship? If they were discreet, Society would not fault either of them. Rafe could continue to manage the estate and would always, she was certain, treat her with kindness and respect. While visiting his true love when he could get away.

The mere thought was so painful she could scarcely draw breath.

Could she lie with him—for he still needed an heir—live with him, talk over household and estate business, knowing his heart was elsewhere?

It was one thing to accept she would have only his

respect and affection when she would also be his sole partner. Quite another to subsist on warmth and honour when she knew his passion was being spent on another.

Could she *share* him? The prospect was so revolting, she had to push it away.

She might create a furious scene, demanding he give Thalia up. But that would likely only alienate Rafe and cause them both embarrassment once Society learned of the disagreement, as with whispering servants and a tidbit of gossip that juicy, sooner or later, it inevitably would.

Not that she would care about being ostracized. But she didn't think she could survive setting in motion something that might lead to a permanent estrangement between them.

What cut deepest, though, was she'd thought… hoped…he might have come to not just like, but to *love* her. Not in the manner of a Grand Passion; she couldn't expect that. But in a warm and cherishing way that, with children shared between them, would be enough. More than enough.

Had she ever encountered the lady before tonight, though, she might well have held out against marrying Rafe. What man could forget such incandescent beauty?

How could someone like her compare? How to entice him enough for him to generate even some small bit of love?

She forced herself to take a shuddering breath, then another. She must stop torturing herself with useless speculation and pull her shattered self back together. She must talk with Rafe and discern how he truly felt about the lost love who had suddenly careened back into his life.

She couldn't address the matter directly, of course. Perhaps, after apologizing for leaving the ball without waiting for him, she could ask if he'd chatted with anyone interesting while she was gone. Perhaps, after the initial shock, he'd recovered his composure and would tell her about the meeting, reassuring her the relationship was well in the past. Pass off the encounter with a jest framed in army terms about being ambushed by an enemy one thought vanquished, but who'd been beaten off once again.

Might he even say that, after the shock and remembered pain, he'd felt...nothing?

Reassuring as that speculation was, it was unlikely. In a thousand years, she would never get to the point of feeling 'nothing' about Rafe, even if she never saw him again.

Still, this had to be faced. After telling him she felt better and apologizing for abandoning him, she'd inquire further about the ball. If he mentioned the encounter, admitted regret and a lingering pain while reassuring her about the strength of their own relationship, she would know her fears were groundless.

But if he omitted any mention of Lady Altorn, if he acted strained or uncomfortable, she would know the cosmic collision had created a seismic shift in their relationship.

What would she do if there had been?

She had no idea. But lying here, staring sleeplessly as the fire in the grate burned down to faint glowing embers, she was filled with foreboding.

Chapter Seventeen

At some point, she must have dozed off, for when Juliana awoke with a start the next morning, faint grey London light showed from behind the bedchamber curtains.

And Rafe was no longer in bed beside her.

As that realization crystallized, her dread deepened. Only a handful of times, when they were at Thornthwaite and he had to meet Sterling very early in the morning, had he left their bed without making love to her. Indeed, he always told her, as they lay in the pleasant warmth afterwards, that early morning intimacy was the best possible start to his day, making him feel optimistic and full of energy to meet whatever the day might bring.

Juliana felt a hollow in the pit of her stomach about what this day might bring.

But if she wanted to replace dread with certainty, she needed to see him before he left for whatever appointments he had for the day—which, had she not feigned sleep when he returned, she might already know about.

She was already half-dressed when Baxter answered her summons.

'Is his lordship still in the breakfast room?'

'I believe so, my lady.'

Relieved, Juliana rushed through her toilet in record time, and ten minutes later, breathless from her rapid descent of the stairs, paused on the threshold. Her first sense of relief since the events of the previous evening steadied her as she spied Rafe still at table, the paper to one side as he drank his coffee.

'Juliana!' he said, standing as she entered. 'I didn't want to wake you. I hope you are feeling better.'

Was his smile a bit strained? Trying not to let anxiety make her see things that weren't there, she said, 'Much improved. It was just…a sudden headache.' *Heartache, more like.* 'All the noise, the heat, the… throng of guests.' *One in particular…*

'I'm so glad you are feeling better. I was concerned, for you are never ill! You didn't encounter anyone who was…unkind or unwelcoming, did you?'

I didn't encounter her. 'No, nothing of that sort.'

'Good, good,' he said, pulling out a chair for her.

Silence fell while she put some food on her plate that she knew she'd never manage to get past her lips. 'Did you stay long after I left?'

'No, I left as soon as I discovered you'd felt unwell.'

'Did your Parliamentary discussions go well?'

'Some were quite thought-provoking. I actually slipped away to the library for a while, to think over several factors in one of the upcoming bills. Which is why Claire didn't find me to let me know you were ill and wished to leave. I'm sorry I wasn't there to take care of you.'

'Anyone else bedevilling you aside from Winston and Claiburn?'

His smile was thin and he looked away, not meeting her eyes. 'Don't worry. I can handle them. I'm sorry to rush off when we've hardly had time to chat properly, but I've got an early-morning meeting. I hope you have a pleasant day.'

He rose, dropped a kiss on her head, and walked quickly out of the room.

Juliana stared at her coffee cup, pushing away with revulsion the plate of food she'd selected. She knew if she tried to force it down, she wouldn't retain a morsel.

Rafe waited for the hackney, chastising himself for having wasted that opportunity for a conversation. He'd had every intention of bringing up his meeting with Thalia; he'd have to soon in any event, as dozens of people had seen them together, some of whom might remember the long-ago affair, and he didn't want someone else telling Juliana about the encounter before he did.

But he wasn't feeling much more settled this morning than he'd been last night and had thought he would escape the house before Juliana was awake. Not yet prepared, he knew if they had more than a brief conversation, Juliana would sense something had upset him. Seeing her dear face, knowing how insecure she was in her appeal as a woman, he worried that broaching the matter before he was completely in control of himself would distress her, perhaps even make her doubt the depth of his commitment to her, even if he produced a fine speech of support.

She was too well aware that words and promises are easy.

He'd have that conversation tonight. He'd be master of himself again by then.

But his visit to the club dragged out late, as he met some army comrades newly returned from the Continent and had been eager to hear the latest news. Caught up in discussion and camaraderie, he'd lost all track of time. By the time the gentleman began discussing plans for dinner and he looked at the clock, he had only time to rush back to Thornthwaite House and dress for his evening engagement—which was a dinner party of Parliamentary gentlemen to be followed by actual discussions about the matters he'd referred to with Juliana yesterday.

He had only a few minutes to look in on Juliana

in her dressing room; she and Claire were to attend a musicale while he and Hart attended the conference.

'So sorry to abandon you all day, Mouse! Some officers from the Tenth Hussars showed up at the club and we became so embroiled in army talk, I lost all track of time. I shall make it up to you, I promise! You and Claire will doubtless enjoy the music more than Hart and I will all the endless discussions. It always seems the most tedious of the members wants to speak the longest.'

He leaned down to give her a lingering kiss. 'Enjoy your evening, my dear.'

'Enjoy yours, as best you can,' she replied. He was conscious of her staring after him thoughtfully as he walked out of the room.

Later that evening at the Hazleden townhouse, Rafe had greeted his host, Lord Hazelden, and was chatting with Hart when the butler announced dinner. He strolled into the dining room, only to stop short on the threshold.

Several ladies were present, already seated. His host's wife—and Lady Altorn.

'I thought this was to be a masculine affair,' he murmured to Hart.

Following the direction of Rafe's gaze, Hart stiffened. 'Sorry. I didn't know *she* would be here, or I would have warned you.

Lady Hazleden is very interested in governmental affairs; I think she fancies herself another Lady Holland. At any rate, she often invites several other like-minded wives to join the group for dinner before the gentlemen go off for their discussions. Don't worry; the ladies will take themselves off after tea, before we begin.'

Fortunately, Lady Altorn was seated at the other end of the table, next to their host, and Rafe was favoured with other gentlemen as dinner partners. Which allowed him to focus on chatting about aspects of the matters that would be discussed afterwards—though he remained acutely conscious of Lady Altorn's presence and couldn't help noting she took the opportunity to send him several searching glances.

Once the meal concluded, their hostess tapped her glass to cue her guests to silence. 'Since you gentlemen will be conferring for the remainder of the evening, we shall all go straight through for tea. So we ladies may enjoy a bit more of your company before you abandon us.'

Following her lead, the guests walked through to the sitting room, where servants were already setting out the tea service. Rafe hoped Lord Altorn would occupy his wife, but he went straight to the side of Mrs Rousley. From the glances they exchanged at dinner and his little touch of her hand as he reached the lady,

Rafe surmised the lovely Mrs Rousely might be Lord Altorn's latest 'interest.'

Rafe turned to face the hearth, as if studying the leaping flames, not wanting it to look obvious that he was avoiding the ladies. But a moment later, he felt a tingling at the back of his neck and drew in a waft of rose perfume he remembered all too well.

'Lord Thornthwaite, pleasure to see you here,' Lady Altorn said, halting beside him. 'I'm impressed that you are taking serious interest in your duties in the Lords.'

'I didn't realize you had an interest in Parliamentary matters.'

'Yes, Lord Altorn was elected to a seat in one of the boroughs his father controls. It's stimulating to be among those discussing plans for the future of our nation. My husband also quite enjoys mingling with political people.' She gave a slight glance in the direction where her husband was smiling at Mrs Rousely.

'I don't always attend these dinners with him, but when Louisa mentioned you'd be one of the guests, I felt I must come.'

Deciding it was better to be direct, he said, 'What do you want of me, Thalia? I'm married now. We can never can go back to the way things were.'

'I know. But can't we salvage…something? Can you tell me you no longer feel anything for me?'

Rafe felt the pull of the beauty who had enchanted

him so many years ago. Of course he felt something—he hadn't yet quite sorted out just what—but he didn't want to encourage her by admitting it.

'You'll have no trouble finding a replacement to admire you,' he evaded. 'Any number of gentlemen, Randolph chief among them, are already eager to lay their devotion at your feet.'

She shrugged. 'Perhaps. But none would be you. No one ever has been. No one ever will be.'

Once, he would have given all he possessed to hear her say this. Part of him wanted to exult at her words, at her desire to rekindle the love that had cost him so much pain.

Instead, to his surprise, her words only fueled the anguished mix of anger, grief, regret and hurt to a hotter pitch.

She might accept the standards of a morally lax Society. She might even feel that, having done her duty by her family, she deserved to seek out such happiness as she could find.

But to go from the blazing purity of the love he'd once felt to the tawdriness of an illicit affair? The idea filled him with revulsion.

'It's far too late to do anything about that.'

She touched his hand. He wanted to snatch it away as if burned…because he had been. Much as he tried to snuff it out, his body…and emotions…still affected by this woman he had once loved so much, he was unable to completely extinguish his response.

'Are you sure there is nothing we can do?'

'Thalia, the young man I was will always love the girl you were then. But I'm not that man anymore and you're not that girl. Life has changed us both and pulled us in other directions.'

She stared into his eyes. Despite the allure of those lavender orbs, he held her gaze steadily.

'You're a man of honour, I see.'

'I always was. That hasn't—and won't—change.'

'You are certain?'

'As certain as I am of anything in this uncertain life.'

She stared at him a while longer, as if willing him to give a different answer. Then she sighed. 'If that is how you feel, I will torment neither of us any longer. I hope we may meet…amicably, at least.'

'I can promise that.'

'But nothing more?'

Desperately wanting to end this exchange, he gave a negative shake of the head.

'Then I see you must be Rafe, my only love, no longer. From now on, it will be "Thornthwaite."'

'As it must be.' He glanced over at her husband. 'Lord Altorn married the most beautiful ornament in London Society, and despite his other "interests," he's not about to let you go. Nor would you want to risk losing your children, your position, your life.'

'Would I not? Sometimes I wonder.'

When he said no more, she finally nodded and

turned to leave him. He watched her graceful form as she walked away from him, drained from the interview, but knowing, after the broad hints she'd given him at the ball, it was one they must have.

He was very glad it was over.

He was a man of honour, as he'd claimed. But even as he couldn't help feeling vindicated, the self-esteem she'd once smashed with her refusal restored, he was ashamed to admit to himself, he had felt…tempted. There was still a remnant left of the ardent young man who would have reveled in possessing the beauty who had once been the whole center of his life. And he would always love her, even if he was not willing to confess that to her.

But he was no longer a feckless young man and he had different priorities. He'd married a wife who possessed more than beauty and grace, the ability to run a household, give grand balls and preside over a dinner table full of distinguished guests. He had a minx who not only delighted him in bed, but enlivened his life with her observations and her unique perspective. One who would be content, as he was, to spend most of her time in the country. Years with the army had taught him he cherished a deep love for Thornthwaite he hadn't realized he possessed when he left England.

He'd made a wise choice, marrying a woman who was a best friend and a delight. A wife who would never subject him to a recurrence of the anguish he'd felt for the woman he'd once loved with such an uncontrollable passion.

He was profoundly grateful that, at the end of this evening, he'd be returning to Juliana.

By the time the political discussions ended that night, Rafe returned home with his mind settled, calm enough now to finally broach the matter of his meeting with Lady Alcorn with his wife—which he hoped would engender only a brief and swiftly ended discussion. Making quick work of disposing of his garments, he threw on a banyan and walked into their bedchamber, where he found Juliana garbed in a dressing gown, seated in a chair before the fire, reading.

'Waiting up for me?'

She looked up, her smile a little tentative. 'You don't mind?'

'Mind? Why should I?'

'You seemed…disturbed this morning.'

Faced with the topic, he found he was not feeling as confident as he'd hoped. 'Oh, nothing, really.' His mind still skittering around how to describe the meeting, he paused, idly picking up an object off the table beside the chair, putting it back without looking at it. 'I had a shock at the ball the other night when I unexpectedly encountered Lady Altorn. You didn't see her?'

'I wasn't introduced, no.' After a pause, into which

Rafe couldn't think of anything to add, she continued, 'It must have been...difficult. After all this time, speaking again to the woman you once hoped to make your wife.'

'Uncomfortable, yes,' he acknowledged, not sure it was wise to add any more. Eager, now that he'd admitted the meeting, to end any further probing into his response, he added, 'But that was many years ago. I ended up with a far better choice. A sage decision I'd like us both to celebrate again tonight.'

She'd sometimes distracted him with passion. He hoped he might now do the same.

He put his hands on her shoulders and leaned down to place a kiss on her head. Skirting the chair, he pulled her up to stand before him, sliding his hands under her dressing gown to cup her breasts and kissing her deeply, his tongue laving hers.

To his relief, she responded instantly, meeting his tongue with her own, leaning into his caressing fingers while moving her hands to clasp his buttocks and pull his burgeoning erection closer. A few minutes later, he parted his robe and lifted her so she could wrap her legs around his waist. She was already guiding him inside as he carried her to the bed.

Chapter Eighteeen

Juliana lay in bed the following morning, staring sightlessly across the bedchamber.

Though Rafe had made love to her last night with no diminution of his usual passion, he'd crept away again this morning without waking her.

Just as last night, when she'd given him an opportunity to acknowledge the pain she'd seen on his face and tell her frankly how he felt, rather than answer, he'd deflected her with passion.

Which was an answer…wasn't it? If he couldn't bear to discuss how he felt about Lady Altorn?

When she'd offered that meeting Thalia again was 'difficult', he'd allowed only that it was 'uncomfortable.' He'd sidestepped answering how he truly felt about her now by saying it had happened 'many years ago', and he'd made a better 'choice.'

Choice. Recalling the word stung just as much as it had when he'd uttered it. As if he were commenting on taking coffee instead of tea.

On the one hand, she'd sensed no hidden excitement or guilty stirring in his description of their meeting. Which seemed to indicate that whatever he still felt, he was not contemplating beginning an affair with her.

Shouldn't that be reassurance enough?

When one was just the superior 'choice'?

After growing so hopeful that he might finally decide he loved her after all, backsliding to becoming the preferable commodity somehow magnified the hurt and the dismay. Which, for a lady who'd married a man knowing he regarded her only as a friend, one for whom she was determined to feel only friendship in return, wasn't rational.

For the magnitude of the pain and the depth of the hurt was now revealing the truth she'd been trying to hide from herself, probably from practically the first days of their marriage. Much as she'd convinced herself that she'd locked away her feelings, they had been lurking far closer to the surface than she'd dared admit. And had risen nearer and nearer to fully emerging the closer she came to believing that Rafe was growing to love her after all.

The moment he affirmed that his former love was definitely in the past had given him a perfect opportunity to vow that Juliana wasn't just his practical choice; she was the *right* one, because he now knew he loved, as well as valued and respected her.

He'd made no such declaration. And if he had not come to love her by now, with all the events of daily living and the passion they'd shared, he wasn't likely to.

Ah, passion. She'd thought to distract herself with it, but in truth, intimacy had only broadened and deepened the love she now acknowledged she felt for him.

Once she'd been convinced she could control her emotions. But her anguish now showed her she'd been deceiving herself to imagine she'd be able to live with a man who was just as compelling and even more exceptional than the young man she'd fallen in love with, and keep her feelings forever suppressed.

Now, her emotions a roiling mess of hurt, grief, and despair tinged with anger, that great, overpowering love had come roaring out, her turmoil having weakened the bonds restraining it.

Unlike the naiad in the fable, she couldn't blind her husband to the beauty of the woman he'd loved. A part of her raged beneath the surface, wanting to seek out the beautiful Lady Altorn and pull out her hair. A surprising reaction for her, who'd never imagined violence against anyone, not even her always-carping mother.

She must be with child, she thought bleakly. Claire had warned that when a lady was *enceinte*, her emotions became volatile and sometimes overpowering.

She could initiate another discussion and try to coerce him into stating exactly how he felt about Lady Altorn and about her.

But love wasn't love if an avowal of it was coerced. Only if he made the statement freely, with no prompting from her.

These last two days had shown her that was unlikely to happen.

So, what to do now?

How could she remain in London, sharing his bed, pining for his love, knowing the woman he had loved, maybe still loved, was right there in the city? How could she act unconcerned, recapture the calm and ease they'd shared before, when she ached with need for him and her heart was breaking all over again?

This, she told herself furiously, was exactly why she should never have married Rafe in the first place. Pain, deeper, more agonizing than she'd felt years ago when she'd first learned of his love for Thalia, scoured her.

But she had married him freely, and there was no one else to blame. Certainly not Rafe.

Now she must deal with the consequences.

How was she to deal with them?

Springing up from the bed, she began pacing the chamber.

Much as her heart ached for his anguish over losing Thalia, she could not find it in her to step aside and let him go back to his former love. Neither could she tolerate the idea of sharing him with her.

Then she remembered the child she was nearly sure now she was carrying. If she could just get through until the baby was born, she'd have a son or daughter upon whom to pour all her love and devotion. If some of it accidentally spilled over to Rafe from time to time, she could dismiss it as the excessive emotion of motherhood.

That didn't answer how she would deal with his feelings for Thalia, if Rafe still loved her. Even sharing a child wouldn't untangle that dilemma.

She paced and paced, but no solution emerged from the bubbling cauldron of pain, uncertainty, hurt, grief and longing that had taken up residence inside her chest.

Time. She needed more time to decide what to do.

She thought again of returning to Thornthwaite, where she might stay alone, reorder her thinking and figure out how to deal with Rafe without revealing either her distress or the unwanted depths of her love. But if she were to depart precipitously for the country, he would probably follow her, and she couldn't yet manufacture the calm and cheerful demeanor that would hide from him what he wouldn't really want to know. A mismatch in their feelings for each other that would, as she'd feared from the outset, make him feel guilty and uncomfortable, shattering their friendship in a way that might be irreparable. So how to get the time alone she needed?

As she crossed the room once again, her attention was caught by the white envelope sitting on her desk. The note from Mrs Earnshaw.

For the first time since she'd spied Rafe in the ball-room last night, she felt a measure of relief. This, then, was the answer to her current dilemma. A place to go where she would have the distance and the tranquility to recover and heal, a place where he would not follow her, at least initially.

By the time she had filled up her new sketchbooks and Parliament was drawing to a close, she could share with him the news of the child. Soothed by her time alone, supported by the joyous promise of that event, she would have figured out how to resume their life together. And decided, if Thalia was part of the future, if she *could* resume it.

Resume their easy, enjoyable *friendship*, she thought, unable as yet to restrain her bitterness over this final death of her dream of his love.

Turning with resolution, Juliana rang for Baxter. She'd begin packing at once.

That evening after returning from dinner and a rout-party, Rafe joined Juliana in their bedchamber. She prided herself that, having figured out a way to resolve her dilemma this morning, she'd been able to conduct herself normally enough throughout the evening that, by the end of dinner, Rafe had relaxed and ceased to send anxious glances in her direction.

She steeled herself against the concern evident in those looks. He obviously felt she was upset by his en-countering Lady Altorn and wanted to reassure her.

She tried to look reassured, bottling up the more volatile hurt and anger beneath a serene façade. Fortunately, she was always quiet in company, never seeking out attention and content to observe from the sidelines, so he couldn't read distress in her minimal participation in the dinner conversation or the games and dancing at the rout.

After all, she had no reason to be angry with Rafe. At herself, for getting herself into the situation. But he'd never deceived or misled her; from the outset, he'd promised only respect and friendship.

It wasn't his fault those qualities now stuck in her throat like sawdust.

Now, for her best performance of the evening.

'A glass of wine?' she offered, smiling.

She must have succeeded in looking at ease, for he smiled back and said, 'Wine for now and I'll hope for better later.'

'Perhaps, if you are a very good boy.'

'Let me show you how good I can be,' he murmured, taking the glass.

She turned away to hide a glaze of tears. Surprising, once she'd frankly admitted her love, how much it hurt to return to the playful exchanges of passion she'd once used to disguise his lack of love. But now she could only go on playing.

'Before you demonstrate that skill, I wanted to let you know that I've decided to accept Mrs Earnshaw's offer of hospitality.'

'Excellent! I can't wait to discover which animals, birds and sea creatures will capture your interest and what marvelous drawings of them you will produce. When did you tell her we would arrive? I should think a fortnight at Thornthwaite would be sufficient after I end my Parliamentary duties before we can journey there.'

'Actually, I've decided to set out immediately. Now, before you protest, hear me out. As the sessions proceed, you'll have ever more meetings and consultations. I've tepid interest at best in the social events here and no interest at all in the making and receiving of calls, shopping and exchanging gossip that occupies most of a Society lady's day. Nor is there much variety in the subjects available to sketch: birds, squirrels and a few assorted insects, since despite their ready availability, I refuse to stoop to drawing rats. You know I detest them and I only sketch the things I love.'

She paused to sip her wine. Rafe was looking at her thoughtfully and hadn't attempted to interrupt her yet, which was a good sign. Encouraged, she continued, 'There will, in contrast, be a world of new creatures to discover and sketch in Cornwall. Many more, I think, than you would have the patience or interest in waiting around for me to work my way through. Remember that day at the Royal Academy.'

He almost groaned before he caught himself. 'I enjoyed watching you enraptured by all the subjects and techniques,' he protested.

'Perhaps, but you can't deny that, had you come on your own or with a party of friends, you would have left far earlier.'

Since that was unanswerable, he didn't attempt to deny it.

'I know you could make good use of your time. And I'm sure Mrs Earnshaw would enjoy having the company of someone who shared her love of Lady Fallsham. But…what about me? What am I to do with myself on those long days—and longer nights—in London without you?'

He looked so forlorn, she almost relented. Almost.

'I think we've already pointed out that much of your day will be taken up either with consultations or meeting other gentlemen at your club. Aren't the rest of the cavalry regiments due back from Calais soon? You'll have so many friends to catch up with, so much news to exchange and so many gatherings fueled by brandy, cigars and card-playing that last until the wee hours, you'll scarcely have time to miss me.'

As he couldn't refute that prediction, either, she continued, 'By the time you are ready to leave London, if you choose to meet me in Cornwall, I should be almost done with my sketching, having filled up my books and probably also exhausted my hostess's hospitality, so our stay there together would be enjoyably brief. Or if you discover before the end of the sessions that there are tasks at Thornthwaite needing your immediate attention, I could meet you back there.'

He sipped his wine, looking thoughtful. Finally, he said softly, 'Won't you miss me?'

Miss the love she longed for that would never be hers? That she'd been foolish enough to think she might have won after all?

The question like a dagger slicing further open still-raw wounds, she dashed away the start of useless tears. 'Desperately. But I shall have to bear up, won't I? I will have my sketching and new worlds to explore to keep me from succumbing to melancholy.'

Words she would need to engrave on her heart and live by.

Rafe shook his head. 'I would like to argue with you, but my days will probably unfold much as you have described. I know London holds little appeal for you, and I promised I would help, not hinder you, in pursuing the art you're so passionate about. You have far too much talent for me to go back on my word now. I can't say I like the idea, but…' He sighed. 'Very well; I'll not stand in your way. But you must return to London at once if you grow tired of Cornwall or summon me and I'll come fetch you.'

He'd put up a bit of a fight, which made her feel a little better.

She had by no means recovered her normal equilibrium, but the burden of distress had lightened somewhat. She would have the time she needed to re-construct her expectations and refashion her emotions. And then, please God, when she did join with him again, she would be able to reveal the joy of a child to ease her into the relationship that would be the most she could expect going forward.

And she'd have discovered whether, or how, she could live with his regard for Thalia.

After all, respect and friendship weren't to be de-spised, she insisted to herself. Many marriages sur-vived on less. She was sharing her life with the only man she'd ever wanted. She had her husband's support for her exploration of the natural world, for her art-work, his appreciation for her help with his estate, and soon, the prospect of a child to bind them even closer.

Should she just cease complaining and be thankful for the blessings she had?

As she finished her wine, Rafe put down his own glass and reached out to her.

'Come here, dear wife, and let me show you just how desperately I will miss you.'

As always, she let him lead her to bed, ready now to submerge her tumultuous emotions once more under the concealing carapace of passion.

Chapter Nineteen

In the evening three weeks later, Rafe sat in the library with Hart, where they'd repaired at the conclusion of a Parliamentary meeting to continue the discussion about the latest matter under study in the Lords.

'…don't think Singletary has enough votes to carry the matter,' Hart was saying, while Rafe sipped his brandy, his attention wandering.

'I believe, after all, he might win women the right to vote.' When Rafe gave no response to that outrageous comment, Hart shook his head in exasperation. 'You're not even listening to me! Where have you been all evening? You barely spoke a word at the meetings and since we've returned here, you've been as grumpy as a bear with a thorn in its paw.'

Rafe turned to his friend apologetically. 'Sorry, I know I've been…distant.'

'You're missing your wife, I expect. It's amazing how quickly a sweet lady can inveigle her way into your heart and home, so that you wonder how you ever managed without her! I hate it when Claire and I must be separated.'

With his friend so besotted with his own wife, Rafe felt he could admit, 'I do miss her rather dreadfully.'

'Well, why not go to Cornwall and fetch her? She's had several weeks to roam about, sketching all the beguiling wildlife she's seen. She may be ready to leave. Or in any case, you can stand to miss the last few weeks of Parliament, if it comes to that. I think we're agreed that the Opposition hasn't enough votes in the House to risk bringing any of their measures to a vote this session. So your absence shouldn't be missed.'

After an initial flare of excitement at the prospect, Rafe sighed. 'But if I go, she'll feel obligated to entertain me or perhaps cut short her exploration there. I did faithfully promise to support her work and give her as much time as she needs. You've seen her sketches, you understand how talented she is.'

'Then go and support her! You're not doing much good, moping about here.'

He sighed again, tempted but trying to resist it. 'I'll consider it.'

'Please do,' Hart said, setting down his glass. 'Now, not to rub it in, but I shall go home to my own delightful wife. Who can entertain me in ways you cannot compete with.'

Rafe smiled ruefully. 'I can well imagine. Lucky dog.'

Hart shrugged. 'You have a perfectly lovely wife of

your own whose charms you might avail yourself of. If you want to enough. Even a wife with whom you only share "friendship" and "affection." That is all you still want to share with her, isn't it?'

Rafe looked up quickly but couldn't read his friend's expression. 'Still—always—a good basis for marriage,' he floundered.

Rising to walk out, Hart clapped him on the arm. 'Just remember, it isn't the only one. Don't let an unfortunate experience from years ago prevent you from enjoying the full richness a life together can offer. Love doesn't have to mean excessive emotion and agony. It can be profound but quiet joy. I'm gone!' he concluded, holding up a hand before Rafe could ask him to cease.

'Thanks for the unsolicited advice,' Rafe said acidly as his friend exited the library.

'No extra charge,' Hart threw back with a grin.

After his friend walked out, Rafe poured himself another glass and sank back into his chair.

There was no denying that he missed Juliana far more acutely than he'd anticipated.

There was the unfulfilled physical hunger, of course. She'd spoiled him so thoroughly with her sensual, responsive nature that he'd foolishly come to take daily lovemaking for granted. The sudden loss of it had been more unpleasant than he'd anticipated, making him wonder how he'd survived all those celibate years with the army.

His dissatisfaction stemmed from much more than just a lack of passionate fulfillment, though. He missed her voice, the charm of her laughter, the surprise of her unusual insights, her calm and quiet presence. She made all the difficulties he faced easier, at Thornthwaite and in London, smoothing his way, never asking for thanks or demanding special attention. Never cajoling for treats or favours, sweetly grateful for a simple sketchbook, a pair of entry tickets to the Royal Academy exhibition or a set of etchings by Turner.

Closing his eyes, he could imagine the feel of her skin under his fingers as she lay on his shoulder in the aftermath of loving. Her faint lavender scent. The sound of her light step in the hallway approaching the library, which always made his heart lift.

His heart. His friend had hinted rather broadly that he'd been letting the long-ago affair with Thalia stop him from fully enjoying the relationship with the wife he now knew suited him much better than his former love ever would have.

Was he—had he been from the first—letting that long-ago pain blind him to the life he might lead now with Juliana?

His initial strong reaction to seeing Thalia again, he was slowly realizing, had been the result of being transported in those first few moments back to the time when he'd been heartbroken and despairing over a future that didn't include her. For, though he'd been briefly tempted by her suggestion that they renew their relationship—certainly her offer had assuaged his bruised pride—he'd never truly considered accepting it. Indeed, repulsed by the idea of replacing what had been a pure, stainless emotion with a furtive illicit affair, he'd been able to dismiss the possibility with no regret.

Would he be able to dismiss Juliana from his life so easily?

The intensity of his rejection of the mere possibility brought him up short. Had he fallen in love with his wife and been too burdened by the pain of the past to realize it?

Love doesn't have to mean excessive emotion and agony. It can be profound but quiet joy.

He'd thought his brother had cheated Juliana by offering her a marriage devoid of passion. Was he not cheating her just as much by denying her a marriage based on a full measure of love?

He couldn't imagine a lady more deserving of having a husband who loved her completely and totally.

The more he considered the matter, the more he realized what a complete dolt he'd been. Secretly burnishing this image of a failed Grand Passion, which he was now coming to realize had been more a young man's romantic infatuation with an unattainable princess who, after a month of squiring her to dances and a few stolen kisses, he still barely knew. It hadn't been a *real* love based on a thorough knowledge and appreciation of the character and qualities of the lady. Then he'd stubbornly held on to that mirage as the definition of love, instead of cherishing the passion he'd been gifted with.

Recalling now the slow, steady development of their relationship since their marriage, he realized he'd long since gone beyond mere affection for Juliana; he *loved* her with a deep, abiding passion far stronger and deeper than the adolescent fixation he'd had for Thalia.

He smiled, then threw back his head and laughed. What an idiot he'd been.

Time to rectify the matter.

But as he jumped up in a fever of enthusiasm, fired by the idea of rushing to Cornwall and pledging his long-held but only newly discovered love for Juliana, he hesitated.

She'd accepted his hand believing their marriage would be based on respect and friendship. Certainly that was what she had expected to share with Ian. Despite her deeply sensual nature, she was often a solitary, self-contained little thing. She might not be comfortable with expressions of great emotion.

He'd promised her as much time as she wanted to sketch and explore. She might not want him hanging about, feeling she must curtail her time in the woods and fields of Cornwall, as she'd felt it necessary to end her day at the Royal Academy exhibition, despite admitting later that she could have remained until closing.

He didn't want to hem her in or put a damper on her creativity. That wasn't the way to treat someone you liked, much less loved.

But then, he was a clever fellow. There was always the magic of passion, with which he knew he could easily distract her. He truly would be happy to accompany her on her forays up on the cliffs or into the woodland shadows. If she preferred to go alone, he could be content to remain at Mrs Earnshaw's house, awaiting her return, eager to view her day's work.

Still irresolute, he wandered into her sitting room and over to the desk, intent on finding Mrs Earnshaw's invitation. He'd need directions to the estate in Cornwall if he did decide to set out.

Somehow, the love he'd so suddenly realized seemed to fill him to bursting—joyous, exuberant, hardly able to be contained. He wanted to see Juliana, be with her, even if he had to restrain himself from expressing his feelings.

The note wasn't perched against the inkwell, where she'd kept it before. He opened a desk drawer, pleased to discover it—and surprised to also find one of her new sketchbooks.

Knowing how excited she was to capture as many

images as possible—and how she'd crammed little sketches into every corner of her previous, inadequate book—he wondered why she hadn't taken it with her. Perhaps she'd forgotten it in the drawer.

He could bring it to her. That should win him an appreciative smile when he arrived, he thought happily.

He'd thought the book empty, but as he lifted it out, he realized that she'd already made some drawings. He flipped it open to find a few pages of studies, smiling as he recognized them as Hart and Claire's son, Andrew, and Claire's niece, Arabella.

Affection for the children was evident in every stroke and shadow, he thought. No rats. *I only draw what I love.*

He turned to the next page and his breath stopped. On that page, the next and the next were more lovingly rendered drawings.

Portraits of him.

She'd captured him sitting in the library, reading, his eyes downcast, a faint smile on his face. In another, his face was outlined against a sunny, cloudless sky. In the last, he reclined against the pillows of their bed, shoulders bare, his face alight with happiness.

Swallowing hard, he closed the sketchbook.

She did indeed love what she sketched; the drawings made it all too apparent. A love she never expressed verbally, but which he now recognized was displayed in all her lovemaking, all the tender companionship

and ardent support she'd offered for the burdens of the
estate she willingly shared with him.

Would Juliana reject his all-too-late declared love,
when she'd so obviously loved him silently, uncom-
plainingly, without asking for anything for herself?
While he dithered on like an idiot about 'friendship?'

He wasn't sure. But he hoped that his lack of per-
ception hadn't worn the fabric of her love so thin that
the essence of it had frayed, unable to be patched together again. He prayed that it wasn't too late now to
vow the complete love and devotion he should have
given her on their wedding day.

Which he would offer, as soon as he saw her again.

The following afternoon, Rafe returned from his
last consultations at the Lords. As Hart had noted, it
wasn't likely that any measures of importance would
be brought forward for the rest of the session, and
in any event, nothing that would generate a vote so
close that his vote would be needed. He'd informed
his friend of his imminent departure for Cornwall and
been grateful that he'd been spared any further observations on his general obtuseness in the matter of love.
He'd left orders with his valet to pack up everything
except the one suit of clothes he'd need for tonight's
dinner. Though he didn't much feel like going out,
since he couldn't set out until the morning anyway,
he might as well keep the engagement and employ his

restless energy in winning some blunt off some less-skilled player in the card room. He'd avoid the ballroom; he didn't want to dance with anyone but Juliana.

He was consumed with impatience to see her, frustrated that he had a several days' journey before he would reach Mrs Earnshaw's home in Cornwall. He couldn't wait to see the surprise and, he hoped, delight on her face when he turned up unannounced.

Or if he saw annoyance, at least he'd know where he stood. And begin that instant, he vowed, to woo her properly, as he should have from the beginning.

He might be a blockhead, but he was a persistent one. He'd start with 'friendship' and 'respect' and continue to expand it as far as it would go.

He'd hurried up the entry, handed off his hat and cane to the butler and was striding towards the stairs when a movement on the landing above caught his attention. He'd about dismissed it as a maid leaving the library when something about the motion of the figure arrested him.

'Juliana!' he cried, a wave of overwhelming joy washing through him. 'You've come back.' Taking the stairs two at a time, he rushed up to meet her.

As Juliana saw Rafe in the entryway, her pulse accelerated and her nervousness returned. She wasn't at all sure what she meant to do was the right course of action, but after having nearly three weeks of solitude in which to ponder her next step, like a moored boat that drifted with the current, she came always back to the same course.

At least he appeared happy to see her. That was a good sign.

Even better, he enveloped her in a hug and then kissed her with such urgency, she nearly forgot what she meant to do.

Before he could sweep her off to the bedchamber, she recalled her purpose. 'Shall we go into the library? I wanted to talk with you.' She blushed, recalling that even being in the library hadn't always guaranteed they'd do nothing but talk—and it was possible, depending on what happened next, that they might indeed do more.

But first, she must utter the words she'd been bursting to say to him for more than a week.

He followed her in docilely enough and remained silent, not demanding at once—as she half expected he would—to know why she'd returned early and what she needed to discuss. Once she'd settled him in an armchair and poured him a glass of wine, too nervous to sit herself, she stood before him.

'I know you were distressed to see Lady Altorn again,' she began abruptly, in her urgency to proceed to the most important part of her speech, forgetting the introductory comments. 'You know how sorry I am that you were not allowed to marry the woman you truly loved. I also agreed to marry you knowing full well how you felt about her and understanding that one doesn't forget a love like that. Knowing that you could promise me only affection and friendship.'

He made as if to speak, but she waved him to silence. 'Please, let me finish. Everyone thinks because I'm quiet that I'm meek and biddable, but…that's not really true. When there is something I care deeply about, I will speak up for it. Fight for it. And I care deeply about you. I had thought to leave London to take time to decide whether or not I could reconcile myself to your loving her while I remained your wife and partner. I've decided that I cannot do that. I will not stand meekly by and allow Lady Altorn to reestablish her hold over you. On the contrary, I intend to use every wile I possess to lure you away from her and make you forget that you loved her first and better than me. Beginning now.'

With that, she leaned over to give him a kiss. With them both having been deprived of sensual satisfaction for weeks, her tentative kiss soon fired in them both a desperate need neither was prepared to deny.

Rafe stood, picked Juliana up and carried her to the sofa. Kissing her urgently, he lay her back against the cushions. And for long, intimate moments afterwards, neither of them said any more.

As they lay entangled on the sofa in the sweet aftermath of passion, Rafe cuddled Juliana close. 'My dear wife, although this confession may induce you to discontinue plying those wiles I love so much, I promise you there is no need for you to counter Lady Altorn's advances. It's true she did suggest we renew our acquaintance—and more—and I confess, for a moment I was tempted. But I rejected her offer in terms so unmistakable, so she could have no doubt about my conviction.'

She raised up on one elbow to stare at him. 'You did? With unmistakable conviction?'

'Yes. Still, I have done you a great disservice.'

'But if you refused her…in what way, a disservice?'

'By wedding you with no mention of love. I suppose I'd thought myself in love with Thalia for so long, I blinded myself to anything else. When in truth, I've probably loved you since we were children. With a true love, based on shared history and interests and affection, not some melodramatic infatuation. Despite my being an idiot too dense to recognize the emotion for what it is, I hope I may still earn your love in return. I…have some reason to hope perhaps you might care for me, too. I found your sketchbook.'

'Oh,' she said in a small voice.

'Can I hope that you may love me, fool that I've been? And if my blind refusal to see the truth right in front of me has withered your affection, will you let me try to revive it? I promise to work at being worthy of your love every day for the rest of our lives.'

He held his breath, tense with hope and dread, waiting for her response.

At last, she chuckled softly. 'Foolish man indeed. Did you not guess that I've loved you ever since you helped me rescue that squirrel? I only agreed to marry Ian because he needed me and you were in love with Thalia. Knowing how deeply you'd loved her, I hesitated to wed you, not sure I could keep buried the love I'd given up on, afraid if you ever suspected, it would make you uncomfortable and ruin the friendship between us. I never expected you would be able to see me as more than a friend. Despite that, I'd decided I would fight for you, not meekly give you up to the woman you once loved. I… I can't quite believe that the woman you love…is me.'

'Believe it,' he said, 'The only woman I have truly loved. My one Grand Passion.'

'You no longer believe marriage is best made between friends?'

He shook his head. 'Forget that idiotic pronouncement. Loving deeply is so much finer, better, more satisfying a basis.'

Chuckling, she moved a hand down to stroke him. 'It certainly is more satisfying.'

Groaning, he bent to kiss her again. 'It's been a long, long, long period of deprivation. You're right; it's time for more satisfaction.'

Suddenly she pushed him away. 'Not just yet. In

the shock of your declaration, I almost forgot the most compelling reason for my intention not to allow another woman to claim you. Not when I'm about to gift you with a child. An heir, I hope.'

It took a moment for the news to register. 'You are with child?' he asked slowly.

She nodded. 'Sometime this winter, I should present you with your firstborn.'

An upsurge of joy filling him, he hugged her tight, feeling humbled and grateful. 'One last thing to make our life complete! I need a son to inherit, I know, but truly I can't wait to have a daughter with big brown eyes and piercing intelligence, who resembles her mother.'

'Let us make a new vow,' he continued. 'No more hiding thoughts or affections. Only open honesty between us.'

'As long as honesty allows me to tell you every day how much I love you.'

'I can certainly agree to that. And now, shall we retire to the bedchamber before a maid wanders in? There's the small matter of satisfaction that needs to be tended to.'

'With all my heart, my love, my life.'

Rafe helped her up and hand in hand, led her to their chamber, filled with a euphoria greater than he'd ever experienced.

They'd made a new vow to complement their marriage lines. Ahead lay the promise of a renewed life together and a brand new life to share it with them.

He could ask for no greater blessings.

* * * * *

Make sure to read the previous instalment of the Soldiers to Heirs miniseries whilst you wait for the final book in the series!

The Unexpected Duke

Why not also check out Julia Justiss's Least Likely to Wed miniseries

A Season of Flirtation
The Wallflower's Last Chance Season
A Season with Her Forbidden Earl

MILLS & BOON ®

Coming next month

THE DANGERS OF DECEIVING A DUKE
Louise Allen

Celebrating Louise's 75th Book!

The kiss was not gentle, but hungry, as though both were famished.

She was not an innocent. She had been married. But this was not right. Not there, not now. Not ever.

That was his conscience, shouting at him against the thrum of his blood, the aching need and desire for her, the answering desire Cat's body was signalling. Her mouth was open under his, the heat, the dart of her tongue and the nip of her teeth acting like a shot of brandy in his blood.

They were as one in passion and, it seemed, in tune in more ways than that, because, in a split second it was over. She drew back, even as he lowered her carefully to the floor and straightened, stepped away.

'That was a very bad idea,' Quinn said, controlling his voice with an effort. 'I apologise.'

'That realisation appeared to strike us both at the same time. No apology is needed.' Cat sounded equally breathless.

She moved away a little, but not, he thought with relief, out of wariness, but to brush the dust from her skirts.

'We agreed that a cat may be friends with a duke, did we not? But friendship is as far as it can go.' Her clothes apparently ordered to her satisfaction, she looked up and met his gaze squarely. 'I am not in the market for a *carte blanche*, Quinn. And no other offer is conceivable, is it?'

Continue reading

THE DANGERS OF DECEIVING A DUKE
Louise Allen

Available next month
millsandboon.co.uk

COMING SOON!

We really hope you enjoyed reading this book.
If you're looking for more romance
be sure to head to the shops when
new books are available on

Thursday 26th February

To see which titles are coming soon, please visit

millsandboon.co.uk/nextmonth

MILLS & BOON

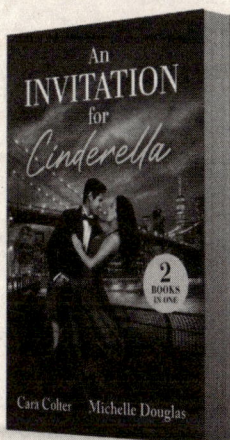

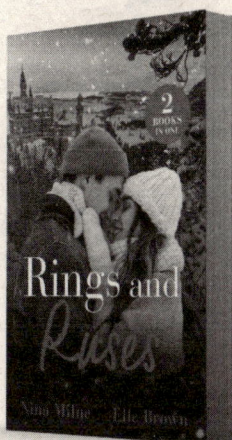

LET'S TALK

Romance

For exclusive extracts, competitions and special offers, find us online:

- **f** MillsandBoon
- **X** @MillsandBoon
- **◎** @MillsandBoonUK
- **♪** @MillsandBoonUK

Get in touch on 01413 063 232